The Bigfoot Files

The Bigfoot Files

LINDSAY EAGAR

CANDLEWICK PRESS

Copyright © 2018 by Lindsay Eagar

First edition 2018

Library of Congress Catalog Card Number pending
ISBN 978-0-7636-9234-6

18 19 20 21 22 23 LSC 10 9 8 7 6 5 4 3 2 1

Printed in Crawfordsville, IN, U.S.A.

This book was typeset in Berkeley OldStyle.

Candlewick Press
99 Dover Street
Somerville, Massachusetts 02144

visit us at www.candlewick.com

For my Finley

Proof

Bean! Come see!"

Miranda had heard her mother call her like this before; she'd heard it at least a dozen times that weekend alone. But even though it was a familiar summoning, even though Miranda was concentrating on a civics essay that was due three days earlier, even though the wind blew through the yellowing trees with a certain seriousness and the congregating clouds outside of the jury-rigged awning threatened rain, she stood up. She stuffed her papers beneath a rock near the barren fire pit and ran.

But first she grabbed the camera.

There were half a dozen others with them in Big Cottonwood Canyon, some of them driving across entire states to get here. They had all seen the same report, an obscure story written for levity, plucked from a credible news site and then trickling through their online community, their forums, their blogs: A pair of young hikers witnessed strange rustlings in the nettle. They had seen an abnormal stillness in the surrounding wildlife, as if the warblers and the foxes and the cutthroat trout were holding their breath as another beast, a king, passed through. They had noticed an unusual darkness in the evenings that concentrated around a figure — something tall, something that was neither human nor animal, but definitely something alive.

Most of all, the hikers said, they saw shadows. Shadows without moorings. Shadows in impossible shapes. Shadows that formed and disappeared in the space of a single blink.

And then the hunt began.

They all wanted to see one. They all wanted proof.

But sometimes, Miranda thought, the others seemed like they wanted the game to keep going more than they wanted to *know*. They liked the hide-and-seek of it, the gathering of intellects and theories, the division of perimeters, the smoky campfire evenings, and the fancy infrared equipment that must be unloaded and carted and mastered.

Even if a creature was bagged, tagged, and hauled around the world on exhibition, many of them would no doubt still scour the media for reports, would still get together for the search. The search was what they lived for.

Not Miranda. She wanted proof.

She and her mother had been hunting for years. She was ready to *know*.

And the time was ripe. In the whispering petals of wildflowers, in the babbling of clear rivers, in the freeway currents across their pockmarked windshield on their drives home after fruitless trips, she could hear it sometimes: *Soon. So very soon.*

That afternoon her mother had left camp to investigate a tree-mounted motion sensor camera that had been activated, then mysteriously lost power—no doubt pushed off the branch by the wind, as often happened. But her mother was giddy at the prospect. "Or maybe—maybe, Bean—Bigfoot knocked it over when he saw the blinking light!"

"What is he, camera shy?" Miranda joked.

Those jokes were easier to make lately. They grew on Miranda's tongue like thorns; all she had to do was spit them out.

Up past the reservoir Miranda went, a thin wind crying through the firs like a vindictive ghost. When the first of a cold rain dotted her cheek, she resisted the urge to run back under the awning with her homework. Instead she focused her mind—

What if this is it?

What if I turn this corner, around this pine, down this gulley, and I see him?

What if we found Bigfoot?

Even from behind the parched autumn grass and the quaking, coin-size leaves of white aspens, Miranda could spot her mother wearing the mad-eyed grin of a person obsessed—it beamed, it was like a new sun.

A knot in Miranda's stomach untied itself.

It's happening, she thought, *and I'm ready.*

"Where?" Miranda flew through the swishing grass and into the clearing, camera poised. "Where is he?"

"Look at it, Bean!" Her mother stepped backward, angling Miranda to see the dampening loam behind a fallen log.

Miranda's insides tangled.

A footprint.

Only a footprint.

Smudged into the dirt, a heel and five toes, clearly human—or, at least *humanoid,* she corrected herself with some bitterness—and fading as the rain hit the ground.

A large footprint, yes. But when Miranda checked herself for veneration, for the stuff that her mother currently oozed like she was able to convert oxygen into awe . . . it wasn't there.

There was nothing there.

Miranda waited while her mother and the others took photographs, while they found the missing motion sensor camera (which had indeed fallen from the tree and turned itself off), while they analyzed the footprint's length and width and tread, while they spoke about the find as if it was the first of its kind and not, as Miranda would have pointed out had she not been too empty to speak, the tenth footprint they'd found that year alone.

Miranda acted polite. Miranda acted smiley. Miranda acted the perfect assistant as they huddled around the footprint like it was a relic. She held jackets and helped frame their "Aha! Discovery!" pictures and nodded when they said, over and over, "Can you believe it?"

Another footprint.

She really, really could believe it.

"We're so close, Bean." Her mother put an arm around her, and a sudden, foreign instinct came over Miranda—to jerk away, to push back, to run.

When her mother was twelve weeks pregnant, she'd seen baby Miranda on an ultrasound—just a grainy white dot dancing across the screen "like a jumping bean," her mother always said, and the nickname stuck.

Miranda couldn't remember the last time her mother had used her real name. Why had that never bothered her before?

The storm finally convinced them to leave the clearing; they peeled away reluctantly one by one until it was just Miranda and her mother—and the footprint, until the mud claimed it.

"This, right here." Her mother gestured at the ground, at the aspens, as pale as if someone had drained them, at the forest all around them. "Isn't this amazing, Bean? We're so close!"

Miranda couldn't hold back. "But we've seen so many footprints. If he's really out there, why haven't we seen him yet? Why haven't we found real proof?"

"Oh, Bean." Her mother again wrapped herself around Miranda, constricting her. "Be patient. We don't find Bigfoot—Bigfoot finds us."

It was only after her mother walked ahead, the sound of her happy whistle piercing through the din of the storm, that Miranda realized what she'd said:

If.

She'd said *if.*

The word came out so naturally, as if it had been perched there on her lips for a long, long time—and her mother hadn't even noticed.

Miranda had barely noticed.

Miranda dragged herself back through the rain to camp, where she found the notes for her civics essay, soaked and torn cleanly in half by the wind. She searched, but the missing sections were hiding somewhere in these woods, these damn trees that refused to reveal anything that was given to them to conceal.

The next day they drove home, where they would unpack and stay only until the next bumpkin farmer announced that he saw an ape-like creature crossing the stream in his fields. Until the next shadow.

Miranda tuned out her mother's circular talking. Something new was happening within her, and she honed in on it. Where there was once wonder, there was now itching, a grain of sand in your eye.

Where there was once fireworks and golden frenzies and the sensation that she was reaching out to touch magic and magic was reaching back—there was instead this tiny, odd anger burrowing beneath her ribs.

"We're going to find one, Bean," her mother said, again and again. "We're so close. Believe me."

Miranda curled up on her seat, feigning sleep. With the hand farthest from her mother, she reached up and pulled out a hair. A single hair. The bite of pain chewed through the hot fog in her brain. It gave her something to hold on to.

And so she did it again.

Another hair, another bite.

Eventually her mom stopped talking and there was, at last, quiet.

Miranda pressed her ear against the cold glass of the window, straining to hear the air currents above the rumbles and grunts of their car—but outside the window, there was nothing.

Outside the window, it was a dead zone.

Soon, soon, soon—that was what she wanted to hear. A reassurance. But the wind on the dark, rain-soaked highway, the air brushing the windshield and the metal of the car door, the sky around the bold twilight stars—all were silent.

Except this one word, echoing in her head again and again—*if, if, if.*

1.

Miranda was good at naming shadows.

She could sense them before they incorporated into solid darkness, before they had decided on a shape—and then she could tell exactly what they belonged to.

You are only a spare desk, hulking outside the principal's office.

You are only a banner, flapping in the gale of the air-conditioning vent.

You are only a hawthorn bush, a streetlight, a bird, the clouds rolling across the moon—you are only me, my shape reflected on the ground behind me.

A peculiar skill for a twelve-year-old to take pride in—the days of checking under beds and in closets for hungry monsters were long over for most of her peers.

But there was still someone at Miranda's house who made a monster out of every unexplained silhouette or indecipherable sound.

And so she had to be vigilant.

And she had to come here, to the school, before anyone else arrived, so she could work.

A house full of monsters was not a place where she could think, no matter how much she tried to hide in the shadows.

She sat in front of the lockers, a spread of homework and books around her. It was a balancing act she attempted most mornings — trying to jostle the various assignments that were all due that day, none of which was even close to being completed.

Pockets of magic existed in the world, Miranda knew, but they came exclusively in the form of moments like these — the hours before the school opened, when the building was an empty shell and the freshly born sunrise made the harsh fluorescent lights in the hallway almost obscene in comparison. Moments when the only sound was her own wheels spinning.

These cereal hours, these foggy mornings . . . Miranda had always been busy enough to need every waking hour of her days, but lately she'd been squeezing out extra time where she could.

She had to.

She had to make sure everything was perfect. Even if

other elements of her life threatened to ruin everything.

She glanced at the clock. Quarter to seven: That gave her only fifteen minutes to devote to each assignment. And even if she did manage to get them finished, that didn't leave time for anything else—any of the other things she had to do to catch up. It wasn't enough time. It was never enough.

Panic jolted through her like cold coffee.

What if I don't get these finished?

What if I have to ask for more time?

What if they won't give me more time?

Too many things swirling, hovering—they gathered in a mist, thick as a curtain. Mind spinning like a second hand on a clock, she took out her phone and opened her to-do list.

To-do list:

Finish study guide for history

Put tutoring schedule online

She twirled her inky hair around her finger. There was something else she was missing, something that was clouding a large amount of her mental storage—

Fall Fling! How could she have forgotten? Her delinquent homework was eating every other task in her brain. The Fall Fling was next week, a dance that would raise money for new projectors in every classroom and simultaneously provide her classmates with three hours of teacher-free socialization. It was her most ambitious project as student body president so far, and she had to get every detail just right.

Confirm student council meeting with administration

Call DJ about extension cords

Order pumpkin spice doughnuts from bakery

Her election as student body president had been a rare historical feat—only a seventh-grader, and yet they had still chosen her. A seventh-grader, to rule even the older grades.

And so the Fall Fling had to be perfect.

That word again, *perfect.*

Her favorite word.

Proofread flyers

Write script for school announcements next week

Her to-do lists never seemed to get any shorter, no matter how hard she hustled; her mind was a video game landscape, every item on her list a bad guy. You kill every one within sight, and it's quiet until you turn a corner and you're ambushed.

A dozen papers around her, two textbooks straddling a folder of exam notes, and eight tabs open on her phone—and the ticking of the clock, which was as loud as her own pulse—

Something inside her unspooled.

What if there are questions on the history test that weren't on the study guide?

What if the DJ cancels?

What if—

She inhaled, concentrating on surrendering the tension in her shoulders, loosening the imaginary cords that bound her, but they only cinched tighter.

What if the bakery loses our order?

What if no one shows up to the dance?

What if I don't get it done in time? Any of it? And then the camp, the leadership camp—

What if, what if, what if?

Alone in the hall, she reached up and yanked out a single strand of hair. A prickle, then relief.

One strand of hair, and she could think again.

Another strand, and she could breathe again.

A door opened down the hall. A shadow emerged.

The custodians, she predicted, beginning their slow tour of the school's floors with their mops.

But it was her guidance counselor, Ms. Palmer.

"Miss Miranda Cho." Ms. Palmer eyed her, jingling her keys in the door of the counseling office. "It's early, even for you."

"Just getting some extra credit work done." A baby fib. "You know how it is—if I'm not ahead, I'm behind."

And she was so far behind.

She gritted her teeth and hoped the counselor would leave her alone.

"Actually, Miranda, I'm glad to run into you." Ms. Palmer paused. "Can we talk?"

The counselor disappeared through the door without waiting for a response; Miranda gathered her things from the tiles, and as she lifted up the pages, she gathered herself, too. The counselor wouldn't interrupt the student body president unless it was important.

Like the camp?

What if Ms. Palmer has news?

She folded up her annoyance and put it into her pocket.

Inside her office, Ms. Palmer's fingers clacked on her keyboard, her computer sluggish as it woke up for the day. She'd finally organized (or had someone else organize) the mishmash of files that were, until today, threatening to overtake her desk. She'd gotten a haircut, too — though apparently a fairly cheap one, as her curls were slightly higher and tauter on the left side of her head. And there was a faint, barely there stain on her collar — coffee or black tea, splashed into the shape of a continent.

Small details. Anyone else would gloss over them, let the details remain camouflaged against the rest of the mundane.

But to Miranda, small details were dessert.

"Have you heard anything?" Ms. Palmer asked, and Miranda's heart thumped crookedly.

"Nothing yet."

Nothing in the mailbox, nothing in her e-mail — nothing at all.

"You're a shoo-in, Miranda." The black wave composed itself—Ms. Palmer was not the type to soothe. "Your application was perfect—you had a perfect term last spring. Perfect grades, perfect extracurriculars, and now, with you serving as student body president . . ."

Miranda hid a sigh. She could live forever in that word, *perfect*.

Three weeks ago she'd applied to a leadership camp for next summer, one of the most prestigious youth programs in the nation. Students who were selected flew to Washington, D.C., for communications workshops, service projects, White House tours, and meetings with important people. The kind of people Miranda wanted to be when she grew up.

Any day now she would find out if she got in. Any day.

"Miranda, I wanted to talk to you about your absences."

Somehow Miranda managed to keep her smile from slipping. She even widened it, a cat's smile.

"I've been reviewing your attendance record. You've missed ten days of school—we're still in the first term." Her eyes bored holes into Miranda. "You're not skipping school, are you?"

"No," Miranda said—but she'd hesitated. "At least, not on purpose."

"What do you mean?"

Here we go, Miranda thought, and swallowed. "Sometimes I have to go with my mom on her work trips. But I

15

always bring my homework and I've never missed a deadline." She didn't mention that sometimes she had to get extensions for those deadlines.

But the counselor wasn't impressed by Miranda's semi-honest disclosure. "What does your mom do for work?" she asked, and the questions formed before Miranda could even blink:

What if she laughs?

What if she doesn't believe me?

What if I tell her and it doesn't make me feel any less alone?

"She's—" A thousand lies leaped to Miranda's aid:

She's a travel photographer.

She's a corporate lawyer with bicoastal clients.

She's an artist with a case of wanderlust that parenthood never cured.

But the truth was written somewhere in her file; Ms. Palmer would find out if she lied. And then there would be more questions.

Ms. Palmer waited. Why did guidance counselors have to look so kind, so dependable? Everything about her seemed soft to Miranda—a pillow to hug, a hammock to fall into. Someone to spill all her secrets to.

Even the secrets she kept locked away from herself.

"Do you know what cryptozoology is?"

Ms. Palmer frowned. "Like the Loch Ness Monster? Things like that?"

"Yes." Humiliation flowed through Miranda's body in a polluted river. "My mom does that. She looks for creatures—last week we were in Ohio."

"What's in Ohio?"

"The Frogman." *Burrow into the ground,* Miranda instructed herself, *and don't stop until you're on the other side of the earth.* "Half man, half—"

"Frog." Ms. Palmer laughed once, a gust of air. "That sounds like a fun job. Does she work for a zoo?"

"No," Miranda said. That would be respectable. "She runs a blog—*The Bigfoot Files.* She charts sightings, organizes searches, that sort of thing." She pursed her lips. Those were all the details she was willing to offer—she already wished she could erase the name of the website from this conversation. The last thing she wanted was for Ms. Palmer to look it up.

"Anyway," Miranda concluded, "she has to travel a lot."

"And you don't have a sitter you can stay with? Or family?" Ms. Palmer didn't ask about Miranda's father. That, too, would be in her file.

No, Miranda had nothing like that. Babysitters cost money, and family, well . . . family members were supposed to be the ones who stuck around when the good times had run out and only the muck was left.

Miranda and her mother had no such people.

"Can you talk to your mom?" Ms. Palmer said. "See if she'd be willing to cut back on her travel, at least during the school year? It's important that you're here for classes—"

"I know." Miranda hated when she snapped, when she knew she was acting like a stereotype of her age. But she hated it more when adults explained things as if they were simple, when in fact they were impossibly messy. They handed her a skein of tangled yarn, then wondered why she wasn't wearing it as a sweater.

Ms. Palmer studied her. "Are you afraid to talk to your mom?"

Miranda was so surprised by the question, she nearly laughed. "No," she said, and it was the truth. Not scared of her mother. Not at all. That was akin to being afraid of a muffin. A crayon. A toadstool.

Ms. Palmer leaned back in her chair. Miranda made herself small as a beetle as the counselor studied her—hands folded calmly in her lap, lungs bringing in air and returning it with a steady rhythm. No detail at all that would give her away. Nothing that would let Ms. Palmer know how much Miranda wanted to reach for a hair.

"You only have two absences left before you face losing credit for this term," Ms. Palmer said, and Miranda's heart crash-landed in her stomach. No credit meant her grades would be suspended. Liquefied. Her end-of-term report card would bear those two dreaded letters—NC—instead of those bright, clean As sweeping down the margin, unbroken, like a mountain chain.

"And you know what that would mean: even if you did get into the camp"—*if*, Ms. Palmer said *if*—"you'd have to turn it down to make up your absences at summer school."

When Miranda was dismissed, she stood on gelatin legs and muttered something resembling a good-bye. She headed back into the still-empty hallway, closing the counselor's door behind her.

If. She'd said *if.*

The hours before school started had always felt like Miranda's secret. A magic time.

Now the building seemed eerie without the kids talking, running, pulsing through like blood cells. The halls were just empty veins, and they felt thinner now, too. Less room to breathe. Miranda's thoughts rattled around in her brain, echoing, colliding into each other, entire universes.

A shoo-in for the leadership camp, Ms. Palmer called her—and the counselor was not generous with compliments.

But she had also said *if.*

There could be no *if.* Miranda had to go to that camp. She had to.

In the meantime, she sank back down among familiar shadows—the shadow of a tower of assignments whose height was incompatible with the amount of time she had left to finish them. The shadow of the teachers with whom she would have to bargain, *again,* for extensions. The shadow of her cringing and squirming and loathing herself for needing the extra days.

Looming over them all was the biggest shadow, the one she could never outrun, the one with a mouth and a spine and a thrumming heartbeat—the shadow of the knowledge that she would never get it all done, she would never get caught up. No matter how fast she worked, no matter how hard she hustled—next week would be Alkali Lake. The week after that—Hope, Idaho. The absences, piling up like beach trash.

Until something changed, every day would be a hustle.

Miranda pulled out hair after hair while she raced through her homework, and on every strand she made a furious promise: No more missed classes. No more extensions. No more meetings with Ms. Palmer where the counselor cross-examined her about her life and about her mother, getting dangerously close to the truth.

Between yanks and sentence diagrams, her mind galloped over happy terrain: daydreams of the leadership camp. Two months of catered meals and clean, matching bedsheets. Two months of grown-ups acting like grown-ups. Two months with two thousand miles and at least that many imaginary creatures between her and her mother.

Perfect, Ms. Palmer had said. And Miranda would be.

2.

School always ended too quickly.

The hours flapped past like hurried birds in a cold sky. All too soon, Miranda sat outside, beneath the old bur oak tree, her backpack full enough with books and papers and expectations that it could sink her to the bottom of a river. She should have unzipped it at once and finished her vocabulary sheets, but instead she leaned her head against the trunk, the scars of previous generations' initials carved into its bark, and allowed herself the briefest, smallest moment to simply breathe.

Breathe and watch the tree.

Boughs, blackened green against the blue of sky. Leaf after leaf, layer after layer, until the canopy was thick enough to bury the clouds.

Anything could be hiding behind these leaves.

She stiffened. That wasn't one of her own thoughts, born of her own mind. That thought belonged to someone else.

Even something as simple as the leaves of a tree had been ruined for her.

She looked around — at real life unfolding before her. At the last of the buses driving away. At the faculty parking lot slowly emptying, teachers and staff going home to cook dinner, to tend to household chores, to zone out in front of the television until bedtime — things normal people did. Stray boys used the near-empty parking lot to cruise on longboards, despite the signs posted everywhere forbidding it.

Miranda squinted — she'd known all of these boys once, back when they were all little and their families had rotated carpools to get them to kindergarten. Back when Miranda's mother worked a nine-to-five, and different moms would sometimes watch her after school for an hour or two.

Back before everyone in her mother's life dropped them like old sandwiches.

Now the boys stretched tall and lurpy, like their bones had grown faster than their skin. She had grown, too, she knew, but somehow when she was around these boys, she felt like she hadn't changed at all. Like she was still freckled and pigtailed, still three feet tall, still starry-eyed. Still telling her outlandish stories—and still believing every word.

She hadn't been that girl in a long time.

One of them saw her and, after a moment, waved. A dash of his hand; he could have been swatting away a bug.

Miranda pretended not to see.

To-do list, Miranda typed on her phone.

Proofread flyer for Science Club sign-ups

Finish bibliography for English

After a moment, she added:

Talk to Mom

It was late summer—or early fall, depending on which side you were rooting for. Pockets of color were visible on the mountains, brushstrokes of faintest yellow and ochre and pink among the dark conifers. Chilly evenings stung when the sun went down, but a faux-July still made for sweltering days.

A small season of its own, this season of change, of transition. Miranda always felt a burst of momentum at this time of year, a gentle push from the gods of new school terms and sharpened pencils and fresh starts.

Not even the click and shift of September could make Miranda excited for this last item on her to-do list. She wasn't *afraid* to talk to her mom. But that didn't mean she wanted to. Indeed, she would rather—well, that was a list that could have gone on for miles, the number of things she'd rather do than talk to her mom.

The oak leaves turned over, a soft breeze finding them above Miranda's head. And beside her, something rustled the well-manicured hedges trimmed along the junior high building. Her pulse spiked and her breathing slowed, her back straightening against the trunk. All involuntary reactions, her body triggered by the sound of twigs snapping and the smell of fresh air.

It's nothing, she told herself. *A squirrel or a bird.*

Her mind knew there was no such thing as monsters, but her body was slower to convince. When a pigeon hopped out between the bushes, she still exhaled harder than was necessary.

It was always nothing.

A trio of girls came out of the science room, one of them carrying a mushy, post-eruption papier-mâché volcano. Two of them were the Martinez twins, Alex and Carmen.

The other girl was Emma.

Miranda had a brief window in which to dodge them—to run back into the school, to hide in the baseball dugout, to climb up into the tree and make a nest, where she would live forever—but her dignity made her hesitate, and then it was too late.

"Hi!" Carmen called.

I didn't hear her, Miranda told herself. *I'm busy, I'm writing in my student planner, I'm working . . .*

And then she heard it:

"Hey, Miranda."

Emma.

She could never forget the timbre of Emma's voice—rippling soft in the air, pretty as birdsong. Even after a whole summer without hearing it, Miranda knew it like she knew her own heartbeat.

The girls walked toward the oak, and Miranda's chances of avoiding them evaporated.

What if Emma told them what happened?

What if she's coming over to confront me about it?

What if they laugh at me?

She put on her official student body president face: engaged mouth, listening eyes. "Oh, hi!"

"Are you waiting for your mom?" Was that a barb in Emma's words?

Miranda skimmed her fingers along the straps of her backpack, letting them dance into the ends of her hair. "No, I was about to start walking." *Their rides will be here any minute,* she reasoned, *and then I'll be free of them.*

Free of conversation. Free of questions.

Free of trying to fill the space between Emma and herself with anything but this discomfort, gathering like dust.

Her vocabulary sheet waited, unfinished in her

backpack. Was there a word for this? A word for people who used to be friends, and then stopped?

"You're walking? All the way home?" Emma lived near Miranda, on the opposite side of town—in fact Miranda could still see Emma's bedroom window from her own bedroom window.

Sometimes, when she couldn't sleep, Miranda would push aside her curtains and wait until Emma's window went dark and her night-light snapped on—the rose-shaped one Emma kept by her bed, the one that made her whole room glow pink as sunset, each plastic petal the intense shade of the floribunda buds in Emma's front yard. Then Miranda would snap off her own light and fall horizontal onto her covers and close her eyes.

Somehow, on difficult nights, it was easier to find sleep if she pretended both of them were looking for it at the same time.

Miranda pushed the subject elsewhere. "Was this your project?"

Emma surveyed her volcano with a wrinkled brow. "Yep. All those hours painting these dumb little palm trees by hand, and Howard only gave me a B."

"Everyone knows Howard is a beast," Alex said. "She never gives As. I made a lightbulb potato and she still docked me points for skipping a step in the scientific method."

"Which step?" Miranda asked.

"Hypothesis," she said. "Our brother did the same experiment when he was in her class, so it wouldn't be fair to guess what would happen, right? I already knew."

The girls laughed. Miranda laughed. Emma glanced at her, happy blue eyes lit up like a carnival sky.

Those eyes.

You can do this, Miranda told herself. She didn't know why Emma was speaking to her now, after all these months, why Emma was so smiley, so warm.

Don't mess this up. Don't do or say anything weird. Nothing like what Mom would say.

"What did you get?" Emma nudged Miranda and sent her heart into a tap dance.

"Um, a ninety-nine."

"Wow," the twins chorused.

A ninety-nine, she wanted to repeat. *As in missing one point.* Not a solid one hundred, Miranda's favorite number, the double zeroes like fat balloons full of air, the roundest, most perfect number in the grading system.

"What was your project?" Alex asked.

Miranda studied the way the blades of grass bent beneath Alex's sandal, the spiky shadows it made on the sidewalk. "Oh. Um, I tracked the spread of an invasive species of borer beetles through a neighborhood's trees."

The twins' jaws dropped. "No wonder!" Carmen said.

"Miranda's brilliant," Emma said.

Miranda glowed with the memory of what it was like

to hear someone say these things in this possessive way. To feel proud of your best friend's accomplishments, responsible for her triumphs, to be equal partners in every high and low of her life, like you have a growth. Like you have a *twin*.

"So you're like a real scientist," Carmen said. "Are you going to invent something?"

"Build a robot?" Alex said. "Discover a new dinosaur?"

"Maybe someday." There was no limit for a girl who cared so much about her ranking in the district-wide science fair that she charted the reproductive habits and egg sac locations of the beetles for six months. Yes, she started plotting her project last spring, while still in sixth grade. A preemptive strike for her application to the leadership camp, and, for anyone who happened to be looking, a chance to do the scientific method right. To show that she could do science the right way.

If you were going for perfect, you couldn't afford any practice shots. Perfect didn't believe in them.

Carmen said, "You should come over! We're making cookies."

"We live three blocks from here," Alex said. "Emma's coming, too."

Emma shifted the volcano in her arms and gave Miranda a ghost of a smile—but her eyes, Miranda noticed, were watching, hyperaware. Waiting.

Remembering.

"I can't." Sweat condensed in Miranda's armpits. "My—my mom's coming—"

"You said you were walking," Emma said gently, and Miranda's insides flailed.

For a politician, she sure was terrible at lying.

Carmen linked her arm through Miranda's. "Just call your mom when you get to our house."

The elbow crooked in hers made Miranda reel. Had it been this easy before, to make a friend?

"What do you say, Prez?" Emma was looking at her, right at her. Hope scratched against her rib cage.

It had been easy to lose a friend, too. Her brain regurgitated the image at her like a sip of foul vinegar:

Emma's face, the last time Miranda talked to her.

Emma's cheeks, bright as fire when she made her escape from Miranda's house.

Emma's steps down the porch reverberating in Miranda's ears long after Emma was gone.

Reality struck Miranda like a meteorite:

What are you doing? You can't go to their house. You can't go to anyone's house.

And no one can come to yours.

She made a big show of slapping her forehead. "I left something in my locker!"

"What?" Emma asked.

Miranda thought quickly. Lying to grown-ups was easy. They were so eager for you to say what they wanted to hear, they'd rearrange your words themselves if they had to.

But kids saw through you. The three pairs of eyes on Miranda made her feel as sheer as the wind.

"Student council stuff," she blurted. There. Nice and ambiguous. And true, if they wanted proof. "You—you guys go on ahead." Why were the words so hard to say? Why did they come with an aching in her throat, an unfairness in her chest? She wished, desperately, that she could be one of them. A normal girl, giggling with friends, gobbling up chocolate chip cookies, inviting people over on a whim. She wished she could be the kind of girl who says yes, who could go enjoy the normal bustle of some-one else's house.

But she would never be such a girl.

"Should we wait for you?" Alex said.

Emma was silent, but the expression on her face—the one that said *this is sad, but not surprising*—said every-thing for her.

"Uh, actually," Miranda said, "I might have a family thing."

And before the girls could spot the punctures in her lies—the way she wrenched her hands, like she was trying to remove them from her wrists—she turned and practi-cally ran back into the school, where she hid in the foyer and watched through the tinted windows as the girls walked away without looking back.

What if that was my chance?

What if she had been reaching out? Testing things? Opening a door?

What if there was a way—?

But Miranda was an expert at knowing when things were impossible.

A door had been shut—Miranda was the one who had shut it, and it would stay closed.

The secretary came through the foyer. "Miranda," she said, surprised. "Don't you have a ride?"

"My mom's on her way," Miranda said. To support her claim, she let the secretary walk her out of the school, back into the golden afternoon light; they paused together where the curb dropped off into the road.

The secretary shifted her purse against her body. "I can't leave until all you students are home."

Guilt crept into Miranda's bones. Her mother didn't actually know school ended at two forty-five. Her mother thought school ended at three thirty.

She thought it, because that's what time Miranda told her school ended.

That way the school was always empty when Miranda was picked up.

"She's running pretty late, isn't she?" The secretary stared out at the street, the sun's rays making ripples of the black asphalt, and Miranda fiddled with the edge of her shirt to keep her hands from migrating to her hair to yank out her guilt.

"Wait, what is that?" The secretary blocked the bright rays with a flat hand. "Is that . . . a dog?"

A vehicle cruised into the pickup lane—a huge, tan vehicle, a cross between a van and an RV. Cartoonish eyeballs circled the headlights; plastic antlers branched out from a dented roof rack. A pink tongue unfurled from the front bumper and dingy brown fringe dangled from the doors.

This was why she couldn't go with Emma.

This, and a million reasons just as hairy and embarrassing.

Miranda screwed her mouth into a tight little pucker, putting away her smile for the day. "That's my mom."

3.

The Critter Mobile was missing one of its hubcaps. It still wore the crusty mud of last month's trip through Jackson Hole—hot on the trail of the borophagus, a hyena-dog hybrid rumored to prowl the shores of Wyoming's lakes. All they'd found was beached carp and trash.

A collection of bumper stickers coated the cargo carrier on the Critter Mobile's roof, overlapping one another in a veritable map of the vehicle's travels: YELLOWSTONE NATIONAL PARK. ARCHES—BEEN THERE, DONE THAT. EVERGLADES—LIVE FOR THE ADVENTURE!

Front and center, above the license plate, was the white I BELIEVE sticker, like an emblem.

"Where were you?" Miranda asked through the open window.

Her mother held up her brick of a cell phone. "I'm sorry, Bean, I lost track of time. Phone died."

"Then charge it." Miranda glanced back at the school. The secretary still stood there, squinting at the van—*What are you waiting for?* she thought. *Go home.*

"I can't find my charger."

Miranda deposited her backpack on the bench behind her, then pointed at the sign of a left-facing arrow with a red slash through it. ONE WAY. DROP-OFF OR PICKUP ONLY. "You're not supposed to drive this way."

"We're fine," her mother said. "That's just a formality."

"It's really not." Miranda's quiet reply was lost in the noises of the Critter Mobile: the fart sound of the captain's seat as she sat down, the screech of the door slamming shut, the sinister whistling in the undercarriage as her mother pulled away from the curb.

Miranda bent way over, out of sight, pretending to fix her sandal; the Critter Mobile always took a few minutes to accelerate, which meant they slunk past the busy soccer fields with the pace and energy of a parade float, scraggly brown fringe blowing in their exhaust.

Kat, Miranda's mother, tossed a handful of spicy Funyuns into her mouth with one hand and operated the long, sticky gear shift with the other. "How was school, Bean?"

"Good."

"Any big tests coming up?"

Miranda waited until they passed the edge of the school's grassy acreage before she answered. "We just had midterms."

"How'd you do?" Kat asked.

"Fine."

The Critter Mobile's driver-side mirror had suffered a fatal injury in the Ozarks last summer, so Kat had to stretch tall and arch around her headrest to see behind her when changing lanes. She did so now, and Miranda watched her, holding her breath. They were technically the same size, but Miranda always thought of her mother as shorter, smaller. Kat added bulk to her frame with sheer, floral-printed flowing robes—capes, Miranda called them, and Kat would argue, "Capes don't have sleeves, Bean. These are capelettes." As if Miranda should not only understand the various kingdoms and phyla of cryptids and monsters, but also demonstrate a working knowledge of the classification of capes, capelettes, robes, dusters, sweaters, and such.

With Kat twisted so, Miranda took in the full effect of her mother's hairstyle. Kat's long black hair was braided two ways: a huge fat braid down one side of her head, and six little snaky braids on the other side, sparkly lavender ribbons woven through the strands.

Miranda worked with other students' mothers all the time. They came to PTA meetings, they volunteered for assemblies, they chaperoned dances—

35

To-do list, she quickly typed while the thought was as fresh in her mind as wet ink:

Confirm that Hannah's mother ordered the linens for the Fall Fling refreshment tables

She loved how those moms dressed—casually in comfortable jeans and T-shirts, or in suburban-mom cardigan sets, or in tailored pants and blazers if they came straight from work. Their purses were subtle, their shoes practical, their haircuts symmetrical. Miranda always wanted to stare, wanted to drink in every detail.

Between Kat's flowery capes, her wild accessories (today's earrings were glittering white unicorns with jeweled lilac stars for eyes), and the giant silver-rimmed glasses that magnified her eyes to gargantuan proportions, Miranda often felt she was being raised by a wispy, human-size butterfly.

"Guess who I talked to today?" Kat said.

Miranda replied on autopilot, "Who?"

"Uncle Bob."

Uncle Bob was not Miranda's uncle.

Kat started calling him that years ago, but he wasn't related to any of the Chos. Bob was one of her mother's colleagues—or the closest thing Kat had to colleagues. He was a pale, perspiring, balding, middle-aged man who kept a portable metal detector on his belt and was a close talker. When Miranda thought of their meetings with him over the years, the memories came along with the scents of the things he'd eaten most recently—microwave taquitos, cheesesteak, onion rings.

"There was a Bigfoot sighting in Washington today," Kat went on. "In Olympic National Park. At the falls in Fable Forest, early this morning. A couple of honeymooners spotted him across the reservoir—full corporeal sighting. Red eyes and everything! He lumbered back into the rain forest before they could get their cameras."

Energy leached from Miranda's body as her mother spoke. Another week, another Bigfoot sighting—and, Miranda thought with new alarm, another trip. Another absence.

She could not miss any more school. She couldn't.

No matter what a pair of bored backpackers thought they had seen.

"Oh, don't worry, Bean," Kat soothed her daughter, misinterpreting her frown. "No photo means it'll stay hush-hush for now—the last thing we want is for *Bigfoot Bozos* to catch wind." She put on a war face. "Someone's going to get him on film one of these days, and it's not going to be them."

Bigfoot Bozos was a reality show in the style of nature documentaries, filming Bigfoot researchers out in the wild. They flew around the country and captured it all: Bigfoot hunters sniffing the dirt for traces of the beast's alleged sulfuric body odor. Bigfoot hunters sitting in lawn chairs for hours at a time with binoculars glued to their eyes, eating cold beans from a can while waiting for the Squatch himself to prance through camp. Editors compiled the footage and added music and sound effects, making the cryptozoologists look maximally ridiculous.

To Kat, the show made a mockery of everything she stood for.

To Miranda, the show was the punchline to the joke she was living.

Kat moved on from the alleged Fable Forest sighting to the latest conference presentations on Bigfoot's post-summer migration patterns to Uncle Bob's theory about Bigfoot's electrosensory abilities — "Just like sharks!" — and she didn't stop talking.

She was still talking when the Critter Mobile lurched into the driveway of their humble single-story house. Miranda got out of the car and shut the door, and still her mother talked, hands waving so energetically she honked the horn by accident.

Miranda followed the sidewalk down to the mailbox, all the while keeping an eye on Emma's house across the street. Emma's garage was open, the curtains drawn — if Miranda didn't know for certain that Emma was currently with the twins, she wouldn't have risked walking outside at all.

What if they decided to come to Emma's house instead?

But she had to check the mail.

It could be today.

She prepared herself and opened the mailbox.

Nothing. So not today.

No mail yesterday, either. Or the day before.

Miranda kept her face steady in case—just in case—someone could see her. In case Emma had already made it home and was watching from her bedroom window.

Inside, though, Miranda roiled.

No news about her leadership camp, positive or negative.

She wanted to know.

A quartet of terra-cotta lawn gnomes stood on their porch—much beloved by Kat, much endured by Miranda.

She kind of hated those gnomes.

It was unsettling, how easy it was to hate things lately. How she'd become quick to the drawing of scorn, swift to be stirred up over things which, not so long ago, had delighted her.

"Hello, Clarence," Kat said, shaking the hand of the bespectacled gnome with the daisies in his beard. "Fine afternoon."

Miranda went inside before Kat started responding for the inanimate lawn ornaments; she couldn't stand the sound of her mother doing a wizened old gnome voice.

A habitat provides clues to the creatures it contains; it cites what foods sustain them, how they spend the darkest, starriest hours, what they do to bathe and wash and keep their skin or hair or scales or fur neat. Careful observation of such a habitat—a collecting of details—could tell you so much about the animals who called it home.

So then this was the Cho household:

Every wall but one was covered over in photos, in maps, in artifacts from their travels. Every spare surface displayed something that had been clawed from the earth or hewn from its slumber in a bog or cut from a tree. A wiry white hair in a glass case (its owner, Kat insisted, a snow Yeti). A yellow femur hanging above a photograph of the Chos in Florida (the bone belonging, Kat would have explained to queriers, to a skunk ape). A segment of petrified tentacle ("a giant freshwater octopus fossil!" Kat called it; "a common prehistoric squid," Miranda argued) on the coffee table beside a stack of obscure wildlife magazines.

Centered on the mantel was a hulking footprint—plaster and rock and embedded twigs. An impression of the first print Kat had ever found. Other mothers kept photos of their children above the fireplace.

One wall of the living room was covered in rainbow splatters of oil paint. On a random, wine-soaked Friday, Kat had forgone ordering dinner and instead started this mural, but abandoned it by midnight, before it could ever become anything other than paint slop. It was still there, a rough, thick layer of abstract clouds and nonsense shapes.

"That part kind of looks like a tail," Kat would sometimes say. "Maybe it wants to be a lizard." As if globs of oil had ambitions.

Miranda knew it would never be anything but a mess.

Another of her mother's projects that would never be completed.

Kat set her keys on the counter and turned to her daughter. "I'm going to update my blog. Do you want to—?"

"I have homework." Miranda said. "Can I use the laptop first?" She was already down the hall, closing her bedroom door when she heard her mother say, "Okay, Bean."

The habitat that was Miranda's bedroom was one of bare white walls, well-dusted crown moldings, and plain blue curtains left to hang beside their window. No posters, no photos, no trinkets. Furniture was utilitarian. The desk was aseptic, a lone history book open.

An environment clean of distractions—but even so, its inhabitant was distracted.

If she tilted her head, Miranda could see the hydrangeas in Emma's front yard, the corner of Emma's roof, the checkerboard lines in Emma's freshly mowed yard. All of them familiar details, recalled in blank moments as Miranda walked to school on dark mornings, between sentences on English essays, before she fell asleep.

Details of a former life.

Miranda could have picked this apart all evening. She wrestled with the idea of calling her, leaving her a message, retracting her earlier excuses, inviting her over. Letting her see Miranda like this.

In her habitat, exposed.

Letting Emma see Kat again. Introducing the two properly, crossing her fingers that it wasn't too much—that Emma would see the footprint above the fireplace, and the assortment of antlers in the garden window, and the speckled eggs in the freezer, and decide to stay.

But Miranda drew her curtains and unzipped her backpack.

She opened the laptop. As its screen warmed and brightened, she checked the number of homework assignments she needed to complete (four) and rechecked the due dates for all of them (tomorrow).

Four assignments. Then she could do it.

She cracked open her notebook and, making sure the volume on the laptop was low, started an episode of *Bigfoot Bozos.*

Kat could never know, but Miranda binge-watched the show. She'd seen every episode.

"My pa saw a squatch when he was my age," a man with a neckbeard was saying, "and his pa saw one, too." He sniffed. "Guess I was just born to believe."

A shaky camera panned an ambiguous forest, then the lime green flash of night-vision goggles, and the logo sprawled across the screen, the *B* in *Bigfoot* shaped like a footprint.

And then the man launched into his list of evidence, all of it limp, and Miranda's laugh was freeing. These same things had been uttered here, under this very roof, multiple times, and they sounded as porous and outlandish from the neckbearded believer as they did coming from the woman in the "I Kissed the Jersey Devil (and I Liked It)" shirt in the kitchen.

This was why she watched it. For catharsis. The show was the closest thing she had to a confidant.

"Everyone keeps telling me I'm wasting my time out here," the man said, "but I know he's out there."

"How?" the interviewer prompted. "How do you know?"

The man shrugged. "I always trust my gut. And my gut believes."

Miranda looked up from her notebook and studied the screen, the swift cutaway to a snarl of overgrown branches and thickets of green and moss and leaves. For a moment it focused on a particular mass, a clump of something in the corner of the trees.

Miranda hit pause.

She stared.

A shadow.

She played it again, and the camera whipped past the shadow to the man. His sweaty-lipped, "Over there! I saw it near them bushes!" had Miranda snorting, rolling her eyes, and scanning her history study guide for the best possible entry point.

4.

You need something, Bean?"

Miranda hovered in the kitchen. Her hands wanted very much to pull out a hair—just one, to settle her dancing nerves. She'd worked for nearly three hours, finishing her assignments and whittling the day's to-do list down to this one last item:

Talk to Mom

She searched for the right words; they flitted away like shy moths in the dark.

Kat was sorting artifacts—when she had too many of one kind of object to store in their house, she sold them on her blog. She finished wrapping the dried scales of a North Atlantic furred trout skin in tissue paper and looked at her daughter.

Miranda cleared her throat. "I was thinking—" The doorbell rang, and her heart kicked against her chest as if it had grown feet.

What if it's Emma?

What if she's ready to be friends again?

What if she's ready to forget what happened?

But Kat came into the kitchen with a long white package.

"It's here!" Out of a snowstorm of packing peanuts Kat lifted something that could only be described as a Contraption. "Do you know what this is?"

Of course I don't, Miranda answered wearily in her mind, *but I'll bet you're going to tell me.*

"This is a scanning pulse detector: part radar, part video recorder." She positioned the thing on her shoulder and aimed at the fridge. "Trust me, if a creature walks past, this thing will catch it one way or another. Isn't it amazing, Bean? Someone on *Bigfoot Files* recommended it."

Every one of her mother's words was a tentacle, covered in suckers, reaching out, feeling for human contact—and it made Miranda want to fold in half, limb and hair, and hide beneath a rock.

"And this," Kat said as she unwrapped a stainless-steel canister, "is for scat samples . . ."

Miranda's attention drifted like flotsam, wandering to the fridge where a printed article hung on a cheeseburger magnet: "Patterson-Gimlin's Bigfoot, Fifty Years Later: The Real Deal, Or Gorilla Suit Hoax?"

Another paper was below it, a newspaper clipping yellowed with age—it might be older than Miranda—about the sighting of a leather-winged, long-beaked prehistoric-looking bird in the Rio Grande Valley, silhouetted against a flaxen harvest moon.

If Kat was correct, the whole world was full of creatures and mysteries and magical things, around us all the time. Things most people couldn't—or wouldn't—see. *Who knew so many of us were blind?* Miranda thought.

She used to think it, too, or something similar. Miranda remembered when she would wake up every day seeing sparkles in the corners of her eye, when she would walk with her hands open and loose because she knew, any second, a falling star could land in her palm. A time when she would check outside every window, behind every tree, and peek into every backyard—just in case. Just in case she caught a glimpse of something that no one else saw.

Kat still held the contraption, as proud as if she'd birthed it herself. "I can't wait to try it this weekend."

"This weekend?" Miranda said.

"Olympic National Park, remember, Bean?" Kat tested all the buttons on her new gadgets. "We're going to find Bigfoot."

And then the right words gushed from Miranda's mouth. "Mom? About this weekend—I'm not coming."

46

Stars belonged in dreams and in doodles and in night skies. Miranda's hands clenched into fists now, tight enough to crush and smother a star even if it dropped into her palm like rain.

Kat filled a mason jar with water and lifted it to her succulents in the garden window—plants renowned for being easy to keep alive, and yet Kat killed a new batch every year. "I know it seems like we just got home, but this could be it." Her eyes twinkled behind her teacup-round glasses. "Uncle Bob's in Tahoe with the Tessie crew. He won't be able to break away, not for days—so it'll just be us. Just you and me, Bean."

Beneath Miranda's skin, her blood sizzled. "Mom, no." She breathed in. "I cannot miss any more school. I've already missed so much!" Ten days, Ms. Palmer had said, a number that still made Miranda's breath snag in her throat.

"We haven't been gone that much—" Kat started, but Miranda held out her fingers and counted.

"Sharlie in Idaho. The Mothman back east. Arkansas for the Howler." Miranda listed every trip they'd taken since summer vacation had ended until she wiggled seven fingers. "Seven trips, Mom. Plus all the driving time, there and back—that's ten whole days of school I've missed. I haven't even made up my late work from Ohio."

Kat considered it. "They'll just have to miss you for a few more days. It's not like you're skipping school for

Disneyland—this is a major scientific discovery, Bean! It's been months since there's been a sighting with such specifics, and this is a new site for us. A real rain forest. It's the perfect habitat for a humanoid creature: freshwater rivers and valleys and high ground—"

"We never find anything!" Miranda burst in. "No matter where we go, it's always the same. It's footprints, footprints, footprints."

"Not true!" her mother crowed. "What about Tennessee? We found the hair of an Appalachian black panther!"

"That was dog hair," Miranda said.

"Quit being such a cynic—as soon as Bob finishes the DNA analysis, we'll know what it really was."

Miranda instinctively tuned her mother out. The DNA analysis would come back with the same results that all the others had: zero evidence of the existence of any new species.

DNA was real science, and in real science, if the facts don't match the hypothesis, you didn't throw out the facts—you made a new hypothesis. You adjusted. You rearranged, you took new observations and tried again. Real science freed itself of all expectations, sorting the evidence as it came.

Which is why Kat would never be a real scientist.

"If I miss any more school, they'll drop my credit for this term," Miranda informed her mother.

"All right." Kat said, taking in her daughter's sullen face. "We'll slow down after this trip. Weekends only—no more absences after tomorrow. And Monday. And possibly Tuesday, and that'll be the last time you miss school—unless we need Wednesday, too. But it'll be worth it, Bean. It'll all be worth it when we find one."

Miranda knew there was no point in bringing up the leadership camp, no point in explaining to Kat that her work trips dangled over the camp like an ax on a string—Kat couldn't comprehend that anything was as important as Bigfoot. She probably thought Miranda could brag about it at school, convince her science teacher to let these trips count as extra credit.

And then this obsession of Kat's, this fixation on creatures mysterious and unknowable—it would billow and strangle and burn everything else in their lives—it had already taken Emma.

Miranda wasn't going to let it take anything else.

"No." She was surprised to hear how quietly it came out; she found she didn't need volume to make her point. Instead she found the old anger, rising like a storm within her—and the more she concentrated on this word *no*, the more powerful she felt. She could topple thousand-year-old trees, she could grind the Critter Mobile into axles and rubber and metallic mulch, she could blow away the whole Fable Forest, shadows and waterfalls and Bigfoot and all—but she would not go on this trip.

The leadership camp, she thought, and it was a beacon in the swirling madness. Anything to get into the camp. Anything to break free from Bigfoot, from this weird house cluttered with fake artifacts and oversteeped dreams.

Free from her mother.

Kat pretended to be wounded. "Other kids would be thrilled to have a mom who lets them miss school for trips around the country."

Miranda resisted a snort. What did her mother know about other kids?

What did she even know about this one?

"I'm not other kids," she finally said.

Her mother exhaled. "All right, Bean. I'm not sure who you can stay with — Uncle Bob is still out of town —"

"I'm twelve years old," Miranda said. "I'm old enough to take care of myself."

Kat shook her head. "This isn't one evening watching a movie alone with a pizza. This is a whole weekend. Maybe longer."

"I'll go to sleep at a decent time," Miranda vowed, "and I won't make any messes or watch anything trashy. *Please.* I can't miss any more school."

As Kat regarded her daughter, the daylight from the living room hit her unicorn earrings, making them gleam. Making their purple eyes sparkle, almost like they were alive — to anyone else they would have seemed alive. To Miranda they were just the gaudy details of the biggest wound in her life. "Promise me, Bean," her mother said, "that you'll make at least one mess, okay? Blow up a potato in the microwave or something. And only let three teenage boys over at a time—they'll eat all my Funyuns."

Miranda spared her mother half a smile. "Your Funyuns are safe with me," she said, holding back a high-pitched glee because she'd won—she'd won!

No trudging through yet another national park, which should be a sublime experience, a chance to celebrate the natural heritage of the country—but was always ruined when they spent the whole time tracking cryptids. No crawling through grime and mud to spy, for hours, on a watering hole that's deader than the school halls after the bell, no pretending to be excited about bushes that appeared to be trampled in a very specific way. No footprints or stray hairs or errant growls in the twilight.

No disappointment.

"Indian okay for dinner?" her mother asked.

"Yes. Good. Anything you want." Miranda went back into her bedroom, where she shut the door and promptly leaped onto the bed, mouthing, "Yes!" silently, so Kat wouldn't hear her celebrating the first time she'd ever successfully turned her back on Bigfoot.

When Miranda was finished gloating, she went back to the laptop.

She had finished her homework, accomplished all of

today's pressing matters on her to-do list, and cleared up the situation with her mother.

Now. Now she could do it.

A nightly ritual, she logged into her e-mail and, with a prickly breath, hit enter.

No new messages.

Her father had given her a cologne-spiced hug and a dry kiss on the forehead when she was five, and then he had left.

Miranda had asked her mother where he was once, maybe two years ago. (She already knew the answer; she'd used the Internet to follow his migration from their home state to the smoggy, hilly San Francisco Bay region. But she wanted specifics, painted details—where he was, how, and why.) Kat offered a vague, "He's . . . somewhere else, Bean. Not here. Isn't that all that matters?" Then she had quickly and clumsily switched the subject to Mongolian death worms.

The divorce had been swift. Void of drama. When it happened, Miranda tried to collect details of the proceedings, but she was too young. Too young to gather the information she wanted—all she knew was that the court had awarded Kat full custody and then her dad had slipped away like a fish in a stream.

"I'll come back." That's what he'd said, in their driveway, when he'd knelt down in the rain to give her a kiss. He hadn't cried, so she hadn't, either.

Wasn't that all she needed to know? He hadn't cried.

If he had been saying good-bye forever, he would have cried.

All this time, and she was still waiting.

So two years ago when Kat's *Bigfoot Files* blog had become successful enough that she needed to maintain it daily, at home, instead of walking to the library, she finally invested in a laptop. Miranda hadn't even waited twenty-four hours before she took the computer when Kat was asleep and searched for her father, safe in the blackest hours of the night, safe in her room.

Safe with the "delete all history" function.

There he was, the very first hit, his name in bold beneath a photo—head tilted back, a laugh uncurling, sleek leather jacket.

Miranda felt like she was seeing herself for the first time. People regularly called her a miniature version of her mother, but she didn't think it was accurate. Surely a person's appearance was more than just their physical traits; surely their internal attributes bled out onto their skin, shaped their faces, shaped their countenances?

In which case Kat and Miranda should look like strangers—and that was how Miranda thought of her lately. A stranger who may have given birth to her, but was her polar opposite in every way.

Her father was a mirror—Miranda saw her own reflection every time she saw his face.

On that night she had peeked at his website, his social media links, trying to act like all of her clicks were accidents, slips, stumbles down the virtual rabbit hole.

He was part of a start-up business—an IT management company with funding from Apple—and he had recently relocated to California because "this is the neighborhood to be in if you want amazing things to happen," he said in the article she knew by heart now.

Memories of her father were crisp only around the edges—soft and soggy in the days and times and years, but sharp in the specifics. She could remember flashes of him:

His hands, long, rough fingers with half-moon nails and a scar on one knuckle, she forgot which.

His space in their garage, where he stored his tools.

His smell, bracing and spicy.

Parts of his voice were fuzzy in her mind—she hadn't been able to find any video or audio of him speaking—but his face . . . it was a somber version of her own, her dark eyes reverberations of his.

Insignificant details, perhaps; it was all she had of him. She hoarded those details like rubies.

Miranda couldn't pinpoint why, exactly, she had written a message to him that night. One moment she was staring at his e-mail address, wondering how she could ever summon the courage to reach out, to uncurl a tentacle—the next, she was hitting send.

Maybe he collects details, too, she had thought. *Maybe he wishes he had details about me.*

For two years now she'd been sending him e-mails — updates on her school life, a celebratory (and subtly bragging) message when she won her big election, random tidbits from her best homework assignments.

Every week, after particularly long and difficult days when the items on her to-do list were self-replicating and her head was filled with the black smoke of a grinding, overworked engine, she would do this — she would carefully, mindfully complete the things she needed to complete.

She would close herself in her room.

Then, in her most hallowed, protected routine, she would open her e-mail, and she would write, and she would tell him how hard she worked, every day, in case that was the type of thing that would make him proud.

There were plenty of things she didn't tell him. How she would give an arm and an ear to get into that leadership camp. How she would give an arm and an ear to get a reply from him.

How she would give an arm and an ear to know when he was coming back.

She never mentioned anything about her mother, or Uncle Bob, or the cryptozoology madness that now infected her life like a pox — the tiny, harmless hobby of Kat's that had snowballed into an entire lifestyle. Just snippets of what his daughter was like now that she was ten. Eleven. Twelve.

Snippets of what he was missing.

Her entire body deflated now, as she stared at her empty inbox.

He'd never written back. Not once.

Kat didn't know this, but right before he left, Miranda had had a dream.

She and her father were in a forest at night, the trees tall and thick as skyscrapers, darkness pressing violently against the leaves, crowding the two of them. She walked between the trees, holding hands with her father, and then suddenly he was gone. Vanished. She cried out for him, but she was alone, and spent the rest of her dream running in every direction, lost, spiraling deeper and deeper into the trees and the shadows.

If she were the type of person who believed in such things, she might consider the dream a premonition, a hint from the universe that someone was about to step out of her life.

But Miranda was no such person.

It was only a dream.

Her father hadn't left *her;* he'd just left.

"I'll come back."

Two years without a reply, and yet. Yet she still believed—

"Bean?" Kat knocked with one knuckle.

56

Miranda slammed the laptop closed.

"I'm going to Bombay House," Kat said through the door. "Be back in twenty."

"Okay."

"Unless you want to come." The doorknob twisted.

"No," Miranda said, a bit louder than necessary. "I've got stuff to do."

"All right, Bean."

Miranda counted her mother's steps away from her door, counted the seconds between the Critter Mobile's squeaky, abrasive ignition and the graceless squeal of Kat riding the tires hard, and then she typed out a new message. A new update. A new tentacle.

And then she deleted the history.

Somewhere, deep inside of her, there was still a filament of light, a thrumming heartbeat.

Somewhere, deep inside of her, she still believed.

5.

There was always more to be done.

Even though Miranda had already accomplished more today than most of her peers (and many adults) did in a week, there were other to-do lists, other plans. If she wasn't ahead, she was behind—and if she could get the itineraries for her student council meeting tomorrow printed and stapled, then she might be ahead.

Out in the living room she opened the desk drawer where Kat usually kept the stapler, but it was empty.

Not empty, but full of silverware.

Forks, butter knives, and a long iced-tea spoon.

Miranda sighed. It was a daily occurrence in the Cho household, to come across such wildly displaced items — Miranda would reach for bread and find a pair of Kat's clean folded underwear instead. (The loaf of bread would be carefully tucked into Kat's dresser, along with the saltshaker and the TV remote.)

She'd even witnessed her mother do it — wander through the house with her hands full of laundry or groceries, and somehow lose everything during the span of one conversation, setting things in cupboards and baskets and onto shelves. It was a marvel, Miranda often thought, that Kat hadn't ever misplaced her own daughter.

Miranda gathered the silverware in a bouquet and headed to the kitchen. There, in the cutlery drawer, was the stapler, along with a toothbrush and a bundle of mail.

"So here's where she's been stashing it," Miranda muttered, flipping through the envelopes, and then chills ran down her back.

What if my acceptance letter is in here?

What if my rejection *letter is in here?*

But each letter in the stack of mail was addressed to her mother.

She let her eyes run over the words on the envelopes: KATERINA CHO, URGENT! PLEASE RESPOND! FINAL NOTICE! FINAL ATTEMPT! The words were stamped on every single envelope in red, bright as blood.

And every envelope was unopened.

Her stomach clenched.

Those were not good words.

She glanced out the living room window. No giant panting van-dog in the driveway, not yet.

And so she slid all the mail out of the drawer and took it into her room, where she tore it open, every stitch of it—opening someone else's mail was definitely illegal, but what if the person who it belonged to would never, ever open it, because she was allergic to responsibility?

They were all bills, statements, notices for their phones, their water, their electricity, everything.

Then she spotted the letter that stopped her breathing altogether.

NOTICE OF FORECLOSURE.

Foreclosure.

They were going to lose the house?

Miranda felt as if a bag of stones had been tied around her neck, and every time she read another statement, a new stone fell in. How long had it been since Kat had made a payment on anything? The numbers in bold at the top of each page were massive, almost imaginary; Miranda couldn't picture those numbers being converted into real money.

Money.

When was the last time Kat had had money?

Heavier and heavier . . .

A week ago she'd dragged Miranda to Ohio for a creature hunt—an unsuccessful one—but they didn't earn any money from that trip. The week before, it had been

Wyoming—and again, they'd come back empty-handed.

"Not empty-handed, Bean!" Miranda could practically hear her mother defend the broken piece of shell they'd found on the shore of Lake DeSmet, which Kat believed was a molten fragment of Smetty, a giant invertebrate that swam in the lake's briny depths.

A shell which, if Miranda remembered, Kat sold on her blog for a decent amount of cash—and only yesterday she'd sold a wedge of white cartilage rumored to be the beak of an ivory-billed woodpecker.

But it was the only recent income of Kat's that Miranda knew of. She hadn't been booked for a keynote address or a lecture at a cryptozoology conference in a long time, maybe six months. That meant most of their trips this year had been one hundred percent self-funded by the revenue Kat received from the advertisements she hosted on *The Bigfoot Files* and the handful of cryptozoology e-books she'd published.

Miranda shuffled through the open mail. Here were Kat's royalty earnings—she put out a book twice a year, and had just released a new one—eighty dollars and fourteen cents.

Eighty dollars!

Eighty dollars was a tiny fraction of the amount needed to sustain a living, let alone satiate all those bill collectors.

Eighty dollars wasn't even enough for groceries.

Another stone around Miranda's neck.

And here, in the stack of mail, was a letter from the Conklin University grant fund, loyal patrons of Kat's cryptozoology research for the last three years:

Dear Katerina Cho,

We are sorry to inform you that the selection committee is unable to provide funding for your project at this time.

A rejection.

No research grant for her mother this year.

And here, a credit card statement:

Miranda's eyes boggled. Were there supposed to be that many zeroes?

Stone after stone, heavy enough to pull her under . . .

Her head swam, her shoulders groaned. All those numbers, the words, the bold print, the red ink — how was Kat paying for anything? How were they surviving?

What if someone from the bank comes and kicks us out of the house?

What if we lose the house and we have to live in the Critter Mobile?

The car was the only thing Kat owned outright.

What if everyone at school sees me in that car? What if they find out about Mom?

Another stone.

What if Mom sees this nightmare as a blessing in disguise? What if she's foaming at the mouth to pull me out of school and monster hunt full-time? Taking the country state by state? Beast by beast? With nothing to tie us down, what's to stop her?

The stones around her neck piled high, enough to dam a rushing river.

And then, creeping, wormlike, a worse thought:

What about the leadership camp?

If her mother couldn't afford the house payment, there was no way she could afford to send Miranda to her camp.

If she got in.

Miranda yanked out hair after hair as she stared at her blank wall; her mind had overheated and now it spiraled, lost.

What was she going to do? How was she going to fix this?

A screech, and a bang. Miranda jumped.

The Critter Mobile was back.

She straightened the stack of bills still in her hand.

"Dinner!" Kat called. "Come get it before it's reheated mush!"

"Be right there!" Miranda hid the mail beneath her pillow and joined her mother at the counter, a hollow smile screwed carefully into place even though her heart still hammered like a windup toy. Until she knew how to solve this, she wouldn't let Kat know she'd found the secret stash of unpaid bills—not until she had a plan.

Her vow of silence was irrelevant; the second the takeout containers were open, Kat did all the talking.

"A new kind of radar," she explained with samosa in her mouth. "Uncle Bob found the machine in a dumpster behind a library and rigged it up. Isn't that wild? One man's trash . . ."

Dumpster diving—that was a new low, even for Bob, Miranda thought, and nearly said it. But then the words flashed in her mind: NOTICE OF FORECLOSURE.

What if we have to go dumpster diving soon?

Miranda kept waiting for a spot in the conversation to open, like a sad carnival game—wait for the spinning wheel, throw the dart, pop the balloon, win the stuffed frog. But she had eaten every bite of her curried potatoes before Kat finally stopped her verbal waterfall, kissed her daughter's cheek, and went to pack her camping gear.

Miranda hovered in the kitchen, wiping the smear of sauce from Kat's empty place at the counter with a rag.

Thoughts of her homework were gone; thoughts of her student council duties, gone. Thoughts of the Fall Fling, important though it was, gone. Her absences, the black marks on her attendance record, gone. The leadership camp flickered in her mind, fading, vanishing—and white-hot frustration blinded her.

How could her mother do this? Ignore the bills, let the overdue amounts stack up like moldy old garbage on a back stoop? What kind of grown-up let things fester like this? How could Kat be so irresponsible?

And how could she do this *to Miranda*? That leadership

camp had been the sun in Miranda's mornings, the sugar in her cereal—the very thing that pushed her through classes and schoolwork and student council responsibilities, even when she felt like she couldn't do it anymore. It had been her beacon on Kat's creature hunts: *Make it through this trip,* Miranda would coach herself during particularly dark moments, *so you can go to your camp. Your camp will save you.*

And now, because of Kat's ridiculous monster chasing, her inability to let this obsession with Bigfoot go, Miranda would have to be the one to let something go. She'd have to give up her leadership camp, see it fly away, off to some other overachiever, and her escape route out of this house—out of this hairy, musky life—would be blocked.

Had her mom even thought of that?

Outside, Kat was unrolling the tent, shaking out stale leaves left from its last sojourn as she sang under her breath.

Miranda stood among the gnomes on the porch, thinking.

The sun was on the edge of the hills, balanced there like a coin. The shadows in their yard stretched themselves taller, almost like hands running from the light.

"Mom?" Miranda said. "About my leadership camp..." She swallowed, her throat dry as bark. Was she ready to hear the answer *no*?

"What about it?" Kat staked the tent in the lawn and crawled inside.

"Can I still do it?"

"Of course." Her mother sounded far away from inside the blue canvas. Kat popped her head out of the tent. "Bean, did you get in?"

"Not yet." Miranda slung and unslung her foot from her sandal, over and over.

"Help me for a sec?" Kat gestured for Miranda to hold up the A-frame while she tightened the lines. Miranda stepped down from the porch and into the grass. "I just wanted to make sure we can still afford it."

Kat frowned. "What do you mean?"

A swarm of evening aphids danced around their feet. "It costs a thousand dollars, remember?"

The quiet seemed to stretch as long as the shadows before Kat answered.

"Yes, Bean. Not a problem." Her mother sounded so cheerful, so assured, Miranda was almost convinced.

She went back inside and shut herself in her room.

What was she going to do?

6.

The evening slowly drained like a pierced fruit. Miranda stayed in her bedroom under the pretense of working on math; instead she shuffled through the bills and statements again and again—the saddest hand of cards she'd ever seen, and Kat would have to play them soon.

Kat was drowning in bills and credit card debt—and so certainly the tuition for Miranda's leadership camp would be impossible. No camp. And also no food, no Internet, no electricity, and no house.

Miranda had to solve this. She had to.

Miranda got out a fresh yellow legal pad. She still had the laptop, but she saved writing longhand for her most serious work, and this was serious. **OPTIONS**, she wrote at the top in big bold letters with her fattest black marker and underlined it.

OPTION ONE.

She tapped the marker's cap against her chin as she thought.

Option one, she decided, was to call the bill collectors directly and ask them for more time. She wrote it down, but it didn't seem a fruitful choice, given the intensity of the red stamps on all those envelopes. FINAL NOTICE, FORECLOSURE, FAILURE TO PAY—those weren't words used by companies who were in the mood to be merciful.

Option two. She wrote, **DO NOTHING**. Let the house go. Let the bank take it back, and figure out a new place for them to live—hopefully somewhere other than the Critter Mobile. Miranda didn't feel desperate enough for this option—not yet—but she knew it belonged on the list. If there was nothing to be done, it would be easier if it felt like it had been a choice.

Option three. **BORROW MONEY**, she wrote.

Not the most responsible action in the world, but an option that adults succumbed to when times were tough.

But who could they borrow money from? Another bank? She knew loans existed, but she had no idea how one actually went about getting one. Plus, she couldn't imagine a bank would be eager to give them money when Kat had this paper mill's worth of final notices.

They'd be better off asking someone they knew.

Uncle Bob?

Miranda wasn't supposed to know this, but Bob had a tax debt from a failed ghost-hunting business he'd started with his first wife. He wouldn't have any extra money to loan; he pinched pennies like a crab.

Uncle Bob was out, then. And that was it. There were no other friends. No family.

Well, that wasn't completely true. Her mother did have some family.

Miranda's grandmother lived in northern California, but she and Kat didn't talk. Not anymore. Not since they built a wall of a silence between them, years ago, after some disagreement—Miranda didn't know details, but it had been enough to burn it all down. They didn't even see her for Christmas anymore.

What if I ask her for help and she says no?

What if she doesn't even remember me?

Miranda fiddled with her marker cap.

What if I ask her for help . . . and she says yes?

Miranda wrote down Grandma Hai's name as an option, followed it with a giant question mark.

She couldn't remember much about her grandmother, only the look of her—a taller, older, more tired version of her mother—and the scents of her house: citrus slices in a cast-iron teapot, first-edition books, dried lavender hanging in the window. Besides those few memories, Grandma

Hai only existed in the rare photographs of little-kid Kat that resurfaced in a junk drawer every now and then, or from random recollections from Kat's childhood—if it was an anecdote with Grandma Hai in a leading role, Kat usually mentioned her with a disdain thick enough to frost a cake with.

But still. Miranda always got a birthday card with a crisp ten-dollar bill from Grandma Hai. She'd never missed a year. She had to be considered as an option.

Right now, she was Miranda's only option.

Outside, Kat had put away the pup tent and was now loading crates into the Critter Mobile's back hatch: nets, ropes, other creature-catching equipment. Miranda watched through the bay window, making sure her mother was fully occupied, then searched through her mother's phone until she found the number.

She then dialed on her own phone with trembling fingers.

"Hello?" The voice that answered was sharp, the sound of a grandmother who believed in the value of a dime, who baked cookies from scratch because she trusted the work, a grandmother who didn't easily forgive an unpressed collar. Or was Miranda already projecting Kat's version of Grandma Hai onto this unsuspecting, hopefully compassionate lady?

Miranda cleared her throat and tried to sound pleasant. "Hello, is this—" saying her grandmother's first name felt like she was speaking to a famous historical figure—"Liang Hai?"

"It is," the voice said, suspicious. "Who is this?"

Miranda paused. "It's Miranda."

The only noises coming from the other end of the phone were the faint tittering of people talking and the clinking of glasses.

"Hello?" Miranda said. "Are you there?"

Her grandmother inhaled, then said to the room, "Hold on, ladies, I need to take this."

Once she had moved to a quieter room, Grandma Hai said, "Sorry, Miranda, you caught me in the middle of my book club." Miranda didn't think she sounded very sorry. "Are you—that is, is everything all right?"

Miranda braced herself. "My mom—I mean we . . . we're in a bit of a pickle."

"A pickle?"

"Financially." Miranda winced as she said it.

"So, Kat needs money," Grandma Hai surmised. "And she couldn't even bother to pick up the phone herself."

"Mom doesn't even know I'm—"

"Making her daughter do her dirty work." Grandma Hai's mutterings dissolved into silence, and Miranda closed her eyes, wondering if shame could be detected through phone lines.

"Miranda," her grandmother finally said, "I'm very sorry you're tangled up in this mess, and it's very kind of you to try to help your mother, but no." Her no was as solid as a war drum. "I can't help. Whatever she wants this time—more of her gadgets, registration fees for her conferences, gas money for another one of her wild goose chases—I am not a bottomless vault. I am not a bank. I won't do it. No more money. No more bailouts. When she called me six months ago for help—that was the final loan."

This new information slapped Miranda in the face like a cold wind. Kat called Grandma Hai for money? "But . . ." She swallowed the boulder in her throat. "I don't know what else to do."

There was a pause. "Sometimes with Katerina," Grandma Hai said, "you have to let her fall on her face."

Miranda was completely deadened. If Kat fell on her face, Miranda would smash down right alongside her.

But after all these years without a real relationship, Kat had called Grandma Hai for money. No wonder Grandma Hai sounded so weary when Miranda told her the reason for the call. No wonder she seemed so uncaring now—how would that feel, Miranda wondered, to know your daughter only looked at you as a human credit card?

A chorus of laughter chimed in the background. *She has more friends than I do,* Miranda thought, and marveled at the things that were possible if you cut Katerina Cho out of your life.

Grandma Hai coughed. "It was good to hear from you,

Miranda. Even considering the circumstances. You—you seem like a nice girl."

"I am." As if to prove it, Miranda added, "Thank you for the birthday cards. I get them every year."

"I know." Her grandmother spoke with unexpected warmth. "I get your thank-you notes. I hope you buy something fun. I'm sorry I can't pick out gifts myself." *I'm sorry I don't know you well enough* is what she really meant, Miranda knew. "You're twelve now?" Grandma Hai added.

"Yes."

"Twelve years old." The pinch of wistfulness Miranda detected in her grandmother's voice vanished with her next sentence. "Well, I'd better get back to my club."

"Good-bye," Miranda whispered. She ended the call and barely noticed when her hand went into her hair. Three strands of hair yanked out, just like that.

Yank, relief. Yank, relief. Yank, relief.

She crossed her grandmother's name off the list and held the marker against the paper, as if to write.

But she didn't, and an hour later she had nothing but an inkblot and a dull ache in her chest as she let her grandmother's voice echo in her mind, over and over and over.

The minutes on the clock passed hushedly—Miranda hated when this happened, when her time was emptied with nothing to show for it.

Her mother knocked. "Bean, are we out of toothpaste?"

"Under the sink," Miranda called.

Sometimes with Katerina, you have to let her fall on her face. Grandma Hai's words danced around Miranda like bonfire goblins, taunting, snarling—easy, so easy for her grandmother to say such a thing. She didn't have to live with Kat anymore. She didn't have to live with the consequences.

Miranda turned over her legal pad so she didn't have to stare at her failure and opened the laptop. Perhaps the Internet would have some ideas. Perhaps she could find a bank willing to talk to a seventh-grade girl.

Instead she looked up her father.

The crinkle of his eyes. His thousand-dollar smile— those teeth hadn't been that straight when she'd known him, she was sure.

The sadness in her was overwhelming. She didn't think, *I wish you had never left. I wish you had stayed and Mom had gone; I am with the wrong parent*—not exactly, but the notions churning in her mind were similar, less-formed versions of those.

"Bean?" Kat knocked again. "Are you turning in soon?"

Miranda had forgotten about sleep. About school. About everything else but this—this person on the other side of the computer screen.

"Not yet," she answered, making her voice calm. "It's only nine thirty."

"I know," Kat said. "I'm going to bed, though. I want to be on the road early."

"Okay. Good night."

"Hold on. We haven't gone over the rules for this weekend." Without asking for permission, Kat opened Miranda's door.

At the sound of the knob twisting, Miranda deleted her history and shut the laptop.

Her mother, oblivious as ever, leaned against the door frame, her hair in a floppy knot on top of her head.

Miranda stared. "What are you wearing?"

Kat's pajamas were a one-piece zip-up with footsies, printed with sweet pink ice cream cones on a candy-blue background.

"Aren't they cozy?" Kat hugged herself, then put on a false stern face. "Now, the rules for this weekend are . . . there are no rules." She grinned, delighted with herself.

Miranda's nostrils flared as she held herself steady. Why did everything have to be a joke, a game with Kat? Why couldn't she take anything seriously?

"Be safe," Kat said. "Be smart."

"I will."

"I'm going to update the blog," Kat said, taking the laptop, "and then go to sleep. Make sure all the lights are off before you go to bed?" She kissed Miranda's forehead, no doubt taking her daughter's silence as gleeful shock at having such a lax, cool mother, and shut the door—

And left Miranda in the wake of Kat's mess, confusion and loneliness knitting themselves on her body like a stifling blanket.

Nearly midnight.

Midnight, and Emma's bedroom window had gone dark long ago.

Midnight, and even the crickets had stopped singing and bundled down, and gone still.

Midnight, and Miranda's skin was tired, and her eyes were dry, and the spark of adrenaline she'd felt earlier, the springing of action to fix this mess of Kat's—that had stopped, and she was only numb.

Black ink smeared the side of Miranda's hand from leaning against her legal pad, poised to write another idea—anything, if only it would come to her.

When her clock ticked into the official hours of tomorrow, she capped her marker in defeat and took a deep breath.

Time to confront her mother. Time to wake her up and tell her she knew what was going on.

Time to hear her mother's excuses, her rationalizations, and her hollow promises to fix what she had done.

Time to tell her mom that there was nothing to be done.

Miranda had already pursued every possible option, but one:

DO NOTHING.

It was all hopeless. The house would be transferred from their possession, they'd be forced to live in the Critter Mobile—at least until they found a shelter or could convince Uncle Bob to let them crash on his disgusting couch. As for her leadership camp . . .

The anger was a hot coal in Miranda's stomach. If she woke Kat up and told her off, if she passed to Kat the blame that belonged to her—then maybe Miranda could finally sleep.

In her bedroom Kat was snoozing sitting up, rumpled against the headboard, her bedside lamp dimmed, glasses askew on her nose. A book lay open on her chest: *Handbook for Monsters.*

The muscles in her mother's face had completely relaxed in slumber; Miranda studied the calm skin, the peaches of Kat's cheeks, the planes of her forehead and chin ironed and smooth.

Miranda waited for the surge.

She waited for a cry to bellow out of her, to wake her mother with, "What is wrong with you? Other mothers' faces would be like clenched fists from worrying about the mortgage payments!"

But her mother looked so starry-eyed, even asleep. She looked so *happy.* Like she was having fun in her dreams, and it made jealousy lick at Miranda the way fire licks at sky.

"Tell me a monster." This was how Miranda used to implore her mother late at night—pushing the clock to its absolute limits when she was supposed to be asleep—and at the slightest request Kat would oblige. She'd launch into a story about the Bear Lake Monster, or the chupacabra, or the king of all creatures, Bigfoot, who reigned in the green, green forests of the Northwest . . .

And Miranda used to be excited for these trips, these hunts for the monsters from the stories, hiding in real life. She'd wake early before even Kat was stirring—Kat, whose blood was so infused with coffee and sugar, she could go from dead asleep to walking and talking in less than ten seconds. Miranda would pack and wait on the front porch in the wee hours of the morning, still in her nightgown but wearing her old khaki explorer's vest, pockets filled—*What if we find something this time? What if we see Bigfoot?*—before it became too hard to believe.

Sometimes with Katerina, you have to let her fall on her face.

But Kat would never fall. Even if Miranda threw the bills in her lap, even if she showed her mountains of evidence proving that her monsters weren't real, still Kat would believe—believe it would all work out, believe she'd disprove science, believe Miranda would continue playing the role of dutiful sidekick forever, losing friends and leadership camps and even their house along the way.

No, Kat would never fall.

But maybe, just maybe, she could be pushed.

Something sparked.

An idea.

A whiff of one, anyway. Idea essence. Idea vapor.

Miranda took the laptop from her mother's bedside table and went back to her room. She checked the foreclosure notice, rereading it with steady eyes.

Thirty days.

They had thirty days until the bank would knock on their door with the legal right to send them packing.

Thirty days to get her mother to grow up.

OPTION FOUR, Miranda wrote on her legal pad, every letter a ritual as the entire plan flickered through her mind on grainy footage.

A DEAL.

She circled it.

And then she drew up plans and wrote lists and printed out articles and highlighted. She dragged every one of Kat's books from the living room bookshelves and cracked their spines, until her bedroom was carpeted in cryptozoology.

She made charts, a map, and in the quiet house, silent but for her mother's gentle snoring in the other room, Miranda went to her e-mail and sent one message.

A tentacle.

The deepest, darkest hours of the night came to keep her company, and Miranda plotted, the house still, the gnomes on the porch holding their breath as moonlight threw shadows past the windows and onto the plaster footprint on the mantel.

It would work. It had to.

1.

To-do list:

Wake up

There is a curious thing that happens in the middle of the night, in the darkness of a still house and in the quiet of a moonlit neighborhood. You suddenly realize that, without fanfare or notification, you have passed into the early beginnings of morning. The blackest hours are spilled behind you like the dregs of yesterday's coffee, and the new day stretches before you with welcoming arms.

Miranda knew this moment well. She had read or studied or worried her way through it many times—but this time, she felt the morning rush toward her, a great river of light flooding the horizon. She set aside her papers and reluctantly closed her eyes, but then dawn arrived, and brought with it an end-of-summer bite that dotted the grass with dew and left the windowpanes chilly to the touch.

Miranda heard Kat wake across the hall. Heard her mother choose a capelette from her closet, heard her mother kiss the jade frog on her nightstand—if only such a superstitious gesture could actually bring them luck, Miranda thought. They needed it.

As she lay there, the heat turned off with a rattle, and the electricity hummed along the floorboards, up behind the walls and the power sockets. Even the silence sounded too expensive to afford.

Beneath her pillow, the mail she'd opened seemed to glow like something radioactive; had they been awake all night, waiting for her? She pulled out the envelopes and stared at them. The red words looked just as serious now in the soft filter of morning, stamped on firmly by someone who meant it.

What if there was another way?

What if she was missing something, something in the details?

She scanned the statements again—those same terrifying numbers, the same impossible hole her mother had dug.

If she wasn't ahead, she was behind.

By the time Kat came into the brightly lit kitchen, Miranda was vertical and dressed, transferring the few food items from the refrigerator to the cooler, burying squeezable yogurt tubes and prepackaged baby carrots in ice cubes.

"Bean!" Kat yawned. "How long have you been up?"

"I don't know," Miranda answered honestly. "Half an hour?" She shut the cooler lid and consulted her phone.

Things to pack, the header read, and with some pleasure, she crossed **Food** off her list. There. She lived for that moment, the temporary lightness.

"It's before six," Kat said. "And you were up late — Bean, you need your beauty sleep."

Miranda whirled to the drawer next to the fridge and found a pack of AA batteries and a roll of tape, which she tossed into an open duffel bag. A body in motion stayed in motion.

"Pretty sure your brain needs more rest than that, too," Kat added.

"Well, I'm awake now." Miranda didn't have time to be tired. Momentum — momentum was what greased her joints and made everyone else seem as though they were running on molasses-slicked sidewalks. Momentum was key. "We still have a lot to do before we leave."

First aid kit and **backup emergency stuff**. Done.

Everything was packed, but there was plenty to do. Plenty of lists.

Lists upon lists upon lists . . .

"Before *we* leave?" Kat filled her cat mug with fresh

coffee and added an absurd amount of chocolate syrup. "Where are we going?"

Miranda inhaled her mom's signature perfume, a blend of chalky candy heart, artificial vanilla, and what she imagined the inside of a cloud must smell like. "Mom . . ." She had practiced saying this speech all night, but now that it was time to speak it, she choked.

She was bulbous, she was an overfilled bucket, she was straining with things she could say, the great hurt she could cause, all of the truth she could pour down now over her mother in a sticky black mass, and it took such effort, on her part, to keep these things stabled, keep them inside.

Look at this place, Mom.

Look at you, Mom.

I can't breathe, with all these footprints on the walls. I am upside down.

Behind her, buried beneath pairs of woolen socks and a spare windbreaker in her duffel bag, the stacks of bills in their opened envelopes whispered to her, fed her lines—

How could you let it get this far?

How could you choose Bigfoot over me?

Like something rotten, she swallowed those things down.

"Mom," she said again. "I know we never—" She stopped, selected different words. "I know the last few trips have been disappointing—we've found some interesting things, yes. But we're still waiting to find proof. Something real. And I know I've been impatient." She pulled in a breath before she said it: "But I've got a feeling about this weekend, too."

Kat tilted her head sideways; her hair, which today was wrapped in two high knobs, gave her the look of a little kid with a cheap headband of costume ears. "What do you mean, Bean?"

Only hours ago, in the obscurity of night, Miranda had watched her mother sleep. Such a strange thing, to see your parent so unguarded, relaxed and free from their grown-up tendencies. Now her mother blinked at Miranda, waiting, eyes enhanced by the glasses so Miranda could see every detail, every shine of light reflecting off the velvety black of her pupils. Not the wise eyes of a grown woman, a mother; rather Miranda had the overwhelming notion that she was staring at the clean, expectant eyes of little-girl Kat. Wanting. Needing.

Looking for the magic.

"This weekend," Miranda said, "I want to help."

Her mother's eyes glittered starry. In any other adult, you'd have to search deep to find a glimpse of the child they had been; little-girl Kat had never gone away. She was standing right here with her daughter.

"You do? Hurray!" Kat clapped her hands. "It's been forever since you helped—"

"No," Miranda said. "I don't mean I'm going to hold

your sample dishes or chase after you with the camera if you think you see a shadow." The words stung, she noticed, Kat frowning as she took them in, and so she put on her smile—it felt too big for her face—and added, "I'm old enough now to really help."

She held up a folder, filled with pages and pages of articles and monster fact sheets, every paragraph streaked with highlighters and feathered with sticky notes. "If Bigfoot is in that forest—*still* in that forest, I mean—" She caught herself just in time—"we're going to find proof. But we've got to do this the right way." She slipped on her old khaki explorer's vest, the well-worn pockets already filled with index cards, binoculars, and a Swiss army knife. "As scientists. I've already repacked the van."

The Critter Mobile had been safely parked in the closed garage when Kat went to bed last night—now it was halfway down the driveway, its back hatch open, filled with bags and storage boxes and tarps, everything wedged together like sandbags stacked to stop a rising tide.

"You moved the car?" Kat looked surprised, but not bothered.

"And I made a plan." She showed her mother her printed itinerary, a weather chart and a master to-do list comprised of ten littler baby to-do lists for the weekend. "I've plotted out every minute of the next seventy-two hours," she explained. "Pit stops, meals, bedtimes—it's all here. It's foolproof. A foolproof plan to find Bigfoot—but we have to do it in three days."

This last detail had Kat raise an eyebrow. "Why three days?"

"I have to be back for school on Monday." Two more absences, Ms. Palmer had said, and then Miranda would lose her credit for this term—which meant today, Friday, would be Miranda's contribution. A sacrifice to the cause. She could afford one more absence.

"That's a pretty tight deadline, Bean." Kat poured a second helping of coffee into her cat mug.

"If we stick to the plan and the research," Miranda said, "we should only need three days."

Miranda had always been an advanced reader, but her mother's face was indecipherable—Kat sugared her coffee and lifted the cup to her face, steam fogging her glasses. Like the coffee had a life force, and if she sniffed hard enough, she could take it for herself.

"Mom? Is this okay?" Miranda said.

Kat set down her cat mug and pulled Miranda into a hug. "It's more than okay!" Miranda's cheek pressed against today's capelette, a pale sea foam green thing that billowed on her mother's frame, a blanket with sleeves. "It's been ages since we had a trip all to ourselves—and we're going to find one this time. You feel it, and I feel it, and we're going to do it together. Just you and me, Bean."

Miranda should have been relieved.

Should have been grateful that she and her mother were so different—that Kat was so easily convinced while Miranda remained a wall, stalwart mortar and brick, immovable no matter how the wind cried.

Instead, Miranda was surprised to feel a tender lump of disappointment. Shouldn't Kat have known her daughter was telling a lie? Shouldn't she have noticed the signs? The way Miranda's sentences curved up at the end, lacing a mechanical, musical excitement into her voice that wouldn't have been there otherwise.

The way her eyes flickered to the duffel bag not once, but three times during the conversation.

The way her hands twitched.

The way her lips pulled together into a line, like she was trying to keep her guilt contained as she remembered—

The e-mail she'd sent. The tentacle.

Then again, Miranda thought, if her mother were more observant, this plan wouldn't work. Miranda would be stuck, helpless on the sidelines as Kat let their lives implode. "Thank you, Bean, for doing all this work. We're unstoppable now that we've got a Miranda Cho to-do list for this weekend." She released her daughter from the hug, but kept her fingers on the curl of Miranda's shoulders. "I can feel it, Bean. We're close. We're so close."

Miranda never knew how to argue with a feeling.

Logic was a rock, a boulder, a mountain with roots sunken into earth. It could withstand earthquakes and mudslides. The end of the world could happen and there would be logic and fact and knowledge—irrefutable, immovable.

But feelings were slippery. They swam; they were viscous; they could fit into any container they needed to fill. How was she supposed to fight against something so spineless?

"I feel it, too." No matter how many times she said this, it would never roll smoothly off her tongue like honey; it clumped on her tongue, as if her mouth knew how far it was from the truth—*though it didn't used to be,* she thought. It used to be the truest, the strongest thing she knew—this feeling of possibility, this feeling that the world would soon split open, that the black thickets would part and she would know, she would *know.*

But that feeling had died a long time ago.

"Let's go, then!" Kat rinsed her cat mug in the sink, then carried the cooler out into the garage, leaving Miranda alone to delete the last item off her to-do list:

Lie.

She would go with her mother. She would act like a real Bigfoot hunter, searching for evidence—*real* evidence, not footprints or shadows, but something concrete. Something irrefutable. Because to bring her mother onto the side of truth she would have to show Kat that no such proof existed—and it never would, no matter how hard they looked.

Then, when all the nonsense had been wrung from her mother and Kat was devastated, Miranda would show her what she'd found in the silverware drawer. The bills, stacked high enough to tower over any excuse Kat could come up with. And then Miranda would gently steer her into a conversation about what to do next. It was right there on the top of her biggest to-do list:

Find Mom a real job.

Getting Katerina Cho to give up creature hunting and find a real job that would pay the bills and save their house—this would be Miranda's biggest project ever. And as soon as she got her mother into an office, a warehouse, a classroom, a ticket booth—anywhere with a steady pay-check and low expectations—Miranda would go to that leadership camp, and she would be free.

All Miranda had to do was pretend to be a die-hard believer for one more weekend. Use all of her research, all of her planning—and all those years she'd spent as the daughter of a renowned cryptozoologist—and then Kat would know.

She would *know*.

The only reason they haven't found Bigfoot, after years of looking, was because there was no Bigfoot.

And then it would all be over.

* * *

Outside, the morning chill was now a memory; the sky had shifted from shades of a wild salmon's belly to a pale blue, the first cool morning they'd had since last winter ebbed into spring.

Across the street, a single light was on upstairs at Emma's house.

Miranda held still, trying to determine if that glow came from the hallway or the bathroom.

What if that's her?

What if she notices when I'm not in school today?

What if she asks me where I was?

A hand snaked up into her hair, to plunder, to take—her fingers pinched the chosen strand—but none of that mattered, she realized. After this weekend, she would never have to hide the truth about her life from anyone at school.

She'd never have to cover for her strange, monster-loving mother again.

Her hand fell back down to her side.

Whatever doubts she might have had about this weekend—about the e-mail, the tentacle . . . they evaporated as she looked up at Emma's house. It would all be worth it.

The light flipped off, and Miranda turned to the Critter Mobile, squeezing the camping chairs into the last pockets of space, and closed the back hatch.

"Mom?" she called. "Let's go!" She wanted to leave

on schedule, but she also wanted to leave before anyone came out of Emma's house. Before anyone saw.

Kat said good-bye to the gnomes and shut the front door. "Prepared for departure, drill sergeant!" She saluted, then her straight posture loosened. "Wait—what about school?"

Miranda froze. "School?"

"Didn't you say you couldn't miss any more classes?"

"It'll be fine." Miranda's throat was suddenly a desert; she swallowed and swallowed and swallowed.

"I don't know, Bean." Kat chewed a thumbnail. "You've been working so hard—maybe this isn't a good weekend. Maybe you should stay here."

Miranda could only stare—was Kat about to throw a wrench in Miranda's plans by being responsible?

"Mom," she said, "I can miss school today. But we can't afford to waste any more time. Every minute we putter around here is another minute Bigfoot is loose in the forest. Anyone could find him—we have to hurry."

"Okay, Bean. If you're sure. But I should call your school." Kat pulled her phone from where she usually kept it—in her bra—and dialed the number.

Just like that. As if she'd done it every other time when Miranda's desk was empty, and her teachers were lecturing, and everyone was questioning her commitment to any of it—to a perfect record, a perfect reign as the youngest-ever student body president.

Perfect.

She reeled when she heard the voice mail of the attendance office blare from her mother's phone.

"Hello, this is Kat Cho, Miranda Cho's mother, calling to tell you that she'll be absent today. Thank you!"

Kat had never remembered to excuse an absence. *Never.*

She pushed her phone back under her shirt and said, "Shall we hit the road?"

Why was Miranda so upset? Wasn't this a taste of what she wanted—wasn't this what the trip was for? To summon forth a version of her mother that would remember to wash the dishes so they didn't have to eat their chili on Frisbees? To bring out the side of Kat that would ground Miranda if she broke a house rule—to bring out a Kat that would make house rules in the first place, and give out curfews, and check to make sure her daughter's homework was finished before the television went on?

To make Kat into a mom who didn't drag her on these trips at all?

As Miranda climbed into the Critter Mobile and screeched the door shut, she let herself smile—a real one. Kat called the school. She'd done it herself, unprompted. Maybe this plan really would work.

Maybe somewhere deep, *deep* down, Kat was ready to put aside her little-girl self and finally act like a real mom.

The Critter Mobile was on and warm, the GPS on

Miranda's phone was blinking and ready to announce a route, but first, Kat angled herself to face Miranda and reached for her hand. "I have to tell you, Bean . . . I'm so excited for this trip, I'm jumping out of my gourd."

"Me, too." The lie fell out of Miranda's mouth so easily, no thought required.

It frightened her, how effortless it was—to make something up. Something utterly believable.

"We're going to find one this time, Bean," Kat whispered. It sounded like Miranda's whisper. "I know it."

Something fluttered up into Miranda's throat.

Something she hadn't felt in a long, long—

She pressed the start button on the GPS, and the soothing robotic voice chased away that golden-soft whisper: "Starting route to Olympic National Park . . ."

Stay in control, Miranda told herself. *This is a trip to get Mom to stop believing—not the other way around.*

The Critter Mobile moved backward out of the driveway, and question after question flocked in Miranda's tummy like geese—

What if this doesn't work?

What if Grandma Hai was right?

What if Mom is too entrenched in this nonsense to be rescued?

What if we lose everything, and my leadership camp is gone, and then I am really, truly alone—

No, Miranda thought. She wouldn't let any of those things happen. She would do this—she was Miranda Cho.

If something was on her to-do list, it got done.

She slipped out of her boots, rested her stocking feet on the dashboard, and scrolled through her to-do lists on her phone, making new notes of extra credit assignments she could do for her teachers when she returned to school on Monday.

Ways she could make up for another absence—her last one. Ways she could prove she was still the same old Miranda. Still perfect.

With her other hand, she yanked out hairs, one at a time, until she lost count.

"Bigfoot, here we come!" Kat cheered as she urged the Critter Mobile up the ramp, merging onto the highway at the exact moment Miranda had detailed in her itinerary.

Indeed, Miranda thought. *Ready or not.*

Here we come.

8.

By the third hour, Miranda was ready to admit this was a mistake.

Kat was on her fifth Bigfoot story and her second cup of drive-through coffee, paying no attention to the weariness reeking from the wilting daughter in the captain's seat beside her. Miranda tried to do schoolwork, to read, snooze, anything—but seconds after she was absorbed, Kat sucked her back out.

"Someone last summer saw a figure twice the size of Bigfoot around Mount Saint Helen's—sort of a super Bigfoot," Kat was saying now. "What do you think, Bean? Could there be a Superfoot out there?" and Miranda nearly erupted, so furious and so quick was the dart of anger that hit her.

Can't she hear herself? Miranda thought. *Can't she hear how she sounds?*

"Anyway, she whipped out her camera," Kat said, "and you can see it on the video—this black figure moving through the trees. It's a little shaky, but it's right there—"

Sometimes Miranda watched her mother speak and wondered if she would actually rustle up dust with how fast she talked, how many sentences she spat out. Perhaps they could be tracked, as they wound up past the city, through dairy farms and onion fields—just follow the trail of chaff, the dull nonstop sound of jabber, the spinning wheels.

"Just think, Bean—all those creatures out there. Just waiting for someone to be in the right place at the right time." She paused to nibble a vine of strawberry licorice, and Miranda breathed out, counted to three, reached for the stereo—

"Oh! I brought this for us!" Kat pushed an ancient CD into the slot and handed Miranda the cover to peruse—a woman with hot pink hair sneered at the camera, swirling galaxies and cold ringed planets behind her.

Kat then proceeded to both sing along off-key and narrate the album's major themes and influences during the guitar solos, and Miranda resisted the urge to swing the Critter Mobile door open and take her chances with a jump into traffic.

Two more hours to the forest, she reminded herself.

Then another hour to the southwest entrance, and one more through the park to their campground. Miranda had a certain site in mind: Tallulah Flats—a five-minute walk to the trailhead, gravel parking for the Critter Mobile, a nice, flat area for the tent, and a row of indoor bathrooms with showers and running water.

Campsites were first come, first serve—another reason to hurry, hurry, hurry.

Only a few more hours until they were unpacking.

Only a few more days until they were making this drive the other way. Back home.

We're already halfway to the forest, she reassured herself.

Only two more sleeps until her mother admitted there was no Bigfoot.

"Time to get gas," she announced after checking her itinerary.

Kat looked at the meter. "We've still got half a tank."

"Really?" Miranda looked at her notes. She'd made the calculations for pit stops herself—oh, but she hadn't accounted for the half hour of idling they'd done in that bottleneck outside of Seattle. "We should fill up now. Gas stations get sparse after this exit."

"If you say so, Bean." Kat stretched to check her mirror. "I need more coffee anyway."

They pulled off the freeway and found a gas station

where a plastic red T-Rex chomped on a sign, large enough to cast its big-headed, small-armed shadow into the street.

Kat parked by a nozzle. "Get me a coffee with three sugars and something sweet—a doughnut. A chocolate one. No, a maple bar. No, both. And something for yourself."

Miranda stared at the wrinkled five-dollar bill in Kat's outstretched hand. "I packed snacks for us." She had a budget in mind for this weekend, one tight enough to cut off circulation. They had to save money where they could.

"Oh, come on, Bean, we're on a road trip! Plus this is all tax deductible." Kat ran a tired-looking credit card through the machine at the pump.

Miranda bit her tongue so hard, she could nearly taste the words.

Instead of arguing, she scurried into the station before she could see how much Kat's beloved gas-guzzling Critter Mobile was going to cost to fill up.

Bigfoot, she thought wryly, *you'd better be worth it.*

Raisinets. Lemonheads. Boston Baked Beans.

Miranda shuffled down the aisles, past the kaleidoscope of gas station offerings, the multi-textured universe of salt and sugar and grease. It was nine o'clock. By now, homeroom bell would be ringing, the halls of the school swimming with students—but no Miranda. She'd been gone so often; would anyone even notice when her desk was empty? Would someone else raise their hand in the hefty silences after the teachers asked their questions? Would someone else give the right answers?

Ms. Palmer—the name was dense in her mind, sinking all the way down into her stomach. Ms. Palmer would notice she was gone.

Miranda battled the thickening guilt with a single thought, sharp as a sword cutting through briars: *I have to pull this off. When we drive out of the forest on Sunday, we have to leave Bigfoot behind, or else I'm missing school for nothing.*

She threw two doughnuts into a bag. There were no maple bars, so she chose one with orange frosting and Halloween sprinkles. Kat would like the little pumpkins, and cats, and witch hats—

Miranda stopped cold, next to the tubes of sunflower seeds in every conceivable flavor: extra-salted, ranch, barbecue.

A car had just pulled up to the closest gas pump.

A silver sports car, chrome hubcaps, tinted windows. Big enough for only two.

The same car she'd seen online, when she was searching for things she shouldn't have been searching for—

Black pepper. Spicy jalapeño . . .

Her father's car.

Miranda crouched down, gut lurching as she peeked

through the hanging bags to watch the door open.

Salted lime. Sweet 'n' sour. Pickle . . .

What if it's him?

What if he comes inside?

What if he doesn't *come inside?*

Nacho cheese. Beet. Sriracha . . .

No one wants to taste the actual sunflower seeds, she thought idly. *They want to pay for flavor. They want to pay to be fooled.*

Sunlight striped the door white as it opened—Miranda couldn't breathe.

What if, what if, what if?

It wasn't him.

She couldn't see the details of the person who was driving—sunglasses obscured most of his face—but it wasn't him.

Now that her heart had stopped its pounding, she studied the car, collecting its details. She could see it now: the way its front was blunt, awkwardly rounded down like a parrot's beak instead of a smooth, pointed torpedo. The way it was more of a dull gray, the color of a grimy nickel, than actual silver.

She rolled her eyes—someday she'd laugh at this, she told herself, at the time she hid inside a gas station because she thought it was—she thought she saw—

"Bean?" Kat came down the aisle and squatted next to her daughter. "There you are! Did you get coffee?"

"Not yet." Miranda wiped her sweaty hands on the seat of her pants—she'd sweat enough to make two small swamps in her palms.

Kat inspected her. "You okay? You look weird."

Miranda blinked, pulled out a hair, and finally the world focused: There was her mother, a grown woman with purple sparkly lipstick and a butterfly clip in her hair, clutching a package of tropical Skittles. Tension returned to her limbs.

"I'm fine." She stood up, led her mother to the java station, where Kat filled up the largest-size cup with coffee and enough sugar to almost make it solid, and Miranda yanked out three more hairs, emptying herself of the embarrassment that had nearly sunken her.

How could I have thought that was his car? What would I have even done if it was?

At the counter, Kat gestured for Miranda to plunk down the five-dollar bill; Miranda did so with some trepidation. Five whole dollars, gone, just like that. For a pile of junk food and caffeine.

"What flavor?" asked the attendant, semi-bored.

Kat frowned. "What?"

The attendant held a cup to the Slushie machine. "Flavor?"

"Oh!" Kat fidgeted with her capelette, beaming. "What? Oh—blue, I guess?"

The attendant pushed the Slushie toward her, along with her change. "Thank you for choosing Gas 'n' Go for all your refueling needs."

As soon as they got back in the Critter Mobile, Kat fanned herself and pretended to swoon. "Wow, that guy was cute. Did you see the way he was flirting with me?"

"He was not flirting with you," Miranda said.

"Uh, exhibit A." Kat held up the cup of blue ice crystals. "Free Slushie, Bean. Maybe he wrote his phone number on the cup." While she checked the domed lid for digits, she drove right past the sign that explained it:

FREE 16-OZ. SLUSHIE WHEN YOU SPEND $40 OR MORE ON GAS.

Miranda opened the trail mix she'd brought from home and leaned her head against the window.

All the proof in the world was right under Kat's nose, but she didn't catch a wink of it.

"So you've been searching for Bigfoot for—how many years, exactly?"

If Kat was surprised that Miranda was asking such a question, she didn't show it; she pursed her lips, thinking. "Let's see, Bean—I went on my first tracking trip when you were six. So that's about—"

"Six years," Miranda said. "Is that around the same time you quit at the dentist?" Kat used to work as a receptionist for a kind-faced dentist who wore her hair in a long gray braid down her back—Miranda had vague memories of seeing her mom behind the front desk, filing and answering phones. It had always seemed a strange sight, like witnessing a zoo animal doing office work.

"About five years ago." Kat ate the last yellow Skittle in her bag and started on the green. "That was a good job, but it was too hard to balance everything once the blog took off. There was no time to go out on searches."

Kat had left the dentist's office and never looked back. Left a consistent paycheck to cobble together a living from research grants, convention speaking fees, and the ad revenue from *The Bigfoot Files*, with a sprinkling of e-book royalties and freelance articles here and there—and, as Miranda now knew, at least one big bailout from Grandma Hai.

Miranda was going to help her mother back into something steady. Another desk job, hopefully something where Kat's extroversion could be utilized, and her tendency to imagine the impossible could be seen as an asset.

But first, she had to write her mother a résumé.

She subtly jotted down the dates of her mother's employment history in a blank corner of her notebook. "So you've only had one job before this?" she clarified. "Just the dentist's office?"

Kat shrugged. "Before that, I had you. That's why I never finished college."

Miranda looked at her mom, recalculating. "I didn't know you went to college."

"I dropped out after sophomore year." She smiled at Miranda, her lips stained blue from her Slushie. "Pregnancy migraines and morning sickness got in the way of homework. I always meant to go back when you were older, but then . . ." Her shrug was cheerful, but something inside Miranda shifted, a spring river thawing.

But then he left.

Miranda catalogued what facts she did know about Kat pre-motherhood, a topic they rarely, if ever, broached: Kat met Miranda's dad and married him at eighteen, even though Grandma Hai didn't approve. Grandma didn't think they'd known each other long enough, and whether or not that was what ultimately sunk their marriage, within a year of the wedding Kat was pregnant, and within five years she was divorced.

Not exactly the fairy-tale ending any mother would want for her daughter.

"You're talking about real college?" Miranda confirmed. "Not some online certification program, or—"

"Real college, Bean. I was a biology major at Reed."

Reed College? Miranda's astonishment reached down to her toes. Reed was a good school—a really good school. And biology was a real science—none of her mother's textbooks would have mentioned Bigfoot—or the Loch Ness

Monster, or the Frogman, or any of the creatures Kat now devoted her life to.

Still, Miranda tried to picture it: Kat, twelve years younger, stars for eyes, bouncing in her seat on dissection day, obsessively checking her answers against the textbooks.

Miranda stopped. The mental images of her mother were starting to look uncomfortably familiar.

"I wanted to work with animals," Kat was saying. "A zoo technician, maybe, or a trainer—I don't know. I didn't get far enough into the program to get specific."

Miranda leaned into the turn as Kat merged onto the freeway. "I've always known what I want to do."

"Then you're one of the lucky ones." Kat put on her blinker and then forgot about it—Miranda listened to its *click-click, click-click* until it became incessant.

She didn't feel lucky.

"But why not study real—I mean . . ." Miranda redirected. "Why not study animals that are easier to find?" Her mother could be tracking giraffes on safari, or studying the critters in the hills beyond their hometown—she'd let any kid in the school come over and be around her mother, if that was the case.

"I don't know, Bean." Kat pointed at a billboard directing interested tourists off the next exit to a museum of pioneer artifacts. "People will line up to stand six feet away from a roped-off wagon wheel, but they don't care that there's been over four hundred reports of a ghost in the museum basement. Or there—" She gestured to the other side of the freeway. "People will drive thirty miles off the main road to go see America's largest string cheese, but if they'd go a few miles farther west, they'd be in the same place where someone spotted the Batsquatch last spring."

She drummed her fingers on the steering wheel. "The world is full of wonders, Bean," she said, "but hardly anybody seems to see it except me."

Out the window, Miranda's eyes found a puffy cloud, fat and soft on one side, fading out to long, white sky-ice on the other. Kat would call it an elephant in the air; Miranda would call it what it was: concentrated water vapor.

Maybe Kat thought she was more perceptive than the rest of the world, but Miranda knew the truth—living with your head in the clouds was easy.

You could look at a cloud and see whatever you wanted to.

Miranda filled in the details of her mother's résumé and considered it. It was pretty bleak—unfinished degree, limited work experience, and this giant gap between a real job and this—this thing Kat was doing now. But Miranda knew it wasn't what you said, it was how you said it. For example, instead of saying her mother had dropped out of college, Miranda could write that Kat "left to pursue better opportunities." Or here—instead of saying Kat worked as a dental receptionist, Miranda could call her a "patient/doctor coordinator."

She stopped writing. There was a rare silence in the car, the murmur of the Critter Mobile's tires on the road pulsing up and into the seats. Kat's eyes were far-flung — something from the conversation had made her pensive.

"Except us, you mean."

"What was that, Bean?"

"Nobody sees the wonder except us."

This statement had the exact effect Miranda was hoping for — Kat burst into a smile, her teeth still tinged purple-blue from her Slushie. "That's right, Bean. Just you and me against the world."

Miranda leaned back into her seat and stared out at the rushing landscape. *I will not let you fall. I will not let you fall. I will not let you fall.*

She recited it over and over until the guilt stopped gnawing and the turnoff for the Batsquatch was only a memory behind them.

9.

Miranda thought she knew forests—how large their trees could grow, how green their leaves could get, how heartbreaking the world could be.

She'd been wrong.

Her mother steered the Critter Mobile off the 101 and onto a bumpy side road, which had Miranda gritting her teeth—the asphalt seemed to be disintegrating beneath their wheels. *Maybe we'll be the last ones to ever drive this way,* she thought. *When we turn off our car, the forest will have eaten the road completely.*

If there was ever a forest that was capable of doing so, it was this one.

She'd seen so many different ones, and in her memory they were all the same—but entering this forest was crossing a threshold, passing from this ordinary world into another, through a portal; she was surprised when there was not fanfare, or a shower of golden sparks, or a shawl thrown around her shoulders as if she was a crusader, returning home to the kingdom she swore to protect.

Something familiar, fidgeting in her fingertips—something awakening, after being asleep for so long.

"What do you think, Bean?"

Any one of these spruces, she thought as they drove, could secretly be a wizard, turning his piney cloak around on himself to hide in plain sight, waiting for the Critter Mobile to pass by so he could attend to his arcane business of gathering lichens and starlight to knit into spells.

Or perhaps that cloister of gnarled hemlocks were witches, clothed in drippy moss, cursed into immobility by a thousand-year-old enchantment, and just as Miranda and her mother curved around the bend, the curse would be lifted, and they would move through the trees, where they could see her—but they would not let her see them. Miranda could try to spin her head around fast enough, but she would only ever catch them in the corners of her eyes.

Such a forest made her realize just how inadequate some words are.

Words like *old*.

The things that were here were beyond old; they were primordial. She could imagine the planet's fish, shaking water off their scales as they emerged from these swamps, covered in algae as they took their first bold steps onto these loamy banks with tiny, capable fins.

She could imagine prehistoric beasts chewing the slender stems that swathed the branches, their leathery hides and long, arching necks camouflaged against the canopies—these trees were old; these trees were a marvel.

Their roots stretched beneath the road and she could almost feel them, their age and their life, crisscrossing beneath the Critter Mobile in a network like power lines—what would they say about her and her mother and the thousands of others who walked beneath their boughs? Would they say anything about them at all? Perhaps Miranda and her mother were too small for something so old to even care about. The notion made her feel wondrous and out of breath and terrified.

She hadn't felt such smallness in a long, long time.

She was aware of the inadequacy of the word *green,* too—why divide the rainbow like this, into only six colors, when green itself deserved an entire spectrum of its own?

There was the dark green of the firs, the verdant green of the liverwort painted on the trunks, the true green of the feathery moss—a green with integrity. There was the murky black-green of the soil, which crumbled like a moist cake, so fae-like against the edge of the tar and the garish yellow lines of the manufactured road. There was the spring green of newborn leaves, the flat green of the maidenhair ferns, the sheer green of the air, the green that was the blending of all the greens . . .

No wonder the human pupil evolved to accept this hue as the most pleasing, the most peaceful, the most sumptuous of colors.

"Bean?" Kat broke through Miranda's thoughts like they were still water. "You okay?"

"Yeah . . . it's pretty." The word was all she had, but she said it, knowing this, too, was another word that was utterly inadequate.

The forest was, all at once, Jurassic, and alien, and fairy-tale—it looked like it held a million stories, one for every fern, every mushroom. And there was room to hold at least one more.

The Critter Mobile stopped at the park ranger's booth near the entrance, where Kat flashed her national parks annual pass.

"Staying overnight?" a short, redheaded ranger asked.

"Yes." Miranda stretched across her mother's lap to answer. "At Tallulah Flats."

"Tallulah's closed due to flooding," the ranger said, checking her map. "You'll have to go north of Quinault."

"But we have to stay near Fable Falls!" Miranda had a plan, and a schedule, and a map—if they had to change campsites, everything would have to be replotted.

"The western access is open." The ranger didn't even blink. "Good elevation, gorgeous views. You have bear equipment?"

Miranda leaned back in her seat, "Yes," she told the ranger, then pulled out her phone and immediately began adjusting her to-do list as Kat took the Critter Mobile into the forest and turned left, not right, at the fork.

Away from her plans and toward the unknown.

"Relax, Bean," Kat said. "Things like this happen. We'll wing it."

Winging it is for birds, Miranda wanted to say, *or for people too flighty to stay on the ground.* But what else could she do? Cell reception was sluggish, but she located the next closest campsite to the falls, a destination called Moon Creek.

"It'll be great!" Kat Cho, ever the optimist, even after half a decade of losing footprints to rain and losing shadows to sunrises. "Moon Creek's supposed to be nice—oh, wow!"

With a jerk, Kat pulled the Critter Mobile to the side of the road and stopped.

"What's wrong?" Miranda searched the shoulder for the deer they had almost hit, the rabbit that had scampered between their tires, the thing that had made her mother stop—but it was all green, green, green.

"Over there." Kat unbuckled her seat belt. "Look at it, Bean. Isn't it beautiful?"

Miranda followed her mother's sightline to a massive red cedar, trunk braided and twisted, creating little pockets and cavities that housed animals—red-breasted sap-suckers were neighbors with Pacific tree frogs and carpenter ants.

A lovely thing, but still . . .

"It's a tree," she said. *The world is full of wonders,* Kat had told Miranda on the drive to the park—was her mother going to pull over and point out every interesting tree in the forest?

"I know," Kat said. "And doesn't it look friendly?"

She jumped out of the still-running car and ran toward the cedar; Miranda grabbed the keys and scrambled after her.

Kat bypassed the moss that grew in rosettes over the knotholes and instead climbed the face of the tree, up and up, twelve, fourteen, twenty feet high, until her baby blue hiking boots vanished in the leaves.

"Mom!" What was Kat doing? Trying to set up a Bigfoot watchtower? Miranda circled the trunk; she could feel how damp the ground was by how much it deepened with every step, like she was walking on a mattress.

"Hello, down there!" Kat shifted so she could peer at her daughter through a break in the branches. "Come up here, Bean—it's an easy climb."

Did I fall asleep in the car? Miranda wondered. *Is this some bizarre stress dream I'm having?* "You come down!"

she called up to Kat. "We have a schedule to keep!"

"This view is incredible!" The leaves and the altitude did nothing to muffle the earnestness in Kat's voice. "We're not going anywhere until you come and see it for yourself!"

Miranda could either begin a game of "who's more stubborn?" with a Bigfoot believer . . . or she could climb. With a groan, she secured the car keys in the breast pocket of her vest and ascended the tree.

Even though the trunk was twisted into a natural ladder, Miranda's hands shook as she went higher and higher. When her eyes were level with the soles of Kat's hiking boots, she stopped.

"It's magical." Kat stood as tall as she could, inhaling through her nose.

She wasn't lying. Every rock; every tree branch; every fallen log, petrified bark made frizzy—everything, covered in moss. It was almost alarming—like everything was sleeping, tucked in for an eternal rest and covered in a blanket of softest green. What about when she and Kat went to sleep tonight? Would the moss creep over them, dusting their cheeks, planting colonies on their eyelids, growing down into their throats?

Her hands itched. "Can we go now?" She had the sudden urge to yank out hairs—not just for the delicious bite, but because she was certain now she was crawling with forest pathogens.

A coat of moss, thickening, stretching, growing over everything in sight . . .

"All right, Bean." Kat finally started back to the ground, helping her daughter make the climb down and out of the drooping green branches. "We couldn't come all this way and not climb a tree," she explained, as if this was sound, scientific logic.

"Now that that's taken care of," Miranda said sternly, equilibrium returning now that she was no longer being held up by the forest, "let's go find Bigfoot."

Miranda had been worried that Moon Creek Campground would be full, and they'd be forced to find yet another site even farther away from the falls—but it was empty. And as soon as she saw it, Miranda understood why.

Algae slimed out of a creek bed and across the dirt campsite, making green-tinted mud; the creek itself was too weak to flush itself clean, but babbling too loudly to be peaceful white noise.

Kat immediately schlepped the tent to the only clearing flat enough to sleep on. "Mud's supposed to be orthopedic, right?" she joked.

Her mother started to shake out the tent, but Miranda cried, "Wait!"

"What?" Kat scanned the ground as if it were covered in snakes.

"We can't set up here—it's going to get so muddy!"

Miranda went through the inventory in her mind—how many wet wipes and paper towels had she brought, and how long would those supplies last if they had to wipe this gunk off their boots and gear every time they went into the tent?

Kat shrugged. "It's a rain forest, Bean. Everything's going to get muddy eventually." She set down the tent gently, as if doing so would prevent a meltdown from her daughter, then seized a clod of mud and threw it at Miranda. "Catch!"

"Don't!" Miranda tried to dodge it, but there it clung, wet and gooey, splattered on her shorts. She gave her mother a look of absolute fury, but Kat just grinned.

"Mom!"

"What? Just getting us properly camouflaged."

Miranda wiped away the mud and shrieked again— something fat and yellow fell onto the ground at her feet. "What is that thing?"

Kat squatted and poked it. "Banana slug." She showed it to Miranda, who flinched. "Gross!"

"Not gross," her mother assured the slug, "cute. I'm calling you Littlefoot and you're going to be the guardian of the camp."

A flame danced inside Miranda, and its intensity frightened her. The sight of Kat introducing herself to the banana slug, lifting it up, trying to feed it a mushroom—it frightened her, too, and not just because this forest, this strange, green place seemed to be bringing out the little girl in Kat.

It frightened her how much she wished she could join in.

But someone had to be the grown-up.

Stay focused. Stay in control. For your leadership camp, she told herself, and felt a little stronger. For the bills. To save the house, to save their entire lives—

No, she corrected. *To build a new one.*

A new life.

She could do this.

"All right," she said, rubbing the banana slug slime onto her shorts. "Let's unpack."

Now that she was here, seeing the trees from deep inside the park . . . it wasn't magical at all. It was only mountains and mist and rain and trees—trees, why did anyone think they had to drive so far to see trees, trees just like any other trees? The only thing remarkable about these trees—which were, she guessed, a little bit *tall*—was there were so many, bunched together. If you put anything together in large enough numbers, it would be impressive. A thousand cakes, a thousand cats, a thousand banana slugs.

The next hour was spent setting up a base for the big search—the tent, pitched at last in the mud; the firewood, wrapped in a blanket to keep it dry until it was cold enough to light; a tarp strung in a circle of spruces, to keep at least some part of their camp dry when the rain began. "That's not an *if*, Bean. That's a *when*," Kat said and peered at Miranda over her glasses.

When everything was set up with a reasonable sense of organization, Kat collapsed into a chair with a fresh orange soda from the cooler. "All right, Bean. Let's get a fire going and break out the dogs."

Miranda had just shaken the pebbles out of her boots and retied them. "It's only four o'clock. We still have time to get to the falls before dark."

"We'll have enough light to get there, but not to get back," Kat said. "We'll go first thing tomorrow morning." She put her hands in her capelette pockets. "I like hearing you so excited, though." Out of a pocket she pulled a melted wad of Junior Mints and popped it into her mouth whole.

"You didn't even check for lint!" Miranda said, a gag on the back of her tongue.

Kat shrugged. "Fiber." She went to fetch the firewood.

Mist gathered thick around Miranda's ankles, curling through the campsite. She looked up, and she heard it—the faint, barely there sound of a song, tinkling like crystal chimes through the green.

She paused. It was a familiar sound—the sound of a music box singing—but she couldn't make out the exact melody.

A shiver dashed up Miranda's spine.

She looked around, and saw the old trees lining the creek bed. These were particularly old grandfathers, some of them bearing scars from previous campers who'd tied ropes around their torsos; the wounds had mostly healed over, giving the trees a gnarled, graffitied effect.

She studied them, as if hidden within their branches were the eyes she would have seen if they were real; she studied the moss hanging off them like beards, the knots that would have been their ears and long, crooked noses . . .

For a moment, Miranda listened to the music box; the song did not end, even when she shook herself, even when she blinked. Another camper, she decided. A little girl who couldn't bear to leave her favorite trinket behind at home.

Nearby, something moved; she caught the motion with the corner of her eye. The hairs on the back of her neck stood on end.

We are being watched.

It was a thought that had prickled in the corner of Miranda's mind ever since they had entered the forest, only then it had been essence and vapor, a dark feeling, a shadow collecting and deepening. But as she thought it now, it felt sharp and corporeal and real.

"You okay, Bean?" Kat asked as she passed, wood stacked under her chin.

The sun shifted behind the horizon; in that snap of

daylight to evening, the music stopped. Miranda hadn't realized she wasn't moving, but now she felt a spell had lifted, and she shook her head.

"Fine," Miranda said. "Just the wind."

But in the silence, a whisper right to her from the shadows, the leaves of those grandfathers rustling in the breeze she'd made up. *What if,* the forest seemed to say.

What if, what if, what if?

10.

Miranda did not sleep well.

The mud, as it turned out, was not orthopedic; as the night progressed it froze and got hard as a wooden slat.

She had packed an air mattress, but the floor of the tent was slicked with algae-dirt and creek water—no matter how desperately she tried to wipe it up, no matter how many paper towels she used, the gunk persisted—and she had wanted to keep the air mattress clean. Earlier, a cheery pink sunset had made an optimist out of her—they would wake up, the mud would go away, the forest would come to its senses and agree to be cooperative. She would swipe clean every dirty surface and spread out the air mattress and finish this trip with a full night's sleep and only an adorable smudge of mud across her forehead.

Now, lying in the dark, her sunniness was zapped. It wasn't smart or discerning to keep the air mattress clean and unused in the Critter Mobile; it was just plain dumb.

If the cold, cruel ground hadn't kept her awake, the sounds certainly would have—a whole forest symphony playing for her, unsolicited. As a game to ward off her restlessness, she tried to decipher them one by one.

That tapping? A woodpecker. That swooping? An owl. That croaking? A chorus frog, and that howling, like something wounded, an unknown animal padding through the mist? That was nothing more than night air, tunneling through the dead hollows of a Sitka spruce.

There was no more starlight music, no twinkling music box melody, and for that she was grateful—even thinking about the ghostly song from earlier made her shiver and pull the sleeping bag tighter around her. The image of those old grandfathers, stretching their rheumatic limbs, twisting over in their sleep—she couldn't shake it away.

In the blackest heart of the night, the forest fell silent. The only sounds were Kat's snores and Miranda's own ragged breathing. And then, sharp and clear, she heard it—the arrhythmic percussion of two rocks or sticks being hit together, banging, banging, banging.

She knew what Kat would say it was. She knew what the Internet would say it was, those websites in the deepest caverns of the web where strange theories floated like scum on ponds . . . but there was a logical explanation. There had to be. And in the morning, when she was clearheaded, she would figure out what it was.

Finally she pretended those sounds were nothing more than white noise tracks on her phone, lullabying her to sleep on a dithery night when Emma's shade was already pulled down, her light already extinguished.

And so this was how Miranda drifted off into the lightest, most fragile sleep of her life, and floated into eggshell-thin dreams of pine needles and soft, sweet growls. She cried out once, when she dreamed of the moss climbing her neck, brushing against her lips. But when she woke, it was only her loose hair, covering her face.

It took several minutes to convince her stiff body to arise and move. The joints in her fingers, her kneecaps, every one of her neck bones—she could feel them all, squeaky and cold as she crawled out of the tent to a clear, clean sky, a few clouds ruffling the horizon. A horizon she could actually see this morning between the trees; the fog that had shrouded everything yesterday in cemetery haziness had dissipated.

Good. She hadn't realized how much the fog had unsettled her until it was gone.

Kat had a small fire rolling, a skewer packed with marshmallows held over the flames. "There she is," she said. "Morning, Bean. Do you want chocolate or extra chocolate?"

Miranda ran her fingers through her hair—the strands were damp, even though it hadn't rained. She smelled like a wet dog. "I packed milk and cereal."

"This is the breakfast of champions." Her mother ate one of the marshmallows right off the stick, then offered the rest to Miranda.

"You burnt them," Miranda said.

"They're better that way."

While Kat devoured enough sugar to power an entire playground of preschoolers, Miranda got herself ready. They would drive to Fable Falls, park at the reservoir, and begin their search at the base of the waterfall, the location of the alleged sighting. Miranda guzzled a whole bottle of water and filled her vest pockets with trail mix and fruit snacks. She planned to cover a lot of ground today, both physically and mentally—she would turn over every rock, look beneath every fallen log, treat this as a real scientific expedition, so when the end of their trip came, and there was still no Bigfoot, Miranda could lock eyes with her mother, muster up a brave, sympathetic face, and say, "Now do you see, Mom? Now can you admit the truth?"

Before she let her mother start up the Critter Mobile, Miranda cleared her throat. "All right. I think we should establish some ground rules."

Kat tilted her head. "What do you mean?"

"I mean we should be very clear," Miranda said, "about what we're looking for."

"Footprints," Kat said automatically. "Stray hairs. Disrupted foliage, stripped bark. Poop of unknown origin—"

"I'm saying let's not get too excited about poop." Miranda pulled out a hair and took in a cleansing breath. "We need to set our standards for evidence high, okay? We need something real. Can you agree to that?"

Kat narrowed her eyes. "Can you? Can you accept it if we find something real?"

Miranda paused before saying, "Convince me."

They drove two miles north of their campsite to Fable Falls, and it was another postcard-perfect scene—water crashing down fat rocks into white froth, then rolling and stretching and calming itself into a still, kidney-shaped lake, a fine mist hanging over the alpine water. Its banks were lined with dried brown pine needles and shingles of gray bark. The unexcitable water was steel blue, licking against round, easy stones that sunned themselves above the water levels, old algae rings telling of the rainy season that would begin soon, and then the water would rise, higher every day. Hermitages of dead logs and sticks bleached the color of bones clumped along the bank near the border of trees. The thought popped into Miranda's head without warning: this is where a Bigfoot would live.

What if—

She shook her head, and the thought leaped away like a pond skater.

"Do you want to start near the water first, or the trees?" Either answer was fine with Miranda; it was the option that was important. The option would make Kat feel as if she were the one in charge. She wouldn't feel Miranda's gentle hand guiding her, leading her to the inevitable conclusion.

"Prints!" The grin on Kat's face should have been reserved for children set loose at a state fair with unlimited tickets.

Miranda sighed.

How well she knew this slow shuffle down the bank to the mud and gunk where the mayflies bred and the bullfrogs stared and the *lap-lap* of the lake was as dull and unrushed as a fountain in a hotel lobby.

At the water's edge, Miranda studied the ground, the way the articles she read the other night instructed, and she did see prints: long, waving lines, left by a snake's gliding belly; the tentative marks of a deer's hooves as it sneaked in for a quick, paranoid sip. And those larger, deeper tracks, the ones that collected their own water like tiny lakes, those were almost large enough to be from—

"What do you think, Bean?" Kat popped up from the other side of a downed tree, brittle from years of lying on its side, the water taking pieces of it for driftwood. The tracks wound down the bank and around the dead tree, becoming less and less pronounced until they disappeared into the lake. Miranda considered them. They were from a creature with a sprawling tread, paws of something that pressed deep into the mud as it drank.

"The gait is about right." Kat squatted, held her palms against a single track, a measurement she'd taken dozens of times. "This is it, Bean."

"Hold on a minute," Miranda said. "You're jumping ahead—you have to make a hypothesis first, then gather evidence, then analyze it without bias. You can't start with a conclusion. Besides," she pointed out, almost giddy, "look closer. These are bear tracks."

Kat was skeptical. "These are bipedal."

"No, look at the heft." The pair of prints made from the creature's back feet were noticeably deeper than the front legs. "A bear came through those huckleberry bushes"—Miranda gestured to the tree line—"down the incline and into the lake, see? Black bears have been spotted in this area—the ranger at the entrance asked us if we had bear equipment, remember?"

Her mother's lips pursed, her nostrils moving independently, like they were taking in more air to keep the body calm.

"Since when do you know so much about bear tracks?" Kat asked, almost accusatory.

Miranda shrugged, her smugness fitting around her

shoulders like a letterman's jacket. "I told you I did a lot of research the other night."

Kat had been to countless places with bears in the ecosystem, had seen a few of them chomping for trout in rivers. She had been a biology major once—she knew how to read tracks.

But her mother would never look down in the mud and see bear tracks, Miranda knew. She lacked the ability to see anything but Bigfoot. Everything she came across, everything she heard, everything she found was always Bigfoot.

Even though it never was.

They examined the rest of the bank, all the way around the reservoir, and their rhythm established itself quickly—Kat would spot tracks, and Miranda would identify them. More bears, a family of deer, a fisherman. Kat argued against that last one, but they could both see the tread of the heels, the gleaming hook of his fly sunken near the inverse of an illegible brand name. Details that were so obvious, you'd have to try *not* to see them.

"I guess that's it," Miranda said, and remembered just in time to sound defeated. "No Bigfoot here." She was hungry, and weary of dirt in all its forms—it had caked beneath her fingernails and in between the peaks of her knuckles when she had, on Kat's insistence, lifted a fish carcass from the mud so as to decipher its cause of death. Bigfoot might have chomped into it and spit out the tough parts, Kat theorized—but when Miranda lifted it by the tail, the hardened remains of the scaly skin slid out of her hands, whole and intact, not a bite mark to be seen.

"If Bigfoot was here, he's moved on," Kat agreed now.

There's no sign of him whatsoever, Miranda wanted to add pointedly. Not a stitch of evidence that suggested a hairy, ape-like mammal was cruising through the trees unchecked—why keep reading clues that weren't there? Why keep faith in something that didn't exist?

"Wait a minute . . ." Kat walked to a stretch of beach where the reservoir thinned and the clear water washed onto sand. She stopped near a fallen branch, a long and skinny one, its dead twigs stripped of leaves and buds and color.

"A branch?" Miranda tied her hair back into a fresh ponytail, itching a bug bite on her wrist from something that had made it past her barrier of repellent.

But Kat crept around the branch, her eyes as wide as her grin. When she bent down to pick up the branch, she did so gingerly, like she was touching something electric. "Not a branch, Bean."

"Then what?"

The not-a-branch was passed into Miranda's hands without asking, and she stopped. "So what is it then?" It was light of weight and soft of touch, almost pliable—she wanted, on instinct, to fan it up and down like a palm frond.

130

Kat waited until Miranda looked back up. "It's a feather," she breathed, "from a bird."

Miranda gave back the not-a-branch so quickly, she nearly dropped it. "A feather? Come on. This is way too big."

"Step one: observation." Kat ran her fingers along the fringe of the not-a-branch as she angled it into a patch of sun; it shimmered iridescent like hairs. "This is a feather and those"—she pointed behind Miranda to more of these odd sticks, which trailed up the sand, among the huckleberry bushes with the crunchy leaves and old spiderwebs—"are feathers."

Miranda kept her face still; somehow the things looked a lot more like feathers when there was a whole pile of them. "Impossible. If these are supposed to be feathers, then the bird would have to have a wingspan of . . ." She did some quick calculations. "Ten feet. Or more!"

"More observations," Kat went on. "We haven't seen a single set of squirrel, raccoon, or muskrat prints—nothing smaller than us. Nothing that could be carried away in sharp, hungry talons—though judging by the size of those feathers, I'm sure even the deer are nervous. Yep, see here—the does keep their babies close when they come here to drink."

Miranda scowled as she looked down at the tracks her mother pointed out—the hooves of mother deer, the hooves of their babies, nearly underfoot.

A bird of this size would eat much bigger prey. A traitor-ous thought.

"And yet another observation." Kat pointed again, this time to the trunk of a thousand-year-old spruce. Sprinkled around its roots were rocklike clumps the size of bricks.

Kat took up a stick and stabbed one of the clumps; it disintegrated into sand and teeth and claws and bits of fur. A terrible sight; the stuff of nightmares.

"Pellets." Kat swigged the orange soda and put the bottle in her bag. "All the gnarly stuff a bird can't digest stays in her gizzard until she regurgitates it in these hard little mouth-poops—"

"Ew," Miranda said.

"—which leads me to step two: form a hypothesis. Giant molted feathers. A dip in common prey animals at a water source. And now, these pellets—still fresh." She pressed into another one with her stick—an entire skeleton spilled out, skull and spine and tail, and Miranda blinked.

Was that a set of beaver's bones? Its square teeth, its flat tail . . .

"My hypothesis is that up there, in those branches," Kat said, and again, pointed—Miranda was growing weary of that finger, that painted, glittering navy nail—to the highest boughs of the wizened tree, "there is a nest of owlets—from the rumored giant owls of the Northwest."

A noise from the crown of the tree.

Miranda looked up, shielding her eyes from the sun. A wad of sticks and moss and other forest debris stuck together in a mass on a high branch—much too high for any reliable estimation of its size, she thought, so there was no reason for her breath to be scant, her heart light in her chest.

No reason for the word *nest* to stick in her mind—there were other logical explanations. It wasn't a nest—it was debris, blown high into the tree during a summer storm. And the feather was not a feather—it was a type of uncommon, deep-woods fern. The smaller animals weren't hiding because of birds; they were shy of the impending humans, and the pellets were—the pellets were—Miranda spun, her mind seeking traction. But she was out of ideas.

"Of course," Kat finished, "if this were an expedition to find giant owls, we would do a lot more research here—we would climb the tree, test my theory, hopefully take a specimen to an aviary specialist and have it properly studied. But it's not. This is about finding Bigfoot, and so none of this matters.

"You can make this about the scientific process, Bean." Kat leaned into Miranda, an arm draping across her daughter's shoulders. "You learned it in school, and you can check those off as we go—I know how you love your lists—but the real scientific process isn't always as clean as that. It's not always about marching through some arbitrary steps. This weekend isn't only about science, Bean."

133

Kat removed her glasses and wiped the sandy grit and splashes of river water off with her capelette. "It's about believing."

Miranda's cheeks burned against the chill of the late morning, and she willed them not to—Kat hadn't put her glasses back on yet; she stared at her daughter with naked eyes, and Miranda wondered if her mother was looking through her. She felt see-through. Did her mother know? Know that Miranda didn't really buy that Bigfoot was real; know that this whole weekend was a sham, a construct, a lie?

"So what's the plan, Bean?" Kat said. "Do we stay here and take another lap around the bank, or head back to camp and regroup?"

"No," Miranda said quickly. "We go to the falls."

"You think that's a good idea?" Kat tilted her head.

"I know large herbivores tend to stay near still water," Miranda said, "but maybe—"

"Maybe there are places behind the falls that would work as a habitat!" Kat finished, grinning, and Miranda weakly nodded. "Great idea, Bean—let's grab the pulse detector and we'll just follow the bank up to the rocks."

As Kat rummaged through the back hatch of the Critter Mobile, Miranda tugged out a hair. "Should we take one of those—those things home with us?" She nodded at the pile of not-branches, gray against the bleached sand.

"Too late for us to claim that discovery." Kat pulled the doohickey from its case and flipped its switch to *on*. "It was all over the cryptozoology forums last year—two universities, both racing to analyze the DNA from feather and eggshell specimens and name the creatures first." With a generous smile, she extended the scanning pulse detector to Miranda, its machinery humming and whirring like something alive. "But we're not here for giant owls. We're here for something else."

The weight of the pulse detector in Miranda's hands, its awkward construction, the thought of how much her mother had likely spent on its purchase—money that should have gone to important bills . . . it all seemed ridiculous again. Comfortingly so. She didn't know what to make of brittle feathers longer than her arm, or muted hoots from the tippy-top of a spruce crown—but she could handle ridiculous. That was why she was here.

But even as she carted the scanning pulse detector along behind her mother toward the crashing Fable Falls, she felt a familiar niggling in the back of her heart, only this time it felt as uncomfortable as a splinter in her palm—something chewing a dime-size hole in all of her reasoning, small enough to keep out everything except for rats and doubt.

You can come, if you want."

That's how it all started with Emma. A sheepish invitation from Miranda, who had to check on the borer beetles in a neighborhood park for her science project, to the new girl with the bluebells for eyes. School had ended and the two girls were lingering at their lockers, which were across from each other in the hall. Miranda had things to do, but she didn't want to walk away. Not now, not when it felt like this, like she and Emma were destined for something. Like they were about to move from being just study buddies in history to . . . more.

So she said it: "I have to go check on my science project." A pause, a moment to gather herself, and then: "You can come, if you want."

Emma could have said no, but she said yes, and that was the beginning.

Miranda was uncharacteristically shy on the walk over. Conversation usually came to her as easy and naturally as breathing; she was the type of girl who had an exuberance, who could always pluck things from the world around her to talk about—but with Emma beside her on this steep incline of the park, she panted and stammered. She was a well, all dried up.

She really liked Emma, who had moved into the red brick house across the street this year.

She really, really liked her.

She wanted to be best friends, but she didn't know— you don't know, do you, whether or not there's such a spot for you in someone's life—you can't know until you ask.

And Miranda wasn't about to ask.

"The ones I need to check are marked here." Miranda showed Emma the map she'd drawn of the park, the one a few blocks from the school, a park built on an extinct volcano covered over with ponds and trees and grass.

Emma whistled. "Did you draw every single tree in the park?"

Miranda tried to shrug. "I like to be thorough." She prayed this would be seen as a positive.

Emma found a sequoia on the map, pointed to its real-life, sturdy-trunked correspondent, and said, "That one."

Miranda couldn't stop a smile.

Wednesdays were vehicle-free days in the park, which meant the girls and other walkers and roller skaters and bikers and joggers were able to use the park roads freely, winding up to the top of the long-asleep volcano; they didn't have to focus on anything but each other and the glory of the pleasant, neutral weather.

"White pitch on the bark," Miranda said, referring to the small blobs of saplike substance coating the trunk. "That's good. That means the tree is fighting back."

"Now what?" Emma asked. "We spray it with bug killer?"

"Nope." Miranda made a mark on her map with a yellow highlighter. "We're here to observe only. See," she explained to Emma, leaning toward her, shoulders touching as she pointed up at the branches. "When the beetles invade, the tips of the leaves turn red — or needles, if it's a conifer. If the whole tree turns brown and dries out, then it's lost."

"Sad," Emma said.

It was — though Miranda had never thought of it like that before. "Don't worry — the trees usually win. There's still plenty of green."

She said "green" but she had fallen into blue — Emma's happy eyes — blue, Miranda only knew blue.

They finished marking all of Miranda's trees, then Emma ran to the playground, to the drawbridge, the monkey bars, all the toys they knew they were about to outgrow, and Miranda followed, light as a leaf on the breeze.

They chased each other around until their legs gave out, then they threw themselves onto the grass beneath a bush of icy purple hydrangeas and Miranda looked at the clouds, then back down at Emma, and then up again at the spinning sky.

And then they huddled in the turret above the big tube slide and talked about impending junior high, the rumors they'd heard about certain teachers, the warnings they'd collected about certain girls and boys; they spoke aloud their great high hopes and fears about the move into this new phase of their lives, and so they left the park buoyed—parched and sweating and grimy with that grit that was unique to the park, a place which was the closest thing the city had to wilderness.

But they also beamed in that way you do when you tell another person a secret about yourself, and you want to pull out hairs and chew on fingernails until they say, "Oh, me, too."

When they reached their street, Emma turned to Miranda. "Want to come over?"

Miranda was so excited she didn't think of the long-term effects. What this meant.

She didn't think about reciprocity.

They were standing still on the curb outside Emma's

house—neutral ground—and so she didn't consider what would happen when she went to Emma's house that day.

She didn't think about how eventually Emma would ask to come over to hers.

"Yes."

And that was her answer, every time Emma asked her over.

Until the day—that inevitable day that Miranda should have smelled long before it arrived, here to ruin everything—the day weeks later when Emma said, "Let's go to your house today."

Miranda—trapped, frozen, a statue, utterly unprepared—managed to say, "We can't, it's being fumigated."

Emma accepted this.

She accepted it the next week, when Miranda said, "Not today, my mom has a cold."

And the next time, when Miranda said, "We have houseguests."

"Mom just had the carpets washed."

"I have a dentist appointment."

"Spring cleaning."

It scared her a little, how quickly the lies came out, but she was soothed every time Emma believed her. Soon Emma skipped over the question altogether, leading them right past Miranda's house and to Emma's front door. In the cold of the mornings, Miranda would brace herself on the way to school:

What if today it happens?

What if today it's all over?

But she would come to her locker and Emma would be there, waiting, a grin on her face—the peaceful grin of friends.

Best friends, Miranda permitted herself to think.

And so Miranda was too distracted by a pair of blue eyes to watch out for the day, the inevitable day—the day when Emma didn't ask and just showed up, without being invited.

11.

Miranda angled her clipboard into the dying sunlight. "We must have passed it."

The signal on her phone was blocked by either the trees or the drizzle, which meant she couldn't use the GPS to navigate them back to camp. She had printed a map of the whole national park, but it wasn't detailed enough to get them past a closed road, orange with construction signs that looked abandoned and edged in spores of licorice moss, and now darkness was falling, along with a discouraging rain and the ever-present mist. Their detour took them through an unknown part of the forest, miles away from Moon Creek, which Miranda now longed for as if it were home.

The darkness, it was turning out to be a funny thing. All day, as they worked and searched around the falls, the gloom had never completely lifted. Sunlight was muted because of the canopy, but with the low-hanging clouds and the clinging fog, it had been twilight-dark in the middle of the afternoon, making their search at the falls futile.

There hadn't been many spots suitable for "evidence" at the falls, anyway — it had been a rocky area, the water crashing down white with a fury and a violence. "Much too sparse of vegetation for habitation here," Kat had said, somewhat crestfallen. "The Bigfoot those hikers spotted must have been just passing through."

Even in the dim overcast, Miranda wanted to keep looking, keep searching — the lack of proof at the falls was the perfect setup for Kat to sail down the river of enlightenment, and Miranda wanted to push.

But now, as the night swooped upon them with only the glazed-over, beat-up headlights of the Critter Mobile to penetrate it, Miranda thought, *This. This is true darkness.*

The world in shadow.

Something darted into the road, a long-eared shape lit up white in the headlights' beams.

"Mom!" Miranda cried.

Kat swerved just in time, and then the thing was gone, just a blur on the shoulder behind them. Miranda gulped down the lump of adrenaline in her throat like a pill.

143

"You have to watch the road!" The words came out of Miranda like angry burps, a reflex of her panic.

"I am!" Kat leaned forward slightly over the steering wheel, though even at her tallest she looked like a junior high schooler. She tipped the last of her Cheetos into her mouth, orange residue coating her chin.

Miranda felt like all the wrinkles meant for her mother were forming on her own skin instead. "Let's just get back to camp in once piece, okay?"

The truth was Miranda had to concentrate to keep calm—to ignore how frightened she was.

What if we never find our way back?

What if we tumble off the road and the trees eat us?

What if we keep driving forever and the moss takes our car and buries us, and in a hundred years tourists come to see the huge, mysterious mound of green—

She pulled in a breath and pulled out a hair.

Her imagination was getting away from her, like an unleashed pet. The forest. It was the forest's fault. The forest was making her imagine the impossible.

Miranda looked at her mother.

Kat hummed, bouncing in her seat as she steered to whatever song was playing in her head. Didn't it scare her, too, that they hadn't passed any other cars in so long? Didn't it bother her, too, the way the edges of the road dropped off, like tiny cliffs? The way the trees sprang up right there on that edge, so close to them, she worried one might suddenly grow sentient and decide to smack them with a frilled branch.

And these weren't just any trees—they were of the massive, archaic variety: Douglas firs, western red cedars, Sitka spruces so tall she couldn't find the tops of them, all of them covered over with velveteen moss, their roots shaded by ferns—all these details illuminated by the Critter Mobile's weak beams in a lighting scheme more befitting the opening sequence to a horror movie than a drive through a beloved national park.

Perhaps it was the trees, then, that had brought forth the memory of Emma at the park with the beetles—a memory that was supposed to be sunken like a stone to the bottom of Miranda's mind. She had sunken it. Buried it. Let it lose itself among the to-do lists and what-ifs and the other memories.

But the trees had summoned it, and it had bloomed, vibrant, a wildflower in her mind until it wilted, quick as winter.

Emma, and the beetles, and the blue, blue eyes . . . it was a brief reminder of what Bigfoot had already cost her.

Out her window, she tried to see past the trunks and get a glimpse of something, anything—anything but leaf, anything but limb—anything recognizable, anything that might guide them back to camp, but it was only green and green and green . . .

Even the night, in the forest, was green.

She shivered, tried to focus past the sound of the windshield wipers, pushing away the gentle rain.

There could be anything hiding out there.

"You okay, Bean?"

"Just a little carsick," Miranda fibbed.

"How about a distraction?" Her mother then launched into a one-sided debate about the topic du jour—the six- to eight-foot-tall bipedal humanoid himself—and Miranda ingested a sigh.

"So the number of reported wood knockings has almost tripled in the last year, but the number of actual Bigfoot sightings has decreased—why, do you think?"

Miranda had only been half listening; her attention was for the GPS dot on her phone, flickering like a dying star. She should keep trying, she figured, keep reloading it until she got something. "Uh, I don't know . . . the weather?"

"The weather." Kat blinked. "Huh. You might be onto something, Bean. Climate change would shorten winters in wooded areas, push back snowlines, decrease the amount of available standing water . . ."

A sharp, venomous barb hit Miranda, and she cut through her mother's words. "That's why he's been so hard to find—maybe we should be baiting him with Popsicles."

The silence wedged itself between them, an unwanted guest.

Miranda knew she owed her mother an apology—she should explain that only half of her meant what she said, a half that was exhausted and worried and wishing for the comfort of their campground, the reassurance of that muddied pup tent and the patched sleeping bag and the cold, hard ground and the side of the sky she had woken up beneath—but at that moment the GPS on her phone gave up its attempts to reload and crashed completely.

"We're lost!" she proclaimed. "We've been driving around for almost an hour!"

"Relax, Bean." Kat sacrificed a steering wheel hand to pat Miranda's knee. "You still have your paper map."

"We drove off that map two detours and five turns ago!" *This is bad, this is bad,* her brain chanted. She yanked out a hair. Another hair. Another. "Have you seen any signs?"

"I've seen lots of signs," Kat said, cheerily. "Falling rocks. Rest stop ahead. Bear country."

Miranda glared at her mother. "You're not help—"

A terrible noise creaked from the underside of the Critter Mobile. The whole vehicle shuddered.

Then it shut off.

"Uh-oh." Kat managed to steer it to the side of the twisting road, kissing its bumper against the foliage.

"What's wrong?" Miranda said. "What happened?"

Kat turned the key—a series of maddening clicks, and then an even worse sound: quiet.

The sound of nothing.

"Probably ran out of gas," Kat diagnosed.

Miranda leaned over to peek at the dashboard. "The light didn't turn on."

Kat snapped her fingers. "I forgot! At the last inspection back in . . . December, I think? They told me the light was broken." She looked expectantly at Miranda, her eyes buglike behind her oversize glasses.

"Are you serious?" Miranda ran her fingers through her hair. She wanted, so badly, to grab a handful and pluck and pluck and pluck—plucking the petals from a daisy, one by one, dropping them into the grass. "Why wouldn't you get it fixed?"

"Because." Kat used this word, this single word, the way a child would—as a perfectly good defense. "I didn't have time. We had to go to Texas, remember? The werewolf in Marfa."

A single hair from her head—the bite of pain, the cold of relief . . .

"Okay, we should probably—" Miranda started, but the end of her sentence dangled, then landed and slid away on ice. There was only nightfall and roots and reaching branches, and those dark hills of green over rocks and dirt and dead tree trunks, looking more sinister in the

148

rising tide of evening. The soft rain on the Critter Mobile sounded like laughter.

She had no idea, no idea how to fix this.

No idea what to do.

"Are you all right, Bean?" Kat angled herself sideways in the captain's seat, facing Miranda. "You seem stressed."

"Of course I'm stressed!" Miranda let her clipboard slide into the canyon between the windshield and the dashboard. "We're stuck on the side of the road in the dark in the middle of a forest with no cell service, no clue where we are, and no one to—" she broke off, leaning around her mother.

A ranger's lodge appeared on the opposite side of the road, on the crest of a long-grassed slope, the trees cloistered around it broken to let an amber glow blaze from its facade.

"Where did that come from?" Miranda was slack-jawed; had she slipped into the hallucinatory phase of desperation?

"They probably just turned on the porch light," was Kat's explanation. "Come on, Bean—let's go see if they have a spare gas can."

But Miranda wasn't sure. She studied the lodge, the way its windows and door and porch resembled eyes, a nose, and a grin, a face leering at her. And the way it just *appeared* . . .

Kat reached behind her seat for a purse Miranda

hadn't seen before, a huge carpetbag printed with cats flying in outer space.

Miranda stared. "What is that?"

Kat ran a hand over it. "My cat bag."

In Miranda's wildest dreams, she could never have imagined an uglier purse. Yet somewhere, a company had brainstormed this bag, designed it, had it constructed and sent out to the stores, and they had done this with a specific customer in mind to buy it.

That customer was her mother.

"Let's just go." All her hesitation melted out of her; the sooner they could find some gasoline, the sooner they could finish this trip—and the sooner she could be done with Bigfoot forever.

She exited the Critter Mobile via the screechy passenger door. The rain was less than a drizzle, even—it was a liquid form of the mist, and it didn't seem to fall from the sky; it seemed to come from the trees themselves. They waded through calf-deep thistle until they stepped onto solid ground—a trail, leading up to the rustic cabin.

Miranda felt unexpectedly warm, even with the chill and dampness of the night; she took off her windbreaker and tied it around her waist. Mosquitoes loitered along the naked skin of their arms; crane flies dove dangerously close to the porch light, casting strange shadows on the front door.

"Ranger Pat Bernard is on duty tonight," Kat read from a nameplate. "Hopefully he can help us."

"You don't know it's a *he*," Miranda said, and knocked.

"A ranger has to be able to fight off cougars," was Kat's logic, as watertight as cheese.

"A woman could fight a cougar," Miranda said. "There was a campaign last year to promote more women employees in the parks programs."

"Man," Kat said. "They look better in the hats."

"Woman." Miranda practically growled the word. "No one cares about the hats."

"What is the matter with you?" Kat turned away from the door; her two knobs of hair that earlier had flounced from her head like antennae now drooped, heavy and wet. "Do you have to turn everything into an argument? Anyway, maybe we're both wrong."

The door opened, and a burly man in a red plaid shirt blinked at them with tiny eyes. Stubble coated the bottom half of his face; a snout of a nose protruded so far from his cheeks it cast its own shadow on the porch.

"Man," Kat whispered. "Told you."

"Shh." Miranda couldn't stand the glee in her mother's eyes. To the ranger, she said, "Hi, sorry to bother you. We're trying to get to Moon Creek campground, but we're out of gas."

Ranger Pat rubbed the back of his neck with a furry

hand. A television flickered behind him in a room paneled in cheap, flexible wood—a football game interrupted.

Guilt scorched Miranda; they'd intruded on his quiet evening.

The ranger finally said, "I might have an extra can in the garage. Let me look."

"Thank you," Miranda said.

"Were you guys hiking the falls?" Ranger Pat asked as he pulled on a jacket.

"Yes," Miranda answered, and was ready to leave it at that—but Kat said, "We're researchers, actually—there was a sighting at the reservoir earlier this week."

The ranger stopped, arms in the jacket only elbow deep. "A sighting?"

"Bigfoot," Kat said.

Miranda could have flung her mother off a cliff.

Ranger Pat studied them, and Miranda grimaced. She knew this look well—he was measuring them, watching for cracks. Searching for the joke. "Well, did you find anything?" he finally asked.

Kat didn't notice the smirk in the corner of the ranger's mouth, hidden beneath the lawn-mown whiskers—she never did. "Not today," Kat said, "but tomorrow feels promising." When the ranger didn't reply—how could he, to such a thing?—she asked, "Can we use your bathroom?"

And now Miranda wished that one of those trees

would truly come alive, would reach over and lift her up and carry her away from this porch, away from the ranger, from the chasm of embarrassment she was currently rushing down like a slide at a neighborhood park.

Ranger Pat opened his door wide, slightly stunned—a common side effect among the people who had to speak to Katerina Cho. Her mother left everyone bewildered.

"Where's your car?" Ranger Pat scanned the road from his porch.

Miranda pointed down the trail. The Critter Mobile was barely visible, parked just before the asphalt road bent out of sight. Its tongue hung limply from the bumper, making it look, more than ever, like some out-of-breath creature, panting on the side of the road, nose in the huckleberry.

"That's a car?" the ranger said.

"That's a Critter Mobile," Kat responded with pride.

Miranda couldn't bring herself to engage any longer; she pretended to be severely interested in her phone until the ranger sauntered off to his garage. Then she added to her to-do list:

Get rid of the Critter Mobile — sell it, burn it, especially that stupid tongue, salvage it for parts

She'd help her mother get a new car—a real one, a grown-up one—when they got back home.

If they made it out of the forest alive.

12.

Miranda took in as few details of the ranger's lodge as possible; they'd intruded on his privacy enough as it was. She itched her palms against her khaki vest. She wanted to get back to camp, back to the things on her to-do list. She still had so much to do—she hated being suspended in time like this, snagged on this stupid situation like it was a rusty nail.

Despite herself, Miranda noticed that a bowl of wavy potato chips sat on the coffee table, along with a half-devoured cheesesteak sandwich, peppers and onions spilling out beneath the crusty bread—Miranda could smell it from across the room. A barely touched glass of some white fizzy drink sat on a coaster. Seltzer, probably—ammunition to ward off the inevitable indigestion from eating that greasy sandwich.

The shame washed over Miranda in waves; so they had kept him from his dinner, too. For a moment, anger flooded her. How could Kat have left the gas light broken? And how could Miranda not have predicted this whole situation?

She perched awkwardly on the arm of the couch—half sitting, half standing, and looked out at the night through the screen door.

The evening transformed every distant tree branch into claws, crooked and spindly, stretching toward the moon, which was white as bone against the bruised sky—but strange colors were made, in this hour. The lichen on the trunks gleaming golden, the spruce tips shone so silver, they were nearly blue.

Blue.

Miranda was pushed backward into another memory—the trees, the trees were doing it, they had reached into her mind and pulled it out—

Then, from the living room, Miranda heard the clatter of a drawer in the bathroom. The memory stopped, just short of surfacing, and fell back into the water of her mind.

Again, a sound came from the bathroom—a cabinet screeching open—and she groaned.

It was worse than babysitting a toddler.

She barged in on her mother, who was, as Miranda suspected, perusing the private contents of Ranger Pat's bathroom storage.

"What are you doing?" Miranda demanded. "This isn't our house!"

"No hair spray or Midol." Kat picked up a prescription bottle from the medicine cabinet, examined the label. "That means no wife."

Miranda pulled out a hair, one of those tiny nipping ones along her neck. "We're not here to find you a boyfriend; we're here to find Bigfoot. Stay focused."

"I was just curious." Kat found the bottle boring and put it back. She fished around in her hideous bag and found her cotton-candy hand cream. "Want some?" she offered to Miranda as she smoothed the lotion into the cuticles of her glittering navy nails.

"No, thanks." Miranda would rather her hands smell like the loamy, musty mud of the reservoir than a candy shop.

"You seem extra stressed tonight." Kat pulled a tampon from her cat bag. "Do you need—"

"No, I don't!" Miranda concentrated hard to keep from detonating. "Are we ready," she asked slowly, "to go find Bigfoot?"

"Sometimes," Kat said after a minute, "you talk like we're going into battle." She adjusted her glasses and straightened her capelette, and left Miranda alone in the bathroom, drawers and cabinet still hanging open.

In the ranger's living room, the television played a beer ad, an obnoxious jingle that stuck in Miranda's head like chewed gum, even three commercials later. Mother and daughter sat on the couch, Kat sprawling across an entire cushion luxuriously, Miranda taking up as little space as possible—trying to breathe as little of the ranger's air as possible.

First thing when they got back to camp, she decided, she would change out of these clothes—she could feel the gritty orange dust from Kat's Cheetos coating her every surface. And then she'd warm her sore back muscles with the heat of the campfire—they ached from carrying that damn pulse detector up and around the falls.

She closed her eyes.

What was going on right now, she wondered, outside her window at home? Would Emma's light be turned off, only the pink haze of her night-light visible around the edges of her curtains? Miranda was so tired from two late, restless nights, she was certain if she only saw that rosy glow, she would fall asleep immediately.

Kat jumped. "What was that?"

Miranda blinked, coming out of her daze. "What was what?"

"A noise. Outside." Kat relaxed back into the couch.

The beer commercial came back on the television, and the two of them watched, silent and spellbound by the addictive music of the capitalist advertising compound.

A new smell invaded Miranda's nose—musk, a hint of fermentation, a smack of fresh pine. *The couch really stinks,* she thought, and breathed through her mouth instead.

Kat helped herself to one of the ranger's chips, then let out a yelp, gripping Miranda's arm.

"Ouch!" Miranda shrieked. "What?"

Then she heard it.

A husky growl, a clogged septum straining for air.

"Bean. Don't move." Kat was frozen as she looked beyond Miranda, all spark and dance and light in her eyes replaced by panic.

But Miranda couldn't obey. She had to see for herself.

On the porch, a huge black bear stood on its hind legs, its wet nose pressed against the screen door, a mountain of fur with glistening beetles for eyes.

If it hadn't been so terrifying, it would have been comical; the animal looked more like a man in a bear suit than an actual bear.

But Miranda got another whiff of that strong, hot musk, the scent of wild animal. This wasn't a mascot. Wasn't an oversize teddy bear. It was real, and it was less than ten feet away from the two humans on the couch, only a screen door between them.

"We're okay." Miranda said this like she was trying to convince herself. "Bears aren't interested in humans. It probably just smelled the food. We're safe in here." Her pulse hammered in her chest as she searched her mind for the research she'd done for this trip—she'd read about bear attacks, she knew she had.

"What about the ranger?" Kat whispered.

In one swift horror-movie motion, the bear slashed a paw across the mesh screen and barreled into the cabin. The wooden door frame fell around its neck and hung there like a strange rectangular collar; the bear bucked into the wall and the door frame splintered into pieces.

Just as swiftly, Miranda's brain spat out the information:

Black bears—do not run. Stand your ground. Make lots of noise and if it attacks, hit it in the eyes and the snout.

She jumped to her feet, grinding her boots into the carpet, prepared to raise her arms above her head and growl.

"Bean, run! Run!" Kat cried, and ran across the living room and into the kitchen.

"Mom!" Miranda called. Her feet weren't supposed to move. They were supposed to stay planted, the way those trees out there were planted, rooted to the earth—but the bear charged forward.

In a split second she made the choice.

And she followed her mother.

"Go!" Kat threw open the door to the garage and shoved Miranda through, leaving the bear inside.

The garage was open. Outside, night had fully steeped

the forest in blackness. A star or two twinkled in the cloudy sky; from this angle, the moon seemed to be a mere ornament, resting on the pointed top of a pine tree.

"You never run from a bear!" Miranda shouted as she sidled around a blue pickup truck, speckled mud caked above the tires. She arched her back to avoid the dirt, and her khaki vest caught on the door handle.

"I know, Bean," Kat panted.

Miranda wrenched herself free with a devastating rip, tearing a hole through the pocket of her vest. "Why'd you run, then?"

The door to the house burst open, falling off one of its hinges. The bear's monstrous head poked out of the kitchen, snout first.

"Mom!" Miranda cried.

The bear tried to squeeze its massive body into the garage, but the pickup truck impeded it—long enough for Kat and Miranda to rush around to the back of the house.

"Mom, stop!" Miranda shouted. "You're making it think we're prey. We have to stand our ground! You're not supposed to run from bears—"

"That is not a bear!" Kat said, and tugged Miranda until the two of them were at a gallop.

"What are you—" Miranda started, but she was cut off by a roar—loud and angry, close enough to send chills rippling across her skin.

Too close.

Miranda stopped thinking, stopped worrying about the ranger, or the Critter Mobile, or Bigfoot.

She stopped thinking about the right or the wrong thing to do, and she ran.

She ran.

Kat ran alongside her, and though Miranda gasped for her mother to stop, slow down, calm down, Kat never did. Miranda peeked over her shoulder once and saw it, the bear's fur highlighted by the moonlight, but otherwise the beast was dark as the night, its eyes glowing, and new energy took over Miranda. She couldn't stop, couldn't run fast enough. She let her fear drive her and her mother deep into the forest, until the cabin was a blip in the distance and the road was gone and all they knew was green.

13.

They ran.

They ran and they ran and they ran. They encountered obstacle after obstacle—logs to leapfrog over, downed trees and fallen branches crisscrossing the ground, old stumps and stones jutting from the earth like the forest's own crooked molars—yet somehow they kept their footing.

They did not run through silence; such a deep, dark forest was certainly full of sounds—blips of water droplets from the canopy, the distant bugle of a Roosevelt elk bedding down for the night, the warble of a lonely wren, singing in the understory—but they ran past it. They ran past sound itself, so it was only a rushing over their ears, an eerie nothing that they heard, and beneath that, there was the faint noise of their panting and the shifting of twigs beneath their feet. The twigs did not crackle, because the forest was too damp, and with every step the ground gave in, pressed down, like their footsteps would leave a relief in the floor—a memory of this night.

A cramp had sprouted in Miranda's side. Her feet slapped the ground gracelessly. She stumbled once; Kat helped her back to standing.

"Is it—still there?" Miranda was breathless.

Kat sacrificed a few seconds of running to whip her head around. "I don't—see him." She slowed to a stop.

The forest was no longer moss-choked and dripping wet and green; the trees were still tall, but they were no longer the behemoths of the old growth. Trunks were thick, straight arrows to the stars; the bushes were a reasonable size. They were in a clearing of firs, branches spiked black like a garden of sea urchins—Miranda instinctively tucked in close to her mother's side; Kat put a wiry arm around her.

"Where is it?" Miranda asked.

Kat hushed her, listening. "I think we lost him."

"What are w—" Miranda started, but Kat clapped a hand over her daughter's lips and yanked her to the ground.

"Can you hear him?" Kat breathed the words right into Miranda's ear, and Miranda strained to listen. There—

a monstrous grunting, a heavy tread of paws, getting closer.

Slowly, silently, they crawled. Beneath the arches of the ferns, through the white starlike flowers of the Oregon oxalis, and into the hollowed-out bottom of a big-leaf maple, the roots reaching above ground, creating a tree that looked like it was on stilts.

Miranda hesitated; what gross botanical disease had rotted this tree from the inside out? But before she could voice her concerns, the snuffling, snorting, seething was nearly upon them, and she huddled in the cavernous trunk with her mother, heart thumping, limbs aching.

The bear ran at top speed, right past the hollow tree, through the clearing and out into the open forest. *What a horrible thing,* Miranda thought, *to know that it is possible for bears to move that fast.* She recalled what it felt like to look over her shoulder and see the beast, see its eyes, looking right at them, and it knew what it wanted: to tear them apart.

A nightmare.

Inside the safety of the maple they stayed, tucked beneath its bowed legs, pressed together on hands and knees. Miranda counted to one hundred before she let herself breathe or move or blink. Then she counted again, and when she stopped, the silence welcomed her. Silence usually was a cold, lonely thing, silence usually made you turn inside yourself for company, made you listen to the wind in your own bones—but this silence snuggled her like a quilt.

The bear was gone. Truly gone.

Kat crawled out of the tree first; Miranda followed, legs shaking. "Any idea where we are?"

Her mother looked around at the trees, at the shadows, up at the sky. She pulled her cell phone from her cat bag and tried to turn it on. "Dead," she pronounced.

"Why didn't you charge it?" Miranda reached into her vest pocket for her own phone. "What's the point of you having a cell phone if your battery's always dead?"

"It's not like there's reception out here anyway," Kat said. "Besides, your phone is only charged because you unplugged mine in the Critter Mobile."

Miranda folded her arms. "It's *my* charger. I needed to finish my to-do lists." The words came out like this, all spiked and arrowed.

"Who bought your charger?" Kat said. "In fact, who bought your phone? Who pays your phone bill?"

It took all of Miranda's restraint not to say, "I've seen that phone bill. No one is paying that phone bill"—but she kept her secrets to herself as she searched for her phone and found, instead, a giant hole in her pocket.

The garage.

The rusty nail.

"My phone!" she cried. "I must have lost it while we were running!"

"Shh!" Kat reminded her.

"My whole life is on that phone!" Miranda went on in her fiercest whisper. "All my to-do lists, my schedule, phone numbers for everyone on student council—"

"We'll get you another phone, Bean," Kat said, placing a soothing hand on Miranda's back.

"Our itinerary!" Miranda went on. "All my research—Mom, we're lost! Really, *really* lost!" As soon as she said it out loud, it felt real—she noticed, suddenly, how this section of the forest was even taller, the crowns of the trees refusing to touch each other up at the top where the leaves broke away into open sky. How the green ahead of them looked exactly the same as the green behind. How the constellations above glittered and blended and made Miranda's head spin.

Kat peered up at the sky, too. "Darn. Too cloudy," she tut-tutted.

"Too cloudy for what, checking the stars like a mountain man?" Miranda's shrill voice echoed off the trees. "Follow the Big Dipper south, then take a left at the giant rock shaped like a fox's head?"

"Bean, listen to me." Her mother's intensity stopped Miranda mid-spiral. "We're out in forests like this ten times a year."

"I know, but—"

"You think Uncle Bob does the trailblazing?" Kat said. "He wouldn't know the North Star from a fairy light."

166

"I—"

"You're usually too busy sulking to notice," Kat finished, "but I'm actually very, very good at my job."

Miranda turned, peeling the pine needles off a branch, one by one. *If you're so good at your job, why haven't you ever found anything real?* Unbidden, she thought of the day they'd spent at the reservoir, the giant branch that wasn't a branch, the smell of dirty feathers in the air. "Okay, then," she said after a deep breath. "What do you suggest?"

"I know you want a step-by-step game plan, Bean," Kat said, "but I need to think for a second."

The sweat on Miranda's neck and back had dried cold. She untied her windbreaker from around her waist and put it on. But it was thin and drafty, and the forest was deep and long and cold. She rubbed her hands along her arms, trying to warm them through the nylon, trying not to think of the sweatshirt draped across her seat in the Critter Mobile. Or her sleeping bag at the campsite, or the extra blankets she'd packed.

As she gave her mother time and space to think, the bear resurfaced in her mind, pacing—its shining eyes, its growls, its stinky, oily musk. Where was it now? How long until it finally smelled them out? She strained her ears, and suddenly a thousand noises were magnified around her. Noises she couldn't identify. A hoot—was that an owl? Or a giant owlet? And was that the breeze rustling in the leaves, or the sound of something chewing?

167

"All right," Kat said. "This is what we're going to do: We're going to wait."

"Wait?" Miranda said. "For what?"

"We're going to climb up into that tree," Kat pointed, her plastic bracelets clacking together, "and stay there until the clouds move."

"So that's your brilliant plan?" Anger sent a flash of fire through Miranda, heating her up. "We perch in the tree like squirrels and wait for the wind to blow?"

"Just until I can see which way to go," Kat said. "We'll be back on our Bigfoot hunt in no time."

Lost in the middle of a national forest with no cell phone service, no car, and no light—and yet her mother still had a singular mind for Bigfoot.

This wasn't how this evening was supposed to turn out. It was seven o'clock—their schedule had her roasting kabobs right now, her eyes burning from watching the campfire's flicker. She was supposed to be relishing in the day's strivings and failures. She was supposed to be counting down to the big moment tomorrow morning when she would finally tell Kat everything. That she knew all about Kat's money troubles, but everything would be okay, because Miranda had a plan. They would abandon their impossible search for Bigfoot and begin rebuilding.

"Okay," Miranda said. "We can wait for one hour. But if the clouds don't change by then, we start walking back . . ." She looked around and chose the direction that looked the most promising. "That way."

Her mother shook her head. "Absolutely not."

"I'm the one who printed out the paper map . . ." Miranda started. She wanted so badly to be the one in charge, even though she knew she wasn't sure, any more than Kat was, where they were.

She was just so used to carrying the weight of responsibility, she couldn't stand the idea of handing it over to her mother. Surely Kat would drop it.

"We are not walking aimlessly into the trees," Kat said. "Do you have any idea how big this park is?"

"One thousand four hundred and forty-two square miles," Miranda said, and Kat laughed—she laughed, and Miranda burned.

"I'm sorry, Bean," Kat said with a shrug unbefitting someone who was lost among trees and creeks and moss. "I've got to put my foot down and be the mom."

For once, Miranda added in her mind. But she trailed behind her mother to the trunk of a pine where Kat laced her hands together in a cradle. "Here. I'll give you a boost."

Begrudgingly Miranda let her mom help her up and settled on the branch. She bunched her windbreaker around herself to little avail—she was freezing. The wind was stronger up here; it bit, and Miranda's teeth clacked loud as a jackhammer. She was starving, too. And tired. Her legs hurt, her joints still twitching from their impromptu sprint through the trees.

Kat nuzzled next to her, slipping off her capelette and draping it over both of them like a threadbare blanket. The pine's bark was thick as corkboard, and its needles dug into Miranda's scalp in a strange head massage.

"They're moving, Bean." Kat pointed up to the sky, and sure enough, the clouds were shifting. Not quickly, not enough to produce any stars, but enough to let in a sliver of moonlight, which cast the trees around them in a pale, ghostly shimmer. With the heat of her mother's body beside her, Miranda's bones thawed.

Since when had Kat become so . . . *sensible*? Miranda hated this feeling most of all—feeling needful of her mother.

How long had it been since Kat had packed her a lunch, or washed her laundry? How long had it been since Kat last tucked her in at bedtime? Miranda had been saying good night at the end of the hallway for years. If her mother ever creaked the door open after that to check on her, Miranda always pretended to be asleep; Kat didn't get to take credit for tucking her in when Miranda put herself to bed. Miranda parented herself.

Her anger flickered back to life. Kat wasn't being *sensible*—it was her fault they were in this whole situation!

"You're not supposed to run from bears," Miranda

said, for the third time that night. Her eyelids drooped, but she forced them open.

Kat shifted. "That wasn't a bear."

"Then what was it?" Miranda knew her lines, but she hated saying them.

"That was a werebear."

"A what?"

"Werebears are like werewolves," Kat explained, "but they shift into bears during certain times—maybe the moon changes them, too, or some other environmental trigger. There hasn't been substantial research, and the folklore about them is spotty . . ."

Miranda made a sound in the back of her throat. "Mom, no! That was just a bear. A regular old black bear."

"His elixir was right there on the table," Kat said.

"What elixir? What table?" Miranda said.

"On Ranger Pat's coffee table. Surely you saw it?"

Miranda reimagined the ranger's lodge, all the details she'd unintentionally gathered. "You mean the Alka-Seltzer?" If she rolled her eyes any harder, she'd fall out of the tree. "He had indigestion!"

"It was the special mix werebears have to drink to keep from transforming," her mother said. "If they don't have their nightly cup, they cross over—"

And Miranda, vessel of patience, liar of liars, nearly bubbled over with the truth. All the truth within her, boiling and bursting and ready to flow like lava, like some awakened volcano, over Kat and her weirdness. "Mom?" she said instead. "I'm too tired for this."

Kat paused. "Okay, Bean."

Miranda turned onto her other side, the new gasp of air between them making her shiver again. "Wake me when the clouds move."

Two weeks in Washington, D.C., she recited to herself to take her mind off her frozen fingers. A meet and greet with twelve senators. An all-you-can-eat bagel and schmear buffet. An impressive leadership camp on her résumé for every Ivy League university to see.

Miranda yanked out a hair, picturing the moment when she'd step onto the plane for the leadership camp; she pictured every detail, every part of the journey away from her mother.

Instead the trees handed her another memory.

A memory of the time Ms. Palmer had caught her pulling her hair once. Right before the election results for student body president were announced, when she plastered a smile on her face to hide the nerves coiling inside her belly like a knot of snakes.

"Bobby pin?" the counselor had asked, her huge brown eyes pinning Miranda to her chair.

"Oh." Miranda had tucked her hair behind her ears. "No, thanks."

"Your hair seemed like it was bothering you." Like

172

Miranda's hair was a creature capable of pestering, like it was one of her mother's monsters.

Ms. Palmer didn't look away. She knew. They both knew that she knew.

But before Miranda could dream up an acceptable excuse, the intercom crackled, and the vice principal shared the big news.

Miranda didn't clap, or cheer, or jump up and down — she sat on her hands and beamed, basking in the excitement and congratulations around her, ignoring the suspicion radiating from Ms. Palmer like a spotlight.

It was only a matter of time before the counselor would bring it up again, Miranda knew, and she still didn't know what she would say — how could she explain that sometimes her fingers found their way up to her head, and she didn't always notice what they were doing until the deed was done? Or how sometimes she felt tight, like an overpacked suitcase trying to buckle shut, and how yanking out a hair made her feel loose and open? How could she explain that sometimes she couldn't breathe until she felt that little bite of pain that reminded her she was alive?

How could she tell her counselor that the worst moments were when she was alone with her mother?

She yawned. With some force, she pushed this memory out of her mind and went back to the happy daydream of the leadership camp, the White House, the hive of people just like her, buzzing as one, the brightness of her future glowing like the sun.

The clouds shifted again, extinguishing all light. There was no longer any difference between her eyes being open and her eyes being closed.

Five minutes and a dozen hairs later, she was asleep.

The day, the one she should have seen coming—the one she should have smelled as it crept along the sidewalk toward her, beneath the blossoms of the apricot trees and the spring sun, hanging low above her house like a beacon—started out the same as a normal day, with a conversation over breakfast about Bigfoot.

"Two separate sightings in Parley's Canyon!" Kat poured and sugared her third coffee of the morning, already plotting a route for them down to Utah. "I'm still waiting to hear from Uncle Bob, but I think we'll meet him in Boise just after sundown . . ."

Cereal sprinkled down from the box, jingling as it hit Miranda's bowl. "It was a real, corporeal sighting? Not just a shadow?"

"The real deal, Bean. They tried to get their camera, but—"

In her head, Miranda finished the sentence along with her mother: "but by the time they pulled it out, the creature was gone."

"Maybe we should wait," she said.

Kat set down her cat mug. "Wait for what?"

Miranda played the diplomat, selecting her words carefully. "Remember last time? We raced off to get to Bozeman and there was nothing. Only footprints—which are exciting," she hurried, plunked down that word, "but what if this time we wait until we're really sure? Until we know that we'll find him?"

"We don't find Bigfoot, Bean. Bigfoot finds us. All we can do is try to be in the right place at the right time." She had circled the canyon on her map with her favorite green glitter pen, and Miranda had eaten the rest of her arguments with her cereal. They would be wasted on Kat—once there was an official sighting, reported through the back channels of the cryptozoology community, Kat could listen to little else but that pulse, that thrumming sound in the air—*what if, what if, what if*?

At least it was Friday. She wouldn't miss much school if they weren't driving down to the canyon until later.

Homework from absences had started to stack up like a dammed river. Miranda sometimes felt like she was trying to run on ice, her feet sprinting and sliding and failing to propel her forward, no matter how fast she moved. And with this load of never-ending makeup work came a feeling, a new one that had been showing up more and more lately—a crumbling, a wavering, as if something she thought were made from hard marble was actually sand, and she could feel it disintegrating beneath her.

Something was coming—a wave—and it would crush everything flat.

Perhaps that's why she smiled and nodded for her mother that morning, because it felt less destructive than arguing.

The humdrum of the normal day filled Miranda like air in a balloon; it buoyed her above those feelings of uncertainty as she went to her classes, where she was praised by her teachers for being right—of course she was right (she had to be right). It buoyed her as she came home after a meeting for student council candidates, prickly with the thrill of the impending election—and then it deflated when she opened her door and found Emma, sitting on her couch next to her mom.

"Bean!" Kat was happy as a puppy with a new rear to sniff. "Finally—where were you?"

"I—I had to stay after." Miranda couldn't stop staring—it was like a nightmare come true, the sight of Emma beside her mother. Her friend among the things on the walls, the fossils, the footprints, the rocks and the clutches of hairs and the fragments of bone.

Miranda knew her house was a weird one, but she hadn't been aware of the extent of its weirdness until Emma was here for contrast.

"Hi." Emma sounded timid. "I'm sorry I didn't call—I needed help with a geometry problem and I thought—"

"Don't be silly!" Kat interrupted. "You're welcome here anytime."

How much did she know? Miranda did a quick scan of the living room—Kat hadn't taken down any photographs or newspaper clippings, hadn't plopped any of her "evidence" down in Emma's lap. Maybe it wasn't too late. Maybe Miranda could get Emma out of this house without hearing the word *Bigfoot*.

"My math book is in my room," she said, and meant to go fetch it alone. But her shadow in the hallway had a twin.

Emma was following her.

"There's a bag of spicy Funyuns in the cupboard!" Kat called after them. "And Capri Suns in the fridge! Rot your teeth!"

When Miranda got to her room, she thought, for half a second, she might be brave enough to do it. To say, "No. You can't come in here. You've already seen too much. Let's go back to your house where everything is normal and pleasant and cozy, where there aren't unidentified animal body parts lying next to magnifying glasses on the dining room table, where there aren't strange speckled eggs in a stale nest in your freezer. Where your mother bakes us cookies and your father cuts your lawn, and we are safe."

But the courage left her quickly as a wink, and so with a bit of recklessness she pushed open the door.

"Wow," Emma said.

Miranda replied, weakly, "Yeah."

If the living room was the cramped, cluttered, oddly decorated habitat of a pair of creature hunters, then Miranda's bedroom was a shrine to the magical and mysterious.

The posters on the wall were so many, they overlapped each other's corners, a collage of fanged deep-sea serpents and hippo-shaped horses with bony tusks and red-furred carnivorous bats soaring across a pink moon. TOUCH THE ELEPHANT KILLER! one poster said; HAVE YOU SEEN THE GROOT-SLANG? said another.

Aside from the painted and plastered monsters, on her desk there were souvenirs from Miranda's traverses with her mother: a Maine lobster in a snow globe, a stuffed armadillo, an antlered cuckoo clock, a lava lamp with a teeny-tiny mermaid suspended in its purple goo, at least one thing from everywhere they'd been.

And then Miranda spotted the shadow box.

A framed box up on the wall, with a glass front, which contained things no kid would ever expect to find in their best friend's room:

Strands of coarse brown animal hair, gathered into a clump.

A peculiar set of vertebrae.

Two sets of insect wings, purple as violets, pinned to cardboard.

Souvenirs from her first real creature hunt.

It isn't that weird, Miranda kept telling herself. Lots of kids liked this stuff—they liked creepy tales about lake monsters and centaurs from mythology and dead mice and live snakes and bugs.

But most kids didn't have a mother like Kat, she concluded. A mother who not only believed in the stories, but chased after them.

"You have a cat?" Emma pointed to the open window, and Miranda nearly died.

On the windowsill, between the two blue curtains curling in the breeze, was the saucer of milk Miranda had forgotten to put away that morning.

"No." Kat was behind them now, crunching a Funyun. "No cat. That's for the fairies."

"Oh," was all Emma said, and Miranda knew her well enough to know she was being polite—but she also knew Emma well enough to know that when she twisted the silver ring she wore on her thumb, she was feeling awk-ward, uncomfortable, searching for words.

Miranda prayed for a natural disaster—earthquake, hurricane, anything to distract from the terrible, terrible awkwardness of this moment.

"Hey, girls, can you come look at something out back? I need your opinion."

Stay here, Miranda mentally pleaded to Emma, though her eyes never stopped tracing the patterns of the rug beneath them, but then her mother added, "You can come, too, Emma. I need all the help I can get," and Miranda closed her eyes completely.

Emma followed Miranda's mother back down the hall, so normal was she, so obedient to heed the parent of the household. Dread collected in Miranda's stomach. She wished she had cut Kat off before she could invite Emma, wished she had said, "Wait here, I'll be right back," and then slammed Emma into her room. Her weird, awful room, yes—but it was safer than letting Emma be any-where near Kat.

"Right out here." Kat directed the girls through the sliding glass door and into the backyard, where she had several white paper sacks on the patio table. "I need your noses."

As soon as Miranda saw the sacks, she went pale.

Those were the sacks from the freezer.

"Here," Kat said, unfolding one sack and holding it under Emma's face. "Smell this."

"You don't have to—" Miranda started, but to her horror, Emma, anxious to make a good impression on her best friend's mother, took a whiff.

"That stinks!" Emma gagged, fanning the air beneath her nose. "What is that?"

"Scat." Kat opened another sack and smelled it, then offered it to Emma. "Does this one smell any different to you? A little sweeter?"

"Scat," Emma repeated, frowning. "You mean, like—"

"Poop. Dung. Doo-doo. I'm trying to figure out if both of these are from the same animal."

The world seemed to stop turning, the very leaves in the willow trees bordering their yard holding still as Emma stared—first at Kat, and then at Miranda.

Miranda was ready to save Emma—the excuse was on the tip of her tongue, she was about to fling it out like a shield, but Emma saved herself.

"Miranda? Um, I—I think I'll see if my dad can help. With the geometry homework, I mean." The smile on Emma's face was hollow, made of glass.

"Okay. I left my math book at school anyway." It was a lie—Miranda's math book was on her desk in her room, beneath a scorpion fossil paperweight, but it was all she could offer Emma.

A lie, and an escape, and an apology.

She followed her friend back through their house, their museum of weird, listening to every gentle step Emma took, the whisper of the door closing, the scuff of her footfalls past the gnomes and down the porch steps, and then she was gone. Miranda focused on this, burning it into her memory, everything about it—the falling, the darkening. Something inside had crossed over to shadow; something inside had forever collapsed.

Then she stomped on their floors, making the things on the living room walls rattle, and out the sliding door she flew. "What is wrong with you?" she cried to her mother. "Why did you do that?"

"I've been analyzing these all day! I needed objective noses," Kat answered. "These are the scat samples from last time we went to Parley's, earlier this year, remember? The mystery bush? One of these piles is from a cougar; I can see the rabbit fur it ingested. But does this other one smell like berries, or nuts? Because that could be the difference between this being scat from a bear or an herbivorous Bigfoot."

Kat held out the bag, and Miranda had to stop herself from smacking it, from setting the furry, fruity scats flying onto the grass, or onto the house, or even onto Kat herself.

Instead, Miranda's hands drifted up into her hair. She scratched at her scalp, and three hairs were pulled free in the motion. "I have homework."

But she couldn't bear the thought of going back into her room; she finished her homework at the kitchen counter as Kat divided her scat and prepared the equipment. Uncle Bob finally called right before dinner.

"Parley's is a go!" Kat cheered, and Miranda entered a sort of fugue state as she numbly gathered her things and helped her mother pack up the car.

As the Critter Mobile rumbled out of their driveway, Miranda wondered if Kat had always talked like this, like she was trying to fill the spaces and would panic if there weren't words for every breath?

Had Kat always been so *much*?

Maybe it required Miranda being quiet to notice.

She ducked down as they passed Emma's house, and even though she wanted to look back in the rearview mirror so badly, she didn't. Instead she rolled down her window and smelled the fresh air.

It smelled like an ending.

14.

Miranda cracked open one eye.

How late had she stayed up studying? She'd left her lamp on, and the sunlight streamed past her curtains, bathing her room in a soft, early morning wisteria light . . .

She closed the eye, pressed the heels of her hands into the sockets of her skull; she hadn't had such a vivid dream in ages. And it had been months since she'd dreamed about Emma.

Something fluttered near Miranda's head and with a jolt, she was wide awake.

A fat, gray partridge was flying straight at her; it veered away at the last second.

"Mom!" Miranda screamed. Her nails dug into the flesh of the tree for balance; the dampness made her fingertips slide, so she grasped for leaves, pine needles, flowers, anything.

"Bean?" Kat ran through the ferns, her hair freshly twisted into two knobs above her ears. "What's wrong?"

"Help!" The bird dove for Miranda again, and she shrieked. Scaly talons gouged at her hair, the beat of wings against her ears. "I'm being attacked!"

Kat circled around the trunk. "I see her nest! You're blocking it."

Miranda scampered away from the territorial bird, down the branch, and into a clump of dogwood. A squirrel darted past her, chittering angrily as it climbed up the Sitka's mottled trunk.

"Where were you?" she demanded of Kat, her head still as foggy as the morning air around her. "Why weren't you there when I woke up?"

"I had to pee, Bean, I'm sorry—I was bursting." Kat extended a hand, but Miranda ignored the offer and got to her feet alone.

"Well, would it have killed you to tell me first?" She stepped out of the bushes and attempted to brush the smudge of mud off her clothes, arching her sore, stiff back.

Kat was studying her, and for a moment Miranda was startled; her mother looked so much like an actual zoologist carefully observing a new species. Then she realized that made *her* the animal under inspection, and she glared. "What?"

"Did I do something wrong? I mean, other than leave you alone in the tree for one minute?" Kat's eyes, behind her glasses, projected hope the color of sunshine.

You made my best friend smell poop—Miranda couldn't say it, because how ridiculous was it for her to be mad at Kat for something that had happened months ago?

"Sorry," she muttered, "just tired."

Miranda closed her eyes and inhaled, and tried to push the dregs of the dream out with her exhale. Was it the forest that had done it? Seized the memory from her brain and pulled until it was taut enough to pluck and vibrate and course through her entire body?

In a final gasp she saw it again, the look on Emma's face when Kat had waved the open bags of scat in front of them—and the pinprick of anger expanded within her. She couldn't wait until they got to the Critter Mobile and drove back to Moon Creek to pack their things. It was Sunday, and they'd done what they came for—they'd searched the area for evidence, and they'd found nothing. For the first time she was excited to watch Kat admit there was no Bigfoot—not just to save them, their house, their lives, but also for vindication.

She couldn't wait to see Kat lose something.

Something important to her.

Above them, the branches of the black cottonwoods and the red alders crissed and crossed their leaves, over-lapping each other in a strange crown; a pop of clear sky broke through the dappled green, and Miranda inhaled again as she saw it.

"No more clouds," she whispered. The brilliant white sun seemed farther away than it did back home, which made the morning light in the forest watery, thin as broth. "We can go back to the ranger. Hopefully he'll still gas up the Critter Mobile."

Kat found a granola bar in her cat bag and split it in two, giving Miranda the bigger piece. "Hopefully he's shifted back by now."

Miranda bit into the granola bar with some ferocity—it was too early for monster talk—and recoiled. "What is this?"

Her mother held up the wrapper. "Blueberry cheesecake."

"Blueberry cheese—" Miranda choked down the rest of it, aware that she was glaring, but honestly—was her mother incapable of eating anything that wasn't coated in sugar?

When she was finished puckering, Miranda glanced up at the sky. In which direction did the sun rise again?

Every tree looked identical, none of them familiar, all of them thick and boundless as giants' calves from a fairyland. The sky had, for a moment, felt open, within reach, just beyond the canopy—now Miranda saw the forest again for what it was. A tunnel of green, a claustrophobic, lushly green labyrinth—was that its heartbeat she heard now? Or the throbbing of panic in her brain?

She tried to make sense of the patterns of the under-story—the lady ferns, the liverwort, the mushrooms—of the scuff marks below her in the soft dirt—which foot-prints were hers, and which were her mother's?

And which belonged to the forest's own mothers and daughters? Its critters, its crawlers? This trail here, this long dust line between the roots of a Sitka spruce—was this marking a snake's path, or the scratching of a field mouse's tail?

Miranda was surrounded by small details—her favor-ite—but she couldn't make any sense of them.

"Let me show you, Bean." Kat knelt beside her, grab-bing a stick. She sketched the geography of the area in the dirt—a pair of squiggly lines for Fable Falls, an upside-down V for the distant mountain, which stuck its lavender, snow-capped peak up out of the canopy like a snuffing nose, a wide circle to show the Fable Forest's perimeter, a few curves for the various rivers and tributaries. Miranda cocked her head—it was semirecognizable.

"Here's the ranger's cabin." Kat drew a square. "Here's the road." She traced an X through the thickest of the meandering lines. "And here's where we are." The spot was far from the cabin and the road, but not as far as Miranda had dreaded. "We need to head west. The sun rises in the east—"

"I know," Miranda butted in. "So we go that way."

Kat reached over and gently shifted Miranda's outstretched arm. "That way."

A flash through Miranda's mind—the stack of unopened bills in the silverware drawer, the Critter Mobile's gas light cold and dark against the dashboard—a montage of her mother's most recent failures. "I don't know," she said. "It was so dark out here last night. What if we ran in circles? We could be anywhere. Your map could be dead wrong."

"Emphasis on dead," Kat joked, and a white hot spark of rage zipped up Miranda's spine.

"It's not funny," she informed Kat. "Do you not understand how bad this is?" The more she thought about their situation, the more terrified she became. "We're lost in a forest. Not just a forest—one of the largest national parks in America. No phone. No GPS. No food or water." She looked down at herself; the dried mud and torn bits of fern and sticks and pods crusted on her boots sending her heart into palpitations. "Everything is back at camp. The equipment, the coolers. My notebook, my research—we don't even have a hatchet!"

She looked up at her mother and she felt like she had been slapped—she knew that face of Kat's, knew the pursing of Kat's lips into a rosebud, the dimple in her left cheek depressing in a crater. Her mother was holding back a snicker. "A hatchet?"

"I don't know!" Miranda said. "All the articles I read

told me to bring a hatchet. To hack up stuff—firewood or something." She refused to feel stupid—what research had Kat done? What did she know about any of this?

"Don't worry about hatchets." Kat stood and stuffed her capelette into her cat bag.

"You're positive this is the right way?" Miranda asked again—she would ask it a thousand more times, or until she was sure her mother was suggesting the right direction.

"Yes, Bean!" Kat called over her shoulder, already walking into the uncurling green.

We're going to be fine, Miranda told herself, almost scolding. *We'll find our way back to the road, and we'll make our way home, and by the time we get there, Mom will have realized what a stupid, dangerous waste of a trip this was.*

A waste of a weekend. A waste of a career, of a life.

Kat only had a moment's head start, but that's all the forest needed to gobble her up.

Miranda practically swam through the branches wearing sweaters of moss and the fronds of ferns, her insides flustering, ready to fly away—where was her mother?—but then she spotted the head, the two knobs of hair bobbing against the kelly and the emerald and the willow greens. "Come on, Bean!"

And so Miranda closed the gap between them, leaving only a few inches of space for their feet to fall and rise and fall again, and she tried to focus on something else.

It was already Sunday. What would she be doing on Sunday if she were back in the safety of home, the routine? She let the list fill her mind:

To-do list:

Study for history test

Reschedule student council meeting

Finalize all Fall Fling plans: parent chaperones, helium

tank delivery, student volunteers to decorate gym . . .

"Shh!" Kat stopped, and Miranda nearly collided with her.

"What?" Miranda's blood froze. "It's back?" She waited for black fur, the scent of musk, the flash of claws in the bushes.

"No." Kat climbed onto a jutting tree root, scoping out the path ahead like a turn-of-the-century explorer. "A river," she said, "just ahead. Can you hear it?"

A river? Alarms clanged in Miranda's brain. "Mom!" she cried. "We're going the wrong way!"

"Not necessarily—"

"I'm pretty sure I would have noticed crossing a river last night!" Miranda had woken up chilled but now felt warm, her toes sweaty in her boots—so they really were lost.

As if Kat could read her mind, she said, "We're not lost. We must have gone farther north than I realized—but this is perfect." She put her hands on Miranda's shoulders, at just the right angle to keep her daughter facing her, to keep her daughter from drowning in her own worry. "The river intersects the road eventually, remember? We can follow the water upstream to the road, then follow the road to the Critter Mobile."

Miranda tried to picture the map—not the one Kat had drawn, but the real map. Was this right? Miranda had studied every river and tributary in Olympic National Park—she knew how many miles long they all were, knew which direction they flowed, but she couldn't pinpoint exactly which river this was and when, if ever, it truly bisected the road, which meant she had to rely on her mother's memory.

She had to rely on her mother.

And it felt about as comfortable as lying on a mattress filled with twigs.

"All right," Miranda finally said, when she had scoured her mind of any other option. "If you're really sure, we'll try it your way."

The river was a wild, rushing, uneven thing, lined in muddy rocks, yellow algae gummed onto the banks. It crashed downstream with a tremendous clamor, crooked in the landscape—and this asymmetry bothered Miranda, like an untrimmed tag in a new shirt, the way the water angled into the western hemlocks that cluttered the embankments.

She knew what her mother would say, if Miranda

commented on it: "That's nature, Bean. It has its own reasons for carving a river this way."

Didn't it want to be perfect, to run straight and true?

"Which river is this supposed to be?" She tried to track its course, but she couldn't make sense of it, couldn't recognize it as any of the rivers she'd seen on the map. Unbelievable! Three straight days with her mother, away from home, and her brain had been reduced to a grainy, black-and-white screen.

Except for those memories, she thought darkly. Except for those random flickers of her former best friend, which the forest seemed to fish from her mind—why couldn't it be useful and retrieve directions back to the Critter Mobile instead?

Miranda surveyed the edges of the river as they approached, watching for signs of day campers or anglers, anyone who could rescue them or at least reassure Miranda that her mother had pointed them in the right direction. That the river flowed back toward civilization.

But they were alone.

Meanwhile, Kat moved along the river like a hyperactive five-year-old, stabbing the mud with a stick, writing her name in the grime on the bank, tossing pebbles near the distant mallards preening their feathers and giggling at the splash and subsequent fluttering of waterfowl.

"Bean, look!" Kat tiptoed down the sloping shore to a

long, arrowhead-shaped rock, which jutted out over the river like a miniature cliff. "A mermaid rock."

Miranda sighed—she was not in the mood to play pretend. Not with her neck still cricked from the restless night in the tree; not with her legs now cramped from their sprint through the dark; not when she still had a thousand other things to worry about.

Kat pressed her foot against the rock; a leaf from her boot tumbled over its edge and into the water, swept away. "That's what you used to call rocks like this, when you were younger. You'd jump on every one you saw. And you'd curl up your legs, like a little tail—" She knelt down and demonstrated.

Despite herself, Miranda softened. "I kind of remember."

"And then you'd sing your mermaid song." Kat hummed a wistful tune, then disintegrated into laughter—but when she looked up at Miranda again, there was such profound sadness in her star-eyes. As if Kat had seen, in an instant, that old mermaid Miranda and the current Miranda, standing side by side, and compared the two, and found the current Miranda to be wanting.

And no wonder, Miranda thought. Mermaid Miranda believed every one of her mother's crazy stories. Mermaid Miranda didn't know any better.

But something wrapped itself around her heart as she

thought this—a second skin, scaly and armored—and squeezed.

"Ew." Kat hopped off the mermaid rock and nudged the jutting bank below it with her toe. Miranda could see now that it was garbage—wrappers and old rusted cans and bits of twine and fishing line, all stuck together in the mud, pressing out into the river, almost reaching the other side. A bridge of trash.

"Everywhere we go, we leave a giant dirty footprint behind." Kat shook her head. "We'll be lucky if Bigfoot ventures this far out in the open ever again—someday soon there won't be any sightings at all. Not with the way humans treat our world—like it's all one giant trash can."

Miranda pounced on the proposition of "no more Bigfoot sightings" and began to weave a response, but her mother shushed her. "Hear that?" Kat slanted her head, one of her hair knobs reaching to the sky, eclipsing the far-flung sun.

There was only the peal of the water, the trickle of a pool collecting somewhere nearby, the movement of the birds as they ended their songs—

Something sharpened. Something large loomed from the trees, and Miranda's stomach turned to water.

"No," was her whisper, but the forest did not listen.

The black bear came through the understory; in that moment the sky seemed to touch the ground, the green rimming the blue. The bear swung its head from side to side, looking very much like it was searching for something in particular.

"Across the river, Bean," Kat coached from behind Miranda. "Come on. Quickly."

But Miranda held her breath, held herself absolutely still. Her fingers twitched; they wanted to rebel, wanted so badly to reach up and take one hair, one tiny hair.

"Bean!" Kat said again. "Follow me now!"

"No!" Miranda barked. "You're not supposed to run!" Didn't her mother remember what happened last night? Didn't her mother know now that she had been wrong?

With a sudden guttural snarl, the bear spotted them.

It charged to the river, its paws grabbing at the slick, moss-carpeted earth.

"We have to run!" Kat took hold of Miranda's vest and tugged.

Miranda's limbs were full of electricity, ready to fly directly up and into the air to avoid being slashed to pieces by the bear. The only things stopping her were gravity and the fact that *you are not supposed to run from bears.*

"Stop!" She swatted behind her at her mother's hands. "You're going to tip me into the water!" *Stay still!* she ordered her legs, even as they trembled.

The bear was close enough now that she could see its eyes, glinting like ebony glass. How could her mother think this was Ranger Pat? A transformed human—a werebear, or whatever she called it? Something from her cryptozoology forums come to life? A legend, a bedtime story, a lie?

This thing racing toward them was pure animal. Muscle and claw and teeth.

Run, every instinct in her said fiercely—and hot on her neck was her mother, telling her the same thing.

But the research she'd done flooded back to her—

Stand your ground

Lift arms to make yourself taller

Fight back with fists, rocks, sticks, or teeth

DO NOT RUN

"Bean!" Kat screamed, her hands desperate and white-knuckled on Miranda's vest. "They can't go into water! You have to trust me!"

The bear was here, it was close enough for Miranda to feel the absorbed sun wafting off its black fur; close enough for her to smell nothing else but its heady musk, that sour stink of sweat and decay; close enough that its teeth—

Miranda stumbled backward.

Kat reached out to help her daughter cross the bridge of garbage, but Miranda pushed away her mother's hands—those hands with the navy blue sparkly nails and the plastic bracelets jangling and the same curved pinky that was on Miranda's hands, her most hated finger—and leaped onto the mess of sticks and trash and slick weeds. Her boots depressed the mud.

Suddenly, the garbage slipped beneath them, the great mass peeling away from the rest of the bank and sliding into the water.

Swimming pools in summertime were friendly, joyfully blue—this water was dark and mean, the sound of chaos churning, the threat of bones crushing.

"Hang on!" Kat dropped to her knees, shielding Miranda with her body. The bear leaned over the mermaid rock and swiped a paw, just missing Miranda's head as the entire detached clump of muck floated away.

The bear paced along the riverbank, its fur gleaming dirty black in the daylight, as if it couldn't make up its mind whether to storm the water after them or not. But it lost its chance—the raft of garbage and mud carried Miranda and her mother downstream, the bear seething, trotting along the shoreline until the water curved—*bless the crooked, imperfect path of this river,* Miranda thought as the bear faded into a black speck against the green.

"This is way better than walking. We'll get a proper tour of the forest now," Kat said, leaning over the raft's edge to watch the water's rush, and Miranda goggled at her mother.

"Are you serious?" she cried, her teeth chattering. "We're going the wrong way down an unknown whitewater river on a floating hunk of garbage, and you think we should be excited about the scenery?"

"Hey!" A passing goose bobbed its head, startled by

Kat's volume. "If you had just crossed the river when I told you, we wouldn't be in this predicament!"

"You're not supposed to run from bears!" Were the trees weary yet of hearing her say this, again and again?

"That isn't a bear!" Kat's voice was raw above the violent swirls of the river. "That's a werebear—you can't stand your ground with a werebear or it'll tear you apart!"

The word *werebear* assaulted Miranda's ears, discordant, jamming the melody of facts, of data, of all things true.

Just as Miranda took in the breath to say, "There's no such thing as a werebear!" over and over until her mother folded in on herself, she heard it—the music box again, gentle as summer rain, impossibly delicate above the din of the water.

"Hello?" She stood unsteadily on the raft and called, gasping, "Hello? Can you hear me?"

Kat yanked her back down to sitting, the raft shifting in the water. "Are you trying to knock us both over?"

Miranda kept crying out, "Hello? Help! Help us! We need help!"

"Who are you yelling at?" Kat squinted down the banks, the water soaking her knees, and Miranda looked as well—but the banks had nothing but pebbles and moss and the occasional bird and trees. Oh, how she wearied of trees!

"You can't hear that? That music?" she asked.

Her mother frowned, listening—but the tinkling song had ended, gone as quickly as it had come on. Whoever it was, they must have floated past. She imagined the kind of girl who would bring a beloved music box out to the woods to wind it up and play its eerie tune for the trees, a birdsong of steel and cogs—the type of girl who loved to hear stories, who liked her monsters sharp of claw and bristly of fur and real, very real.

No doubt Kat would've liked her.

"Now what do we do?" Miranda said.

Kat said nothing as the rapids pushed them farther down the river, farther into the forest, with only each other to hold on to.

Tell me a monster."

The black-haired girl sat up in the dark, hugging her blanket-knees on a queen-size mattress on the floor.

A bigger version of the girl jumped in the doorway, a woman with stars for eyes. "Bean, you scared me." She unbuttoned her flannel shirt and draped it over a desk in the corner of the small bedroom, a desk covered in clean laundry from earlier that morning, still nagging to be folded.

Two entire lives, crammed into that bedroom.

"Please?" the girl begged.

"You're supposed to be asleep," the mother said. "You already got a story from Grandma."

"Her stories aren't as good as yours." The girl's lower

lip couldn't possibly pout any lower; her mother was a fiddle, and the girl knew exactly how to play her. "Tell me a monster. A creature. From tonight."

The mother changed into pajama pants and sat on the edge of the mattress. "All right. Tonight it was Bigfoot."

"Again?"

"Again." The mother released her hair from a tight braid and shook it out, littering dried leaf bits and twigs across the bedspread. "But this time, it happened."

"You saw him?" the girl gaped.

The mother showed the girl an image captured on her thermal binoculars—a blurred red outline against cold, black trees. "It was him," she said, "I know it was him."

"I wish I could see him." The girl lay back onto the bed, her eyelids heavy, the creature already swimming around in the darkness, waiting for sleep to come so he could dance through her dreams all night.

"Maybe you will someday." The mother kissed the girl good night and went into the kitchen where she put a kettle on for tea.

An older version of the mother and daughter already sat at the table—the grandmother—drinking from her own mug of steaming tea. Her eyes, once stars, were now more like mirrors, clean from all manner of spot or grime, reflecting spotless versions of the people who peeked in. She kept her eyes in her lap as the mother poured her tea and added three sugars.

"You quit?" the grandmother said.

The mother said nothing.

"Why? That was a good job for you. Flexible hours for Miranda, and they paid you well, even without a college degree. How could you do this? Why do you have to be so irresponsible?"

The mother sighed. "Mama, I—"

"Can you get it back?"

"I don't want it back," the mother said. "It's perfect timing."

"Perfect timing for what?" the grandmother asked. "What are you plotting?"

"To hunt full-time." When the grandmother didn't respond, the mother went on. "I have money saved up, I have my equipment—if I don't do it now, I'll be stuck in that office forever, and I'm close. I'm so close, I can feel it—just a little more research and time—"

"This isn't about just you anymore." The older woman had a particular talent: she spoke words of all manner of consonants and shapes, and yet her lips stayed a bold purple line. "You have a daughter to think of."

"This is for her as much as it is for me." The mother waved her hands in the steam curling up from her tea. "She needs to see that anything is possible."

"She needs to have a mother who provides for her." The grandmother stirred her tea. "You're putting yourself before her welfare."

"So I should give up on my dreams?" the mother said. "That's now a requirement of parenting?"

"That *is* parenting," the grandmother said.

The mother folded her arms. "I'm building a better life for both of us."

"And this is the life you want? A life of camping and travel and searching for these—these monsters you claim are hiding in plain sight?"

"Why do you have to say it like that?" the young mother said. "Like it's so ridiculous? All animals started out this way, didn't they?" The mother paced the kitchen, every one of her movements made more frenzied and overdone by the comparison to her mother, sitting calmly, still as a pond. "The squid—people thought that was make-believe. Same with the kangaroo. The oar fish. The Komodo dragon. The okapi. They all had to be found—discovered by someone, someone willing to look past everything we see every day and find the extraordinary."

"And you think you are this person?" the grandmother said.

The mother shrugged. "What if I am?"

The grandmother straightened. "And this is the life you want to build?"

"Yes," the mother said.

"Then you will have to build it somewhere else." The grandmother placed her hands flat on the table, facing down, so the tops of her knuckles and her wrinkled fingers were exposed, blue veins protruding, the skin worn paper-thin by nothing in particular, just living.

"What are you saying?" The mother's eyes flashed, a warning, stars hurtling through the night.

The older woman held steady—though, if you knew to look for it, you'd find the trembling of her chin. "You've already borrowed more money than you could ever hope to pay back—"

"I'll get you your money, if that's what this is about," the mother practically growled.

"How? Your savings will go faster than you think."

"I'll be fine," the mother said. "I've got—"

"And those?" The older woman pointed at the black case for the thermal binoculars in the living room. "How much did they cost? This is an expensive career you're getting into, and for who? Who's going to hire you? How are you going to earn money when you work for no one but yourself?"

"I'm going to—"

"How will you do this, Katerina? How?"

"If you'll just—"

"I know it was a shock, when he left." The grandmother reached out, put her hand on her daughter's hand.

For a moment, they could hear everything in the kitchen—the mineral drip of the faucet, the whisperings of the dishes, asleep in their cupboards.

"Not to you, right?" The mother pulled herself away.

"Didn't you say it would happen? You knew it was coming?" Her jaw hardened to steel. "It was exactly what you were hoping for."

The grandmother's mirror eyes went cloudy. "I didn't know it would happen. I believed it might, but I never wanted it for you, Katerina. That—that pain. But I can't support this lifestyle. I told you—if you live under my roof, you must be working or going to school." She picked up her tea. "I will give you three months. Then you need to find your own place."

But the star-eyed woman and her daughter were out in a matter of days.

One week later, the mother found her first footprint. She took a mold of it and sent the plaster to a university. The university sent it back with a letter listing the requirements for a research grant application; it was meant to be a deterrent, not an encouragement.

But the mother didn't hear "no." She only heard "not yet."

She set the plaster footprint on her living room mantel in her new cheap, tiny box of a house as a reminder—a reminder to keep walking forward.

A reminder that some things were true, whether people believed in them or not.

The daughter with the serious eyes had overheard the conversation between the mother and the grandmother from her mattress on the floor. And for all the stories of monsters and creatures and mysterious things that hid in the shadowy places of the world, this was the most unsettling—to hear her mother snap like that, to hear her sound like a child. To hear that fear in her grandmother's voice.

To hear the silences, and to feel a new coldness descend on the house.

But most unsettling of all was the moment when they pulled away in their rented moving truck, and the daughter looked back at her grandmother's house—she did not recognize the living thing, standing, solemn, in the doorway as they left. She had never known her grandmother to be cold, not until this moment.

That was the moment she realized it—they would probably never see the grandmother again.

But for a while they were happy—the daughter was allowed to go on all the creature hunts, which were no longer sequestered to only weekends, but ran into first days of school and trick-or-treating and birthdays. Every time they left their driveway in the new-to-them squarish van, the daughter would tilt her head into the cool glass of the window; she could feel something, out there, beyond the wind. Tendrils reaching, a hint of gold in the sky.

Something magic.

"Do you think we'll find him this time?" she'd ask the mother.

The mother would adjust her mirrors and say, half

looking at her own reflection, as if she were talking to herself as much as to her offspring, "We don't find Bigfoot, Bean. Bigfoot finds us." Then, with a merciful wink and a grin that could outshine the sun, she'd add, "But we're close. I can feel it. We're close."

Close or not, he never found them.

And they never found him.

They'd find footprints, or hear far-off noises, or spot shadows, "evidence" that was always exciting to the mother, who was searching for reasons to believe.

But things shifted that night on the floor in the grandmother's house. The daughter began to see holes in everything until, eventually, she saw her mother for who she really was.

A mom who sold her own future and the childhood of her only daughter so she could hunt for monsters.

A mom who traded it all in for bedtime stories.

15.

The debris held together as if it had grown from the earth that way, old cups and chip bags and cardboard tangled together with cattails and sludge, but it proved to be the perfect raft. It only jolted them once, when the river suddenly dipped its elevation to match the decline of the land—Miranda hadn't realized she was dozing until the bump knocked her awake.

It was the lull of sailing, the warmth of direct sunlight on her face, the way her windbreaker was bunched up perfectly beneath her, and her mother's shoulder . . .

She yawned.

Her sleep hadn't been deep enough to make a dream, but she'd had one anyway. Another hiccup of time, another memory regurgitated like a pellet, and this one was full of teeth.

Things were still green, yes, but less uniformly so—the pines were now straight, triangular-shaped, acres of perfect Christmas trees. The distance between their roots and the places where they sprung from the ground—it was comfortable. Breathable.

Moss no longer blanketed every surface, only the fronts of some older trees, the tops of the branches, the sky-facing parts of the rocks. No longer a moss monster that would take over their bodies while they slept, but rather a dusting.

Like frost on winter's first morning.

It embarrassed Miranda, to be so relieved by this.

They kept their eyes peeled for people—park rangers, canoers, for anyone who could rescue them.

But they were in true wilderness now.

"Look." Kat pointed.

Almost a mile downstream, the river bent through a ravine, trees and salmonberry bushes and cattails parting to let the water through. Mount Draco came into view, majestic and proud—and getting closer.

Miranda's heart skipped. They had come so far so quickly.

"The water curves right around the mountain," Kat said.

"So you think we should try to go around the

mountain, too?" Miranda's voice wavered. "That'll put us miles away from the Critter Mobile—"

"Give me a minute," Kat said calmly. "Let me think."

Miranda tried to picture it on the maps she had studied—she recalled that Mount Draco was, yes, surrounded by offshoots of creeks and streams and pools—but she couldn't remember where they led.

She couldn't remember.

"Yes. We'll stay on the river and go around," Kat finally said. "The water on the other side is nice and quiet. We'll be able to climb off there and swim to shore."

"Wait." Miranda frowned. "How do you know?"

"Oh—we camped here once. A long time ago." Kat removed her mud-splattered glasses and tried to wipe them clean on her capelette, which was also dirty.

"Me and you? Or you and Uncle Bob?"

Kat locked eyes with her daughter. Without her glasses to magnify them, her eyes were naked, child-size. Miranda could see straight past her mother's irises to her soul, if she wanted to. But Miranda didn't.

"Me and your dad." Kat put her glasses back on.

"Oh." A small word, all Miranda had to offer.

"It was years ago," Kat said. "Before you. A lot of the terrain has changed. There are more trees now. Fewer squatters. But I do vaguely remember Mount Draco."

Miranda was quiet, considering the forest around her—it felt haunted now, with memories she hadn't even been alive for. What had her father thought of these pines, these birds, this sky? Was he a good fisherman? What would he be doing differently, if he was the one trapped on this raft with Miranda instead of Kat?

"We should come back here in the summer," Kat said, "when the yew trees are in season and the nights are warmer." She smiled. "Let's do it. Just you and me, Bean."

Miranda was only half listening.

Something had been knocked over, a switch flipped.

He had to be smart, she had decided. Book smart. A fan of graphs and charts and numbers, everything laid out just so. He must see the world this way, because that's how Miranda was, too. Miranda must have gotten it from him—where else would she have gotten it from?

"Thirsty?" Kat offered Miranda the orange soda from her cat bag.

"Gross." Miranda shook her head. "It's probably warm. And flat."

"Well, it's all we have." Kat gestured to the river. "Unless you like delicious, refreshing algae water."

"Green tea," Miranda blurted. Nine-year-old Miranda, bored during a hunt for the Bear Lake Monster, had decided to set up a booth selling lake water. The water had been full of bacteria and floaters, but she'd promised it would quench the thirst of any brave takers.

Kat giggled. "A quarter a cup," she recalled. "Uncle Bob went broke."

Miranda caught herself smiling, but wiped her face clean of emotion before Kat could make a big deal out of it—before she could take this and turn it into a mother-daughter bonding moment.

That was not what this trip was for.

Mount Draco loomed closer, and the river picked up speed. A log rolled into the water and was immediately ground to smithereens in the rapids.

Miranda's fingernails dug into the mud of the raft—beneath them, the water churned chocolate brown and steely blue and hunter green, the white mirror of the sun on the surface shattering, then reforming, then shattering again.

"Okay, Bean, I'm going to need you to stay calm."

"What? Why?" Then Miranda saw the mountain, and her jaw nearly fell off its hinges and splashed into the water.

The river did not go around the mountain; it went through it.

Cut out of Mount Draco's rocky base was an archway, under which the river flowed into a cavern so long and deep, they couldn't spot the daylight on the other side. The water dropped six feet before surging into the cavern—a short fall, but a dangerous one, especially considering their raft was made of sticks and trash.

What had she read about Mount Draco? She knew it had caves and tunnels, pockets of dead space.

She knew what lived inside those caves—white-nosed bats, Larch Mountain salamanders, scorpion flies—but she couldn't make her brain summon the details she needed.

What if our raft capsizes?

What if we are smashed to pieces in the wake?

What if there is no way out of the tunnel, and we disappear under the mountain forever?

And then she was out of time for questions.

"Hold on to me!" Kat didn't wait for Miranda to do it; she wrapped one arm around her daughter and clenched the mud-slicked weeds of the raft as it pitched down and dipped beneath the surface.

The world was muted, all those chirps and forest scuffles gone as the water plugged Miranda's ears and shocked her with its cold.

And then the raft bobbed to the surface and passed through the archway into Mount Draco's black cavern.

"Are you . . . all right?" Kat said, coughing.

Miranda choked out a "yes" as she rubbed the river out of her eyes.

They were alive.

Inside the mountain it was dark as night, but with the last swell of sunlight, she caught her mother's silhouette. Kat was chewing on a sparkly blue fingernail. It was an old childhood habit, Miranda knew, one that Grandma Hai had insisted Kat break; her mother was as shaken as she was. Miranda felt a little better knowing this, though she couldn't explain why.

Thankfully, the water was less violent inside the cavern. No more swirling vortex of death—this was a lazy river meandering beneath a fake plastic mountain at a water park, Miranda told herself, and their mud raft was an inflatable inner tube, carrying them away to relaxation. Miranda breathed out, trying to exhale the daggers in her lungs.

The river curved around a cluster of stalagmites, and the cavern opened, brightened. Tunnels in the mountain's side let rays of sunshine through, like windows broken into the burnt orange rock. The water deepened, shifting in color from the cold, earthy blue of a mountain stream to the eerie green of a subterranean lake.

Miranda leaned over the edge of their raft and peered at her reflection in the olive water—an exhausted, grimy version of the Miranda she knew. What would the student body think if they saw their president now? She finger-combed her wet hair, pulling free a few strands that refused to conform, delighting in the tiny pain.

"Bean," Kat whispered. Miranda's hands dropped to her lap. "Are you seeing this?"

Sunbeams pierced the cavern's darkness in rich aureate arrows, hitting the walls and setting off a rainbow of sparkling glitter.

Mount Draco was bleak and crackling gray on the

outside, snow from ancient blizzards hardened on its peaks—but inside, every color of the spectrum glistened. The very air was jeweled.

The mountain's big secret.

"Mineral deposits?" Miranda asked.

Kat's face was covered in a constellation of little white reflected lights. "Or a dragon's hoard."

Miranda rolled her eyes.

"You'd better be careful," Kat said, "or you'll roll those eyes right out of their sockets."

"Sorry." Miranda looked for herself in the water again, but it was too murky. Clouds of black silt, stirred up by their raft.

Dark shadows against the green.

"Hey, Bean. Remember Hilda Wolf?"

"Who?"

"Hilda Wolf! You know, she snapped that famous picture of Bigfoot by the horse trough? On that farm in Oregon?" Miranda made no indication that she knew or cared—Kat went on anyway. "She had a theory about Bigfoot and caves—something about their vocal reverberation and echolocation." Kat glanced around the cavern. "He could be in here, right now. Watching us. Hiding."

Miranda removed a twig that was stuck in her bootlace. "How exciting." Her voice was flat as the water, but she was too worn-out to fake any enthusiasm.

"It could happen, Bean. Someone spotted him here at

Mount Draco just last year." Kat fiddled with her plastic bracelets. "A hiker saw him just before sundown—"

"And let me guess," Miranda said. "He tried to take a picture, but his battery was dead. Or he did get the picture, but a bat flew across the camera lens at the exact moment he snapped it. Or he developed a sudden inexplicable tremor in his hand, so the picture turned out blurry."

Even though the cavern was the most beautiful thing she'd seen on their trip so far, Miranda could not be more relieved to see the end of the cavern ahead—daylight pouring through another archway, the glimpse of a calm, clean-looking shoreline visible in the distance.

Their last minutes in the dark.

Miranda's last chance, before the sunshine chased away the shadows, to say something she hadn't been able to say yet, in the light of day. "I can see how some people wonder . . ." she chose her words carefully, "if there really is a Bigfoot. If he's real, why there isn't proof?"

Kat laughed. "There's so much proof!"

"Like what?"

"Footprints—" Kat started.

"Are easy to fake," Miranda said. "All they prove is that someone with a plaster mold was stamping around in the dirt."

"Hair and scat samples—" Kat tried again.

"Which, so far, have only come from known, already-discovered creatures."

"There are some photos and video footage—"

"And they're never in focus, or they're obviously people in gorilla suits." *Admit it, Mom*—the words were there on her tongue. She could taste them, the yaw of the consonants, their sharpness. *There isn't any real, hard, scientific evidence that Bigfoot exists!*

Kat was quiet for a moment, their raft sailing along the green. "Eyewitnesses," she said. "There have been hundreds of accounts every year for centuries. People spotting large, hairy, simianlike creatures all over the world—but especially in the Pacific Northwest."

"That doesn't count. You can't trust people." Miranda realized she'd been shaking her head for about a minute straight, but she couldn't stop. "People see what they want to see."

"If you can't trust people," Kat said, "you can't trust anything."

Miranda focused on the upcoming shoreline, the way the sun hit the water. Back at camp, tucked at the bottom of her duffel bag, was the stack of opened mail—the bills, the notices, splattered with red ink in envelopes with jagged edges. If she had the bills here, she could pull them out now, let them win this argument for her: *You see where Bigfoot has gotten you?* she would say. *You see where trusting people has gotten me? I trusted you to be responsible, Mom, and now we are in trouble.*

"None of that matters anyway." Kat picked at the long

strands of grass that trapped a rusty tin can to the mud on the raft. "We're going to find proof enough for all of them this week."

This *week*? "No, it's already Sunday." Miranda's insides clenched. "The trip is over. As soon as we get back to the Critter Mobile, we have to pack up our things and start driving."

"But we barely got to search for clues!"

"I told you, I can't miss any more school. I already missed Friday." Tears prickled her eyes. All for this stupid trip, so she could save their house—and save her mother. "We're never going to make it back, anyway. If we don't drown in this stupid river, we'll die of hypothermia or get eaten by that bear."

"Werebear," Kat corrected, and explosions went off in Miranda's head.

"Stop it!" Miranda's shout reverberated in the cavern. High above them, bats rustled among the stalactites. "Stop calling it that. It's just a bear!"

"We're lucky werebears are rogues." Kat continued as if Miranda's words had gone straight into a vacuum; her hands were now caked in mud as she tried to unearth the tin can at her knees. "Can you imagine if he ran in a pack?"

Orange flames. Billows of black smoke. Buildings collapsing.

"It's. Just. A. Bear." Miranda's teeth gritted together so hard, they could have shattered like panes of glass. "Just a regular, run-of-the-mill, terrifying black bear with some sort of territorial grudge against us—"

"You know what?" When Kat finally looked at her daughter, there was steel in her eyes. "If you don't want to believe me about the werebear, fine. That's your choice. I can't make you. But you need to realize," she said as she yanked up the final blade of grass trapping the tin can to the mud, "some things are true whether you believe in them or not." She freed the tin can with a yank and their raft shifted beneath them.

A bellow sounded in the cavern.

"What was that?" All Miranda's anger liquefied into cold, trembling fear. She scanned the cavern for black fur, black claws, a dripping black snout . . .

The garbage under them shifted again. Another growl, like a famished stomach, amplified in the rocky enclosure.

"Bean," Kat said. "We've got to get off."

"No!" Miranda said. "We're almost to the shore—"

The raft slowed in the olive water, then spun around—spun *against* the current.

"We'll swim for it." Kat held out her hand. "You have to trust me, Bean—come on!"

"We're fine! The raft's just caught in the weeds." Miranda's own heart didn't share her faith—it thumped for attention, hopping and scratching and meowing in her chest.

"Bean, this isn't a raft!" The tin can at Kat's feet rolled into the water with a splash. "It's a—"

Before she could finish, the raft shook like a sopping wet dog, and Kat was thrown off. She landed in the water with a splash.

Miranda screamed.

Then the raft dove into the river, with Miranda still clinging to its back.

16.

Miranda's lungs were on fire.

The raft—the thing that wasn't a raft—moved along the bottom of the river. Flashes of colored lights from the mineral deposits penetrated the green water as they took laps around the cavern, the thing trying to shake Miranda off, her hands clenching its weedy tendrils in panic.

Don't breathe in, don't breathe in.

The part of her mind that still held on to a shred of logic repeated this over and over, but it was getting harder and harder to keep her mouth closed. Her body craved oxygen, burned for it.

No oxygen down here! her mind shouted —

Or maybe there was?

That's how the mermaids do it, right?

Something in her brain itched. That last thought didn't feel right.

Maybe sweet relief is only an inhale away?

Which thoughts were good thoughts, and which thoughts were only surfacing because she was starved of air?

Which thoughts were like her mom's thoughts?

The thing abruptly stopped, shuddered beneath her. Miranda convinced her hands to release their death grip. She was finally free, but too weak to kick or swim. Just tired skin and bones drifting through the river alone.

Her eyes fluttered open and closed. Muted rainbow lights and soft green water the color of moss.

And then—

Then she saw it.

She saw it, and her eyes focused.

The thing.

The thing that wasn't a raft.

It wasn't a raft—

Because it was a fish.

A giant fish, one eye blinking dully at Miranda—a long, cylindrical eye, like an old tin can. Her mother must have ripped its other eye clean out of the mud.

Mud that wasn't mud, because it was scales—huge mud-slicked scales covering its garbage-studded body, weeds poking out of its face.

Weeds that weren't weeds, because they were whis-kers. Like a catfish's whiskers.

As for the garbage in the mud—soggy pizza boxes, plastic soda bottles, dozens of cigarette butts—Miranda couldn't tell what was truly litter and what was just the strange scale pattern of this impossible creature.

A creature.

How could they have thought this was part of the riverbank?

Through the sea of green, Miranda watched its bot-tom lip droop, its teeth like broken bits of mismatched glass—emerald green, root beer brown, amber orange.

Her eyes rolled into the back of her head. This was it. The last of her oxygen.

She drifted down, down into the water, down . . .

A pair of arms wrapped around her middle, and she was rocketed to the surface where she gasped for air and found it at last.

"Swim, Bean, swim!" Kat shouted in her ear, her voice rattling around inside Miranda's head.

No, Miranda thought, groggily. *Get out of my head. You can't come in here.*

But Miranda obeyed, kicking her legs, newly ener-gized with every breath she took.

The fish, the thing—whatever it was—made a wide revolution in the river and headed out of the mountain cavern toward the light, where its shadow faded from the water. Off to find another lazy, shady spot in the forest to park itself.

The river carried them under the archway and out of the cavern, too, to the other side of Mount Draco.

Here the water was quiet and low, pooling in a natural reservoir of gunpowder blue. Geese dipped their white-flecked heads in the shallows for water bugs; an abandoned beaver's dam unmade itself in the anemic current, spiky black splinters beaching themselves on the pebbles.

Miranda clawed her way to the bank and lay there, plastered to the ground like a starfish. "What . . . was that?"

Kat sat up beside her, unwinding her inky hair so it dripped down her back. "I didn't get a good look at it—some kind of overgrown sturgeon?"

"A sturgeon?" Miranda said. "That thing was the size of a car!"

"Maybe it's a new species." Kat slipped off her capelette and wrung an entire lake out of it. "A fish disguised as garbage—some kind of survival tactic, now that humans are so prevalent in the park . . ." She flapped on about twenty-first-century evolution and urban camouflage as Miranda's cold dread was replaced by annoyance.

Miranda, who had read practically the entire Internet's offerings on made-up animals, and who had spent her whole life with her mother, hearing her stories, dragged

226

along on Kat's searches, and still—she'd never heard of such a thing.

Such a fish.

Miranda shook her head to empty it of the last dregs of river water and absurdity.

No such thing.

No giant river fish made of trash and mud, swimming through the stream systems of Washington state.

No monsters. No Bigfoot.

Animals and insects and plants that had been discovered through the proper channels, living things with places in the animal kingdom, with scientific names, and labels, and photographic evidence—those were acceptable.

Everything else was complete hooey. Fodder for people who had to invent things in order to make life livable. People who couldn't live in reality the way it was, who needed to paint it over in make-believe and bubbles and barbed tails and unicorn horns.

People who couldn't face facts, because the facts hurt.

People like her mother.

Kat peeled herself off the bank and extended a hand to Miranda. "Well, Bean, I've got good news and bad news. The good news? I know where we are."

Miranda ignored her mother's hand and pushed herself onto shaking legs. The barking ache of her limbs; the pounding of her head from the sunlight, so blinding after the darkness of the cavern; the scrunched-up, empty

227

feeling of her gut, emptier than the school halls in those early mornings—all of that was nothing, lost against the new worry resting on her shoulders as she surveyed her mother. "What's the bad news?"

"We've got about two days of walking until we're back to the car."

Was it her heart, hitting her chest bone so hard that the sound ricocheted through her insides? Or was that droning the sound of the forest, alive and whispering and breathing—

"Two days! But I can't miss any more school! I'm going to lose my credit, my grades—I'll have to make it all up at summer school, and then I'll have to give up my camp—"

What if we run—

What if we find—

What if we—

What if—

Her mind whirred, but couldn't produce a finished thought.

"I'm so sorry, Bean." Kat brushed the dried sand off her bare legs. "I didn't know the river would push us along so quickly—or maybe it was the fish—"

"It wasn't a fish!" Miranda focused on this, hung all her fury on this detail. Whatever she had seen, or thought that she had seen—it wasn't real. "Human minds put faces on things. If there are hints of eye sockets or noses or smiles, we think it's a face—it's called *anthrop—anthromo—*" The word slid around in her mouth like bald tires on a snowy road.

"Come on, Bean. You saw it yourself," Kat said. "There were fins—"

"Our own minds put a fishy face on that glob of garbage," Miranda said. *"Anthropomorphization!"* She spat the word out with relish. "It's called *anthropomorphization!*"

Kat snorted. "You sound like an encyclopedia."

"Better than sounding like an episode of *Bigfoot Bozos.*"

Her mother looked like Miranda had shrunk her down to three inches tall, but Miranda didn't care—she was right. It was a childish impulse that came over her, but she wanted to hit, or stomp, or run right for the trees—run until she had outrun reality itself.

Two days of walking—that meant they wouldn't drive home until Tuesday, or even Wednesday—and then she'd have more absences on her record. No other way to make up those suspended grades except summer school.

Her heart wobbled.

The leadership camp.

Ms. Palmer . . .

She was going to be so disappointed.

Miranda would explain it to her as best as she could—no. She'd demand that Kat go in and apologize.

Explain. Tell the counselor that Miranda would now miss out on her dream because she wasn't willing to give up on hers.

Make Kat tell the counselor that she was the one who had made a huge mess of everything.

Not Mom's mess, a voice hissed from deep within. *You did this. You're responsible. You agreed to let Mom follow the river; you hopped on the raft and jostled it loose; in fact, you're the one who insisted on coming in the first place, remember? Mom was perfectly willing to let you stay home, but you had to butt in and fix everything . . . and now it's all ruined.*

Your fault, your fault, your fault . . .

"Bean, listen to me: If we get moving and cover as much ground as we can in the daylight, we might be able to make it back by Tuesday morning."

"So?" Miranda launched the word at her like a dart. "I can't even miss my first class. I have to be there when school starts at eight o'clock, on the dot."

Kat scrunched her eyebrows. "I thought school started at seven thirty."

"Who cares?" Miranda burst, though her stomach lurched when she realized Mom had nearly caught her lie. "There's no way I'll get back in time."

"We will if I drive all night tomorrow." Kat reached into her cat bag and passed her daughter the bottle of orange soda. "I can get you there, Bean. You're going to have to trust me. Now drink this—don't think about how it tastes, just drink."

Miranda considered her mother as she chugged the soda and nearly gagged—cloyingly sweet and flat.

But she did feel a little better.

Kat took the bottle from Miranda and refilled it from the stream. "I know most of the gear you packed is back in the Critter Mobile, but did you put any iodine tablets in your vest?"

Miranda clutched her vest with both hands. "No."

"A filter?"

Again, Miranda said, "No."

"What do you have, then?"

Miranda zipped it up, defensive. "Just . . . some survival stuff."

"Space blanket?" Kat asked. "Steel wool? A lighter?"

A space blanket would have been useful. And a lighter—of course! Why hadn't she put that on her list?

Your fault, your fault, your fault . . .

"What's wrong?" Kat said. "You have homework face."

"I—I'm just realizing," Miranda said, concentrating to keep the words from bumbling out in a hysterical swarm, "there's a couple of things I forgot."

Kat reached down to pull a burr from the laces of her boots, and Miranda's chest clamped tight.

"We're not going to make it, are we," Miranda whispered. Not a question—a premonition.

"I told you, Bean, if I drive through the night—"

"Not that," Miranda said.

"Then what?"

"I mean we're not going to make it. We're going to die." Miranda's hands shook. Her legs shook. She couldn't breathe correctly. The leadership camp, their bills, Bigfoot—forget all of them. They weren't even going to survive the trees.

The moss.

The green, the green, the green—

"Bean!" Kat scolded. "Don't talk like that."

"How can we possibly make it out of here alive, Mom? I didn't bring iodine tablets. I didn't even think of them." Her throat was dry as sawdust, her entire body wrung of all moisture. Every inhale was a labor.

Kat gripped Miranda's shoulders. "We are not going to die," Kat said. "In fact, I don't want you to say that word again."

"But—"

"We'll probably be a little dehydrated when we get to the car, and we'll definitely be hungry," Kat went on, "but there are other ways to purify water than boiling or iodine tablets."

Something lightened the tops of Miranda's shoulders, like a great bird had swooped down and clutched some of her fears and flew away to drop them in the river. "There are?" That's right—there were. A light came on in her brain, shining on the Internet research she'd done on how to find water in the wilderness.

Kat dug around in her cat bag and found a large steel tube. "Yes! I knew I left it in here. My filter straw—it will filter water while we drink."

Miranda nearly laughed. There was actually something *useful* in that disgusting bag.

Kat plopped the oversized straw into the orange soda bottle and drank. "Refreshing! Now you."

Miranda studied her mother as she sipped. Kat looked, for a moment, so certain, so sturdy—wise, even, the way the sun cut across her face, highlighting her crow's feet, the new lines in her skin that she hadn't seen the other night when she hovered over her mother's bed. There were years in her eyes, something Miranda had never noticed before. Years of experience, years of the ups and downs of living. A few scars from old wounds, and the patience garnered from tending those wounds.

This was what a mom was supposed to look like, Miranda thought. This was what a mom was supposed to feel like. Like Miranda could topple over a cliff, right now, and Kat would somehow defy the laws of physics and be at the bottom to catch her.

"Stop worrying." Kat spoke tenderly. "We're going to be just fine."

Belligerence warmed Miranda like a fever. "I'm not worrying—"

233

"You are." Kat's face grew serious. She pointed at Miranda's right hand, which was buried in her hair just behind her ear. "You've pulled out six hairs already."

Miranda lowered her hand. She hadn't even noticed that her hand was in her hair.

She'd done the dance so many times, her fingers knew the steps by heart.

"I wasn't—I was just—"

"We should make an appointment to talk to Ms. Palmer about this when we get home. It's starting to show—right here." Kat reached out, running her fingers along Miranda's hair as tenderly as if she were stroking the fine down of a newborn's cap. Miranda pulled back and touched the spot herself—

And she recoiled.

Her fingertips found scalp. Bare scalp.

Had she really pulled out that much hair?

Deep inside, something was sinking fast.

A rock thrown into a lake, a sparrow shot in the wing.

"Bean." Kat held her daughter's chin. "It's going . . . to be . . . okay." Then she let Miranda go, and forged ahead through the bushes, taking the lead that belonged to her.

Here was the impossible, unimaginable creature—this version of Miranda that wanted to fly into her mother's arms, and unwind, and cry. That wanted to let Kat stroke her back and pat her head and tell her, over and over, that everything would be okay.

234

This version of Miranda that could believe her.

"Coming?" Kat said, about twenty paces ahead. "We don't want to waste the sunlight while we have it."

The strangeness that filled Miranda, making her light, was one she didn't easily recognize without the bite of pain that usually preceded it.

Relief.

Relief that her mother was here.

Miranda shoved her hands into the pockets of her vest—hands that were squirming, itching to reach up and yank out hairs—and followed her mother away from the river, away from the mountain, away from the shingled shoreline, and out into wild forest, where the trees grew as thick as they were tall, wrinkled and old, and where the very idea of trails or paths was as unthinkable as the idea of an eight-foot-tall biped, hiding in plain sight.

17.

Here in the old growth, more colors joined the green, and the expansion into a jeweled world made Miranda's head spin. The woods teetered in that space between the seasons, beginning the display of the autumnal gamut—pinks and crimsons, pale oranges, electric yellows.

Miranda gathered the details greedily, hungry for the variety: the salmon leaping from the streams, the way the chanterelles glistened between roots of hemlocks, the salt collecting on the lichen of a logjam.

White freckles on a deer and her almost-grown baby, their red coats browning for winter. The cool, frosted gray of dogwood berries, ripe for harvest.

And the black of shadows, which belonged to all seasons.

The chill had already leached many branches, making them stark outlines against the watery sky. Minimalist versions of themselves.

A nip in the air bit the end of Miranda's nose and ears and fingertips.

The world tumbling through fall and then into winter.

Her favorite and least favorite time of year, this time of transitions.

Her favorite, because fall was the transition into a new school year, the season of fresh starts and new classes and crisp boots and new jeans. A chance to level up. A chance to be a new, improved Miranda.

But the details of her fall weren't cider or pumpkin flavored; they were tinged with memory. Hard memories.

Memories that were not green, or russet and gold and scarlet, but colorless.

The concrete of the driveway, cold even through her boots as he knelt in front of her. Yesterday's rain still staining the sidewalks. The plaid pattern of his tweed luggage. Their lawn, crisp on the edges, strewn with dead leaves curled over on themselves.

A season of good-byes.

But this was dangerous, to balance on the edge of such a memory as this—the forest was already too eager to push her backward into them. And there were some memories that would gladly have her, were she to fall into them.

Some that would take her.

Some she would not survive.

She thought instead of how they'd cruised so far downriver, through a whole mountain, and how they now had to hike back up through the old growth, circling back to where they'd started—stranded on the side of the road in a van dressed as a panting, doggish creature.

Two days, Kat had said.

That meant they'd have to spend at least one more night out here.

They had no tent. No sleeping bags. No matches, or blankets, or cocoa—Kat didn't even have long pants. The weather was fine now, the cold only leaving teeth marks. But as soon as that sun went down, it would no doubt draw blood.

Miranda stopped walking. She could hear something, faint and hissing beneath the crunch of the floor.

Like the woods were speaking to her.

Not the whispering of *soon, soon, soon.*

But something . . . off.

Something crooked.

A warning.

"Hey, Bean." Kat cut through the silence. "Remember that poem I used to read to you, the one about the leaves?"

Before Miranda could halt it, the lines scrolled through her mind—

"Come, little leaves," said the wind one day

"Come over the meadows with me and play
Put on your dresses of red and gold
Summer is gone and the days grow cold."

The illustrations were as clear as if she had the book before her now—a knobbly brown tree carved with an old man's kindly face, reaching across a meadow where tiny fairies wearing dresses made of veiny autumn leaves twirled and danced in curlicues of wind. Even before she could read, she'd study those illustrations, and then her dreams would be hand drawn in pen and ink, painted with pale, delicate watercolor strokes . . .

"Kind of," Miranda told her mother.

When Kat tried to recite the poem, she got stuck on the second line; Miranda stayed quiet.

"You used to love fairies," her mother said.

As if Miranda could forget. Oh, how she had wanted to see one! To catch one. To *be* one.

"You wore those damn fairy wings everywhere—to the store, to kindergarten, to bed—until the tulle fell off the wire. And you were always drawing fairies, cutting wings out of paper for your dolls and stuffed animals."

An ache hit Miranda's chest as her mother talked.

"You would leave little notes for them," Kat said, her smile wistful.

"With a saucer of milk," Miranda piped up, half-surprised she had a voice at all, "because you told me that fairies wouldn't come without an offering."

239

"That's right. They bathe in milk to keep their skin clean and fresh." Kat said this with the same cadence as Mrs. Howard reciting facts about the solar system, and Miranda's spine stiffened to hear it.

"I waited for them to come every night," Miranda said. "Every single night." A golden leaf fell in her path, sun shining through and highlighting its lines. "I can't believe it took me so long to admit the truth."

"What truth?"

Miranda dodged the leaf before it could brush against her. "Fairies aren't real."

"Oh, Bean." Kat reached for her; she dodged this touch, too. "I know it seems like we need to see things in order to believe in them—"

"If we could see things, it would be easier to believe in them." Miranda didn't know why, but tears stung the corners of her eyes.

"But that's not how it works," Kat said. "Belief doesn't follow our rules. It's bigger than us—"

"Why is it so ridiculous to want hard evidence of things?" Miranda said. "Not a footprint, or a folktale, or another sighting from some backwoods farmer who makes his own moonshine? Real proof."

Kat walked a few loamy steps before she answered. "Sometimes we're lucky and we catch a glimpse of the magical." As she turned her head to meet Miranda's eyes, her onyx hair, dried now, and fluffy as goose feathers, caught the light and held it, casting a golden halo above her. "Most of the time, though, we're just flailing in the shadows, stumbling around, trying to find the light switch."

Miranda's mind fixed itself on the last time she ever poured milk, in their best dusty blue dish. The last time she ever carried it up to her windowsill. The last time she fell asleep with her feet on her pillow so she could keep one eye on the night.

The last time she realized that being stupidly hopeful was a choice.

There is no light switch. What you see is what there is. That's what she would have said, if only she'd been brave enough.

"Look, Bean."

After they had been walking for, at Miranda's guess, an hour, Kat stopped at a huge cottonwood, little bits of its bark peeled away in stripes.

"Bigfoot." Not even the smear of dirt could hide the glimmer of glee in the corner of Kat's mouth. She ran her hands along the torn bark. "Classic territory-marking behavior. He rubs against the trees and the bark falls off—"

"Ridiculous." The word escaped before Miranda could stop it, and for a moment she saw the icy cold of Kat's eyes, the hyperaware, vigilant, mother-essence sternness.

"You're right. It is ridiculous." Kat pointed at the tree.

"This isn't from Bigfoot's bark marks—the tree's stripped all the way to the top. Much too high for the hairy guy." She spread her palms on the tree, tracing the bare spots as tall as she could reach.

"Bigfoot is scared of heights?" Miranda said, more to herself than anyone.

Kat suddenly took her daughter's hand and placed it on the tree. "Can you feel that?"

Miranda scoffed, but held her fingers still.

And found herself mesmerized.

She'd never felt a tree like this before, its armor removed—it was surprisingly soft. Vulnerable. She kept her hand there, pressing in.

Something pressed back.

She gasped.

A pulse, inside—did trees have heartbeats?

"Something's moving in there," she told her mother, who placed her hand beside Miranda's, pinkie overlapping pinkie so they were both touching the bare tree and each other.

"Oh," Kat whispered, and the thing inside the tree fluttered, gentle as a feather. "Do you know what this is?"

Miranda's breath snagged in her throat—the tree felt so lovely and alive. "What?" she whispered back.

"Bugs," Kat said in her softest, most tender lullaby voice, and Miranda ripped her hand away from the tree as if it were on fire, spell broken.

242

"Gross!" Miranda rubbed her fingers against her vest, wiping away the invisible petri dish of bug germs.

"Thrums." Kat walked to a neighboring tree with similar stripes. "They burrow right into the heart of the tree and make their nests. Then when the eggs hatch, the larvae eat the tree from the inside out."

"I've never heard of a thrum," Miranda said, but her mother barely heard her. Kat was pressed against the tree in reverence, the sensation of thousands of heart-eating bugs beneath her fingers. "I had to research all kinds of tree-predator insects," Miranda went on. "I read about hundreds of varieties. My paper cited twelve peer-reviewed sources—don't you think I would have come across something on thrums? Even the tiniest reference?"

Kat turned away from the tree to face her daughter—why did Miranda suddenly feel like she was the one doing all the talking? Taking up all the silence, all the air for herself, her words?

"So, what then?" Kat said. "I'm just making this up?"

A plunge into freezing water. Was it here? This moment that she'd been waiting for all weekend—no, for much longer than that?

"No." Miranda reached for the truth, the words she had stored for this very instant, but they scattered like pine needles blown down by wind.

"Then what? I'm just horribly uninformed? I'm stupid? Or both?" Kat went on.

Stand your ground, stand your ground, stand your ground, Miranda thought. *Say it. Say it now. There's no such thing as —*

"You are a bright, brilliant girl," Kat said, "but you do not know everything." There was a bite in Kat's voice, almost enough to be a yanked strand of hair. "All right. I'm going over there to pee"—Kat gestured to a cluster of ferns—"and then we'll get going. Sound good?"

She left her daughter with the stripped-bare trees, and Miranda tried to breathe away the ghost of the conversation that she hadn't had. The one where she said, "Thrums aren't real, and neither is Bigfoot."

A twitch.

A movement, a bending of light.

Miranda squinted, drew closer to the tree—

A bug, perched between slats of bark, its wings holding still enough to look fake. Any instinct Miranda had to flick it away dissipated as she studied it. A bug that supposedly burrowed past a tree's thick bark, then viciously chewed away the insides like it was made of bread—such a thing should have fangs, or leathery wings, or demonic eyes.

But it wasn't abhorrent; it was beautiful. Its furry, spindle-shaped body was dusty red, with a pair of gray triangular wings, gauzy as one of Kat's capelettes and iridescent in the late afternoon sunlight.

This wasn't what wood-boring insects looked like.

244

Borers had long, hard, shield-shaped shells, and this insect was so . . . so pretty. Delicate.

Miranda lifted her hand to the tree. The bug transferred itself into her damp, beating palm, and the woods seemed to silence themselves, time swooping into slow motion as the bug explored the back of her wrist and the pad of her fingers.

"Are you real?" she whispered, and the wind of her words startled the thrum; it spread its paper-lace wings and she watched it soar through the air and vanish against the leaves.

"What'd you say, Bean?" Kat came back around the tree.

"Nothing." Miranda brushed her hand on her pants. "Just—I'm ready to get walking again."

"I have to tell you," Kat said, "our hike's going to get a lot harder from here." She reached into her cat purse and passed Miranda a granola bar: caramel and sour apples. Miranda's entire face puckered. "Switchbacks, downed trees to climb over, thickets with thorns."

"I'll make it." Miranda unwrapped the granola bar and gave the trash back to her mom.

"You're tough," Kat agreed. "I know you are. But just—if you need help, it's okay."

"I won't." Miranda stepped over the bulging roots of the cottonwood tree alone, ready to leave this entire moment behind.

Her mother had been wrong.

There was no such thing as thrums.

Whatever Miranda thought she had seen skittering across the tree—it had been a trick of the light. The feel of it on her palm had been the tickling of a crumpled leaf, brushing her as it fell.

This forest was wily, it was tricksy; it snatched her memories and replayed them in her mind, and it distorted the things she saw with its mist and its gloom.

There was no such thing.

But as Miranda walked, she heard a whisper, like a restless stream. A humming behind her.

In the distilled afternoon light, the barren stripes of a barkless tree glowed golden. Miranda stared at it, the humming growing louder and louder, a heartbeat.

"Look, Bean." Kat had draped Spanish moss on top of her head, tendrils hanging down either side of her face. "Troll hair."

I may not know everything, Miranda thought, choking down the granola bar, *but I know better than to believe.*

18.

It did get harder.

Her mother, right again.

The hike shifted from a stroll through fallen leaves and dead needles to a rugged scramble up a clump of fir trees; the colossus white bark pines and the spruces, blue as the sea, crisscrossed their branches, stealing the afternoon light. The fern-filled understory hid holes in the soil, roots lifting like cruel legs trying to trip the humans who stumbled, exhausted, through the greenery.

Miranda's lungs grasped for breath, her thigh muscles aching as they moved. She had no way of sensing which direction they were heading; they could have spiraled back around themselves, for all she knew—she could only trust her mother.

But, oh! How lovely the forest was, and how other-worldly. From this altitude, the park was pristine—groves of trees shot to heights of two and three hundred feet, dripping in club moss. The sky, empty of clouds, bent down, brushing the tips of the pines.

The smells of fall in the trees were the mustiness of cedar root rot, the cool spearmint released when hands brushed a branch of evergreen, and that unplaceable, undeniable scent of cold.

"Drink it in," Kat whispered to Miranda as they watched a pair of Roosevelt elk amble past, the velvet on their crowns of antlers peeling away to the bone underneath. "We'll probably never see anything like this again."

Miranda straightened. "What do you mean?" Did Kat mean there wouldn't be any more trips? No more creature hunts at all?

"I mean this has been a very different trip than our usual one, hasn't it?" Kat said. "We don't ever see this—this wildness." She gestured to a flourish of happy-capped mycelium, sherbet-colored against the damp soil. "It's something else."

It certainly was. Miranda could admit that.

Even the fungi were stunning, each type more strange in shape and texture than the last—the long necks of the honey mushrooms, the purple ridges of the pig's ears, crinkling like chenille, the white flutes of the elfin saddles. . . . It reminded her of an underwater reef, the way nature filled in every nook with an experiment in design.

"Hey!" She plucked a mushroom growing in the braids of a western hemlock's root system, and held it up for Kat to see. "Chanterelles! We can eat these."

Kat picked one, blew away the dirt from its cap, and ate it. "Delicious!"

"Is this what it takes to get you to eat vegetables?" Miranda joked.

"I'm afraid so." Kat took as many chanterelles as she could find and cupped them in her hand. "Come on, Bean. Gotta keep walking."

A few hours later, when they paused to stretch their calves and retie their bootlaces, Kat frowned. "There's something weird about this forest, Bean. It keeps . . . making me think about things. Things I haven't thought about in a long time."

Miranda sat straight up. Tried not to breathe.

"Like when I'm trying really hard to think of one thing, it gets so slippery and just slides away, and I find myself thinking of something else. Something I don't want to—" Kat exhaled, her cheeks puffing out. "What do you think? Could this forest be magic, Bean? Enchanted?"

I find myself thinking of something else. . . . Miranda tilted her head up, stretching her neck, and let the memories that the forest had pulled from her mind roll down

249

her back. Not an enchanted forest, no—there must be a perfectly reasonable explanation for why she'd been thinking so much about . . . her.

"Let's think about it logically," Miranda said carefully. "It could be the elevation, making our brains fuzzy. Or it could be dehydration. Or it could be some component in the rain, some chemical from the mist . . ." She heard her own reservations as she talked, the way her theories were punctured even before they came out of her mouth. But what else could it be that was guiding their thoughts into deep, dark, misty caves of memories that were supposed to be buried forever, lost to rocks and time?

Enchanted forests were for fairy tales.

When her mother abandoned the subject to talk about tree octopi and whether or not they vied for territory with the Squatch himself, Miranda wondered, just for a moment, what kinds of things the forest was drawing from her mother's mind, what kinds of memories.

But she left this thought behind when they started walking again, and thankfully, the forest kept it there.

When the sun sat golden, liquid-like on the distant purple horizon, Kat squatted at a clear, swollen stream and filled their bottle with water. "I think we'll stay here tonight." She gestured to the clearing around them, a circle of Douglas firs and redwoods, trunks wide and lined with snags and knots. Battle scars, as Miranda thought of those defects—old wounds that now provided homes for squirrels and birds and all manner of tiny woodland creatures.

"I'm not tired." Truly she was—but she worried that if she stopped, she might not want to stand up again.

"Night's coming fast." Kat ran damp hands through her hair, collecting the strands into a neat bun on top of her head. "If we power down now and get up at dawn, we'll cover more ground than if we try to fumble our way through the dark."

Her mother . . . actually made sense. Still, Miranda's overworked brain prepared a list of what-ifs to rapid-fire—

What if it rains?

What if we die of exposure?

What if a wild animal sniffs us out and devours us in the night?

Kat dug a hole for a fire in the middle of the clearing, then hauled wood into the hole; Kat seemed so certain, so capable, so un-Kat-like, that Miranda pushed her what-ifs into the stream and watched them drift away.

Her mother hauled wood into her fire pit, whistling, and Miranda watched, aware that she was standing idle while someone else did all the work—and so she filled her arms with sticks.

Kat crossed the clearing and took what Miranda had gathered. "We don't want any spruce, if we can help it." She showed Miranda what she had collected. "See if you can find more of these little dead pieces, for kindling."

That's right—spruce was a soft wood, Miranda recalled from the pages of survival techniques she'd printed out. It would burn fast and make more smoke than heat.

As Miranda searched the area for bits of dried black wood, she felt lighter. It was as if she'd been carrying, all this time, a massive backpack full of stones—and a few had spilled out into the ferns.

They'd make a fire. A good one.

Together.

Kat packed a few larger branches on top. "There."

"How are you going to light it?" Miranda reminded her mom, gritting her teeth to fend off her guilt for not bringing a lighter or a box of matches.

Kat removed her capelette and held it to her mouth. She bit into the yarn until it was severed, then unraveled a string about three feet long. She tied the string to both ends of a stick, like a bow, and twisted another stick in the middle of the string like an arrow. She dug with her nails into a flattened piece of wood, creating a divot, and into this she put the stick. Then she began sawing her makeshift bow back and forth, the string twisting the stick in the divot.

Doubt had Miranda biting her lip. After her mother had been rubbing the stick against the divot for a long time—too long, in Miranda's mind, she said, "Are you sure—"

252

But Kat caught a spark. She blew on it, babying it, until a teeny orange flame unfurled in the tinder. She transferred the flame to the kindling in the pit, and soon a respectable fire blazed forth.

A few more stones tumbled off Miranda's back.

She waved her hands over the fire, the surge of heat prickling her skin.

So her mother took care of the fire. But even as Miranda thawed, she looked around at their pitiful camp and more doubts crept in. "Are we going to sleep on the ground? What if we freeze? What if wild animals come in the night? And how are we going to find dinner in the dark?"

Kat threw a branch onto the flames, pine needles crackling as they burned. "Your job," she said, "is to relax and let me handle it."

"But—"

"I am going to build us a shelter, right here, by that tree." Kat pointed to a cedar, one of its branches broken and hanging like a busted limb. "I'm going to cover that branch with debris, then bind it all with yarn from my capelette so it insulates us. Then I am going to make a delicious dinner of chicory and mulberries." She pointed again, this time to a row of bushes just past the clearing's boundaries. "And we are going to sleep all night, nice and warm, and as soon as the sun comes up, we'll get back on our way."

Miranda couldn't help herself: "And if—if animals come?"

Kat smiled. "Animals won't come. I promise. We're so dirty at this point, we don't smell like anything but forest. And if they do, I'll fight them off."

Miranda was legitimately impressed. If she had been in charge, they'd be clawing beneath the trees for clean water and sleeping on beds of poison ivy. Kat walked around the perimeter of the camp, dropping mulberries and chicory into her outstretched capelette for dinner. "Mom, I—where did you learn to do all this?"

Kat shrugged. "We used to camp like this all the time. Before Uncle Bob's tent trailer. You don't remember?"

"No."

"We used to go a couple times a month," she said. "Throw some granola bars and a tarp into a backpack on Fridays after work and get outside. Away from the city." She sipped her water through the filter straw. "Away from normal life."

Miranda saw a crack and dove right in. "You and me, and"—she dared to say it—"Dad?"

Kat hesitated, the fire snapping. "Sometimes. In the beginning. He would come when he could break away for the weekend. But later, it was just us." She looked back at Miranda. "Just you and me, Bean. Under the stars."

Beyond the clearing, something howled.

A long, lonesome howl.

Miranda scooted closer to the fire, eating the mulberries one by one, letting her empty stomach reacquaint itself with the sensation of food.

"Bean?" Kat's eyes were hidden by the reflection of the orange fire on her glasses. "Thank you for coming. I know this wasn't what you expected—it wasn't what I expected, either—but thank you for being here. With me." She inhaled. "Especially since I know you don't—I know you're not—"

Katerina Cho, at a loss for words—Miranda had never seen such an impossible thing. "That I what?"

Whatever she was expecting, it was not this. "I know you're not a believer," Kat said. "Not anymore."

Miranda couldn't speak.

All those moments this weekend when she'd hidden the truth behind carefully dressed lies . . . all those moments she'd spent wearing a smile, crossing her fingers that her mom couldn't detect the truth—and Kat had known. She had known.

What else did she know?

"How did you figure it out?"

Kat's smile was equal parts happy and solemn. "You're so passionate about everything you do. But with this . . . I could tell your heart wasn't in it. I could see you were just going through the motions." She nibbled a stalk of raw chicory, thinking. "I have to ask you, Bean—when did it happen? What made you stop believing?"

255

Miranda watched the flicker of the flames against the dirt. It was funny. The harder she tried not to think of something, the sharper it formed in her mind—and the more a dozen other things just like it splintered off, memories glowing bright like a tree strung with lights, each branch searing—

"Just grew out of it." She paired her answer with a shrug, and hoped her mother wouldn't see the way her eyes blinked extra blinks, her hands tugged on her fingers.

It wasn't a complete lie. Even before the catastrophe with Emma, the doubts had been boring holes, eating her heart from the inside out. Her box of dress-ups had grown dusty long before they'd grown too small. Her stuffed animals had long been retired to the basement, her bookshelf rotated—mythologies and fairy tales weeded out, replanted with simple novels and useful books like atlases and history. Books grounded in reality.

"You really don't think there's a Bigfoot?" Kat's voice was tiny. A little girl speaking.

Miranda couldn't believe it—this was it.

The conversation she'd been waiting to have, the moment she'd been building toward this entire weekend, and her mother had just unlocked the door and swung it open.

All Miranda had to do was to walk through.

But Kat's voice . . . that little-girl Kat speaking, that

music box melody of wistfulness in her words—Miranda's appetite for being right weakened. Her need to shatter everything Kat believed in waned and quieted as she looked across the fire at her mother.

"I'm not sure," she said gently. "If there is a Bigfoot, I'll need a lot more proof—not footprints, not stray hairs, not shadows. Something real. Something scientific."

That word again. *If.*

She'd said *if.*

Miranda was not supposed to be saying *if.*

"You know how sometimes you wake up in the middle of the night," she said, "and you think you see a monster in your closet? But then you turn on the light, and you see that it's just a sweater, draped over a chair."

Kat said nothing, but kept listening.

"When it's dark again, it's hard to see the monster. Because now you know the truth. Now you know it's a sweater—and no matter how much you want to, you can't make yourself see it for anything but what it really is. You can't make yourself believe."

Kat pressed her lips together, but still didn't say anything. She poked at a flame-eaten log, and it collapsed into ash.

The howl came again. Miranda snuggled close to her mother and ran her hands along the sleeves of her windbreaker.

What if that was a wolf?

What if there's a whole pack?

What if they come to our clearing in the middle of the night and tear us apart?

"Don't worry." Kat saw her daughter's face. "It won't bother us."

And Miranda believed her.

They munched their berries and roots and stared at the fire, Kat prodding it back to full strength whenever it dimmed. Miranda's head tilted back; above them, the night sky unfolded, glorious without the pollution of the city. The light from the millions and millions of stars in the Milky Way created a faint glowing cloud, hazy pink against the glittering blue.

Eventually Kat broke the silence. "If you didn't come on this trip to help me find Bigfoot, why did you come? You were pretty upset about missing school."

To-do list:

Come on Mom's trip and let her search for evidence

Let her search and search and search and find nothing

Show her the bills

Demand that she answer for them. Demand that she stop the wild goose chase. Demand that she give up Bigfoot and become a new, responsible version of herself with a real job —

"I wanted to be supportive." Another truth that was

also a lie. *I won't let her fall,* she'd been telling herself—but she'd wanted to push, hadn't she? Push her mother until she fell, so that Miranda could catch her.

"What about you?" she asked her mother, shining the attention back on her like a spotlight. "Why'd you let me tag along if you knew I don't believe?"

Now Kat tilted her head sideways, the closest thing Miranda had ever seen her mother get to being sheep-ish. "You're going to get into that leadership camp," she said, "and be gone for the whole summer. Then in a year, it's high school. And after that, college. I wanted one last weekend with you, where it was just you and me. Before you are too busy or too—too—not here."

Miranda's entire face prickled, her ears burning. Hers was a mother who pulled the ridiculous Critter Mobile to the side of the road in order to climb a giant tree, just because it looked friendly. Hers was a mother who let Miranda—skeptic, doubter, unbeliever—come on a trip of dreams, because she was already missing her, even before she was gone.

And Miranda had come with her so she could open her duffel bag and throw those dreams into the fire and watch them burn.

She suddenly couldn't stand to be here, sharing a space with her mother—not without imagining how Kat would look when Miranda made her big, cruel, dream-burning

259

move. All this time, she'd expected her mother to thank her. Now, she couldn't stop picturing that moment with tears. With Kat's tears.

"I'm thirsty," she told Kat. "I'm going to go refill the bottle."

"Don't wander off," Kat said, and it was the wrong thing for Miranda to hear her say—the type of thing a responsible mother would say.

Miranda's hands twitched.

She walked through the mulberry bushes, eyes locked on the silhouette of Mount Draco, silver against the night. Her chest was open and heavy, a thousand stones weighing her down as she knelt at the water's edge.

Her fingers were supposed to be dipping the bottle into the stream; instead they were in her hair, plucking out strands while she tried to think of some way to fix it all—some way to save them both, save the house, but without having to make her mother turn on the light and see the sweater draped over the chair. Without ever having to see that look on Kat's face.

What if Kat finds a decent job that pays the bills and keeps creature hunting on the weekends?

What if you let her still have this?

What if you let her still believe?

She could do it. She could find a way to make it work—to make Kat face the music about their financial situation, while still letting her have her monsters. Of course she could. She was Miranda Cho.

And the truth was out now. It felt like a different forest than the one they'd entered on Friday. A different world. Now that Kat knew how Miranda felt about all of it, about Bigfoot and the weekly trips and the cryptozoology work—things could be different. They could live in a different household, one where reality sat at the table. No need to help Mom sort scat samples, no need to pretend to be impressed by a footprint. Kat could indulge in her hobby while Miranda did her homework, studied for tests, applied for college . . .

Just get back to the Critter Mobile, get back to camp, and show Kat the bills.

Then go home and start the new life.

She looked down at the stream, a handful of pale evening stars rippling in the water, and her eyes caught something on the bank.

Something pressed into the damp soil, its outline only visible as the distant light from the campfire flickered across it.

She blinked.

Her entire body seized.

A giant footprint.

19.

Bean? Is everything okay?" Kat pushed through the mulberry bush as Miranda jetted to standing. "You said you'd be right back—"

Before Miranda could block her view, Kat spotted it.

As if she had a radar for this type of thing.

"Is that—?" The violet night reflected in her glasses, making her truly starry-eyed. "Oh, Bean, it is! You've done it!"

"It's just a footprint," Miranda said when she finally found her voice. Footprints were nothing. So many people had found footprints, taken photos, had plaster molds created. They were nothing.

Not even a footprint larger than any possible human foot, something inside her whispered.

"Hind was elevated when the foot made contact," Kat murmured as she hunched over it. "Look, here—the mud is deeper here in the middle. That points to a significant flexibility in the midtarsal joint." She looked at Miranda and stopped. "What?"

Miranda was hypnotized by Kat's use of words like *midtarsal,* the way Kat inspected this footprint like it was a readable map. For a moment, she had forgotten who her mother was—forgotten that they'd found footprints just like this every couple of months for the last five years.

No. Not like this.

Calm down, she told herself. This was just another footprint. Another coincidental indent in the mud—it could be anything.

(Not like this.)

The empty imprint where a rock used to be.

(Not like this.)

A hiker who jumped down from a tree and landed, improbably, with one foot directly in front of the other.

(Not like this.)

"A hoax," Miranda said. Yes, that was it. Some prankster with a mold was leaving prints in the forest, just to play around—that had to be it. What else could it be?

(Not like this.)

Her mother held her hand next to the footprint—it was a kitten's paw in comparison. "I don't think so. Dammit! I wish I could put this on the blog." Her smile was so giddy, her teeth white against the smears of dirt on her cheeks. "Wait here," she said, "I think I have a tape measure in my cat bag."

Alone with the footprint, Miranda shivered. Above her, a streak of light pulsed across the dark sky—the world was full of wondrous things, indeed, but not everywhere. Not everything. This was only a hole in the mud, and yet when Kat saw it, she immediately jumped to the most far-fetched, ridiculous conclusion—that this was absolutely created by an eight-foot-tall biped ape hybrid living in the woods.

It was an almost enviable gift, Miranda thought, to be able to see such magic wherever you looked. The more Miranda studied this mud, the more she could see its irregularities, the way the sides of the divot curved up and out, making it look bigger than it actually was.

And yet.

Maybe it was the way the moonlight glinted off the water pooled in the footprint's heel.

Maybe it was the subtle ridges in the mud, which reminded Miranda of the ridges found on human toes.

Maybe it was the obvious bone spur on the outside of the foot, the strange bulge that told of a life trudging through forests, stomping over logs.

All of it, convincing.

Convince me, she'd said to her mother yesterday by the reservoir.

Please.

Miranda's heart was a hummingbird now, frantic against the cage of her ribs—*no. No, this was never part of the plan.*

Finding something like this was never part of the plan.

Miranda's legs moved. She lifted her boot and sank it deep into the mud, swiveling until only the big toe remained, flooding with water and washing itself away.

There.

Nothing to see.

Nothing to believe.

When Kat came back to the stream, a piece of yarn in her hand to measure the footprint and bring home verification of its length, she stopped when she saw the mud.

"Bean!" Kat crumpled the yarn into a wad. "What did you do?"

Miranda shifted under her scrutiny. "I slipped. I'm sorry!"

She was not sorry. Smashing the footprint felt like a victory, addicting and sweet.

"I know you think I'm chasing air, Miranda, but you ruined one of the most perfectly complete footprints we've ever seen."

"I said I was sorry." If Miranda couldn't see it, she didn't have to think about it. She didn't have to feel the struggle between her eyes and her brain to reconcile what she'd found here—and it already felt impossible.

Comfortably impossible. They were exhausted. The moonlight had been playing tricks on their eyes.

Kat's nostrils flared. Above, the stars flinched.

Here it comes, Miranda thought. The breaking of the fuse, the fireworks, the battle of the Chos, and this time Miranda was ready. She would win.

Miranda Cho always wins.

But Kat exhaled, and softened. "Try to be more careful, Bean." With that, she headed back to the fire's warmth, her usually peppy steps seeming somewhat weary.

Kat knew that Miranda had ruined the footprint on purpose—and yet she didn't yell, didn't punish, didn't do any of the things that Miranda would have done.

How could Miranda feel so much like an adult—the responsible one, the one seeing things clearly—and so much like an impatient, frightened, tantrum-throwing child at the same time?

As she trudged back to the fire, the thought cartwheeled back into her mind—that was a really, really big footprint. Had it really been so large—so much larger than any human's foot that she'd ever seen or heard of?

What if—

But Miranda smothered the question like a flame.

Night pulled a blanket over the forest, old and dark.

Dark enough that it was no longer safe to leave the clearing. The fire's glow was their bounds.

The mulberries and chicory that Kat had gathered actually filled them up. Not a pizza, by any means, but Miranda was one good night's sleep away from feeling refreshed and ready for another full day of walking.

Unlike Kat, who glowered at the fire, slumped down against a log, pinkie nail in her mouth, as if things inside her brain were churning too quickly for her to do anything but stare.

If Miranda dug down, deep inside herself, she found a smidgen of regret for stomping out the footprint.

What was the harm, a part of her asked again quietly, in letting her believe?

But there was harm. She knew it the second Kat set eyes on the footprint—which was arguably a persuasive one, much bigger and more detailed than any they'd ever found before. Kat would never be content to limit her creature hunts to the weekends, to toil away at a desk job while others were free to make miraculous discoveries, to chase down dreams. She'd quit her last job for this very reason. Any so-called evidence she found would be used to justify spending more time in the woods and mountains and wild places of the world, more money on fancy equipment—always more, more, more.

Kat was no better than a little girl who thinks she's a real superhero, or a real princess. A little girl who thinks that all those presents really do appear under the tree courtesy of a red-suited, white-bearded man who magicks himself around the world in a single evening. A little girl who thinks that fairies will come bathe in the saucer of milk she's left on the windowsill, and kiss her human cheek while she's pretending to be sleeping, and perhaps let her catch a glimpse of their wings.

But all games of pretend must end. Including this one.

Because Miranda was not the parent. *She* was the child.

Kat was the parent. And Miranda needed her to grow up.

Believing was dangerous. Miranda knew this now more than ever after seeing the footprint.

Believe in one impossible thing and more will follow, until you are living in a reality of your own choosing.

Until you are alone in that reality, too busy trying to hold on to your nonsense theories and your hollow feelings and your footprints.

Another howl punctuated the air.

It sounded closer this time.

"We're fine," Kat reminded Miranda when she tried to rub the goose bumps through her windbreaker. "Moon dogs won't come near the fire. Not at this stage of the lunar cycle."

Miranda felt like a wrung-out dishrag, her aching body flung onto a log before the fire, and so she didn't argue. She didn't say, "Do you hear yourself? Moon dogs?" She let Kat's babble wash over her, a hateful lullaby soothing her to troubled sleep. "They don't have corporeal bodies like regular feral dogs. They're just vapor and mist—that's why they run so fast. They can go right through the trees. They're called 'moon dogs' because they reflect the moon's phases—when the moon waxes, they grow more and more real, and they hate this. It's painful to them to be real, to have a body, and bones, and flesh, and fur."

Miranda sat up a little, her eyelids a tad less heavy. She'd forgotten what a good storyteller Kat was.

"They hate that they can't just run through everything," Kat went on. "Hate that they have to move around things, hate that they feel so ugly and heavy—so they howl the night of the full moon, and every night after until the moon starts to wane. They wane, too, until they're back to their usual invisible selves."

The memories fell from the branches above Miranda like leaves, fluttering over her. Memories of when she was little, years before she renegotiated her entire bedtime routine and cut the tall tales out of her evening. Back when every day ended with one of her mother's fantastic accountings.

Before Kat decided her own imagination was so potent, she could actually find these made-up beasts in real life.

"Tell me a monster," Miranda used to beg, "tell me a creature."

Kat seemed to recall this, too. "I guess this is just a

bedtime story for you," she said, "since you don't believe."

It was dark, but not too dark to see the hurt on Kat's face as she planted thorns in her words, which Miranda thought was something only *she* did.

Something *she* made up.

It stings, she thought, *to be on the receiving end of such words.*

The howl again, a sad, stretched-out sound, and it had a primal effect on Miranda—shivers down her spine, hair spiking up, an urge to run for cover.

Kat pursed her lips before she said, "Your dad actually saw one once."

Miranda's heart slammed into her rib cage.

No, she thought right away, *he would never believe in that nonsense.*

He's like me, and I'm like him.

"We were camping. Right before I got pregnant with you." Kat smiled warmly; Miranda had never seen her respond to a memory of her father with anything other than a carefully curated neutrality. "Your dad left the tent in the middle of the night to pee, and the moon dog walked through a tree right in front of him."

Kat stared at the fire. "I was so jealous. He got to see one, and I never did." She exhaled out her nose. "Then a few years later, he was the one doing the disappearing." Her chuckle was forced. "Just like the moon dog. Now you see him, now you don't."

The atmosphere in the clearing sharpened. Stars brightening, mist evaporating.

They were going into places they had never been before.

"And he didn't—he never said—" Miranda couldn't figure out how to phrase this exactly.

He never said when he was coming back?

He never said when he would come for his daughter?

He didn't leave a note for me explaining why he had to leave? The words formed in Miranda's mind, but refused to leave the station.

Her mother, gratefully, understood. "No," she said. "When he said good-bye, it was for forever."

Inside, Miranda's stomach hollowed itself out until it was so empty, she could've dropped a penny down into it like a wishing well, and the coin would bounce off the sides with an echo.

"Well," Miranda said. "I don't believe that."

"Oh, Bean." The tenderness in Kat's voice was like a knife in Miranda's stomach. "It's not something to believe in or not believe in; it's the facts. He gave up custody. He wouldn't even hire a lawyer."

"Maybe he knew it was a lost cause." A flame grew in Miranda's chest. "Everyone I know with divorced parents say the moms always get custody. Everyone knows it." It was true. A boy in her math class had divorced parents, and even though his dad had paid eleven grand to hire the best lawyer in the state, his dad only got joint custody. Every other Thursday, and one weekend a month — that was how often he saw his dad.

Still, Miranda wanted to scream every time that kid complained about having to split the time between his parents. *At least you have a dad!* she wanted to scream. *At least you're not scouring the Internet to see if he's changed — grown a goatee, gotten a piercing, changed his signature shirt color from blue to green. At least you're not scraping for details about your father between the couch cushions, details you desperately need because even though they are small, you can use them to build a larger picture — use them as proof that he's real, that he exists, that he's out there, and he's coming back for you someday.*

"I'm so sorry, Bean." Kat opened her arms wide. "So, so sorry."

"Why do you always call me that?" Miranda said. "Why'd you name me Miranda if you weren't ever going to use it?"

"Miranda," Kat said, and the name in her mouth was a fresh downy quilt, a sunny meadow, a mother's heart in sonic form. "I don't know what else to say. I'm sorry. I was sorry the day he left, and I was sorry yesterday, and I'm sorry today. A girl deserves to have her dad in her life."

"Then why did you let him leave?" Miranda burned as soon as this question left her mouth.

How horrifying, to expose herself like this — but the

more skins she shed, the quicker they flew off. She was pink and raw and blood and guts and veins and all her wiring exposed—and she was electric. She was not to be touched. She fired the questions at Kat like cannons. "How could you let him do it, Mom? How could you push him away? Was it all this—all this Bigfoot stuff?"

Your fault, your fault, your fault . . .

"That had nothing to do with it." How could her mother say this so calmly, so easily—as if she really believed it? What else could it have been?

"How could you let him go, Mom? How?"

Target hit. "What was I supposed to do, chain him to the house?" Kat said.

"Yes!" Miranda cried. "Or throw your arms around him, or cry, or threaten to follow him wherever he goes—" She choked on the last of her words. These were the things that she would have done, if she had known what was happening.

In a flash, she saw it all happening again, an instant replay:

Her father, waiting patiently at the end of the driveway for Kat and Miranda to get home from their errands. Kat saw him, his packed car, his suitcase, and swore under her breath. Why was Miranda remembering that now?

A hug for the bean, a whispered good-bye in her ear. . . .

"You should have stopped him," Miranda said to

her mother now. "When he told you he was leaving, you should have—"

"I didn't even know he was leaving, okay, Miranda?" Kat shook as she said this. "He waited until I was gone for the day, and he packed his things. He had been planning to leave for months and never said a word to me." Her chin trembled. "Like he had to escape from me."

Maybe he did, Miranda thought.

Maybe it's the only way I'll be able to get away, too.

"You think I didn't do anything, but I did. I begged him to stay. Then I called him after he left and begged him to come back." The fire lit the tear that streaked down past Kat's glasses; Miranda ignored it. "He wouldn't even take my calls. I called him for *years*. But he left. And he's not coming back."

Miranda's head shook; her heart pulsed shock waves through her body. "You're wrong. You're wrong!"

But Kat's comments had broken on the ground, spilling everywhere. "He didn't fight for us. Not for me, and not for—"

"You're lying!"

"I pushed for joint custody, and he said no. He relinquished his rights." Kat was still quiet, still unbearably composed, but Miranda couldn't listen to any more. She stood up and walked away from the heat of the fire.

"Bean, I'm sorry!" Kat called. "If I could change it all, I would."

274

Miranda heard this, and even though the truth of it—the rightness of it—burned into her like a brand, she didn't stop, didn't turn around.

Kat stood up. "Miranda, come back!"

Miranda's mind was a black scribble as she walked into the deepening cold.

"It's too dark! Miranda! Stop!" Kat shouted.

But Miranda didn't stop. She took off at a run, scampering over bushes and fallen trunks like she had been born and raised in this forest.

Born and raised to be alone.

Kat chased after her but Miranda soon lost her, and in the darkness, her hair blended into the shadows as a cluster of storm clouds passed in front of the full, fat moon.

If she ran fast enough, she could outrun the truth.

With every step she took, her mind recited it, a spell to make the hurt go away:

All her mother's fault.

Her fault, her fault, her fault.

20.

The forest, at night, looked like a completely different land—a fairytale landscape, something from one of her old encyclopedias of fantasy animals that lived on her nightstand when she was little.

Before she knew any better.

Back when she could still believe in things like fairies and mermaids and Bigfoot—before everything got complicated.

When did it get so hard to believe?

Exhausted, hands trailing at her sides, she stumbled through the trees like she was midfall, but she never went down. Her legs kept carrying her farther and farther, her mind spinning a web of the same two thoughts—

She's wrong.

What if she's right?

She's wrong.

But what if she's right?

She's always wrong.

Not like this.

She's always wrong about everything.

What if he left on purpose? Left knowing he would never come back?

What if he didn't just leave Mom . . . What if he left me, too?

Her heart pounded so hard, it made her cough—a flutter in her chest that rolled and tickled up her throat. Tears fell, and she couldn't find her breath—so her body sobbed to get it.

The darkness was oppressive, sticky. The trees' shadows crisscrossed the earth in strange nets. Beside her, the sound of hooves thundered—some great animal, running parallel? But it was only a white hare, she saw, who dove into its burrow beneath a spruce and watched her pass, ears trembling.

She slowed near a grove of cedars and scooted to a sitting position, letting her back scrape down a crooked trunk, her face wet. Cold air sank its fangs into her skin.

The night cry of a bird echoed around her.

An ordinary owl?

Or a giant owl, screeching for dinner?

Anything seemed possible now, the forest opening wide as if she had stumbled through a portal into a new world, anything but the thing she wanted most of all. Anything but him.

The dam that held back the ridiculous creatures of the cryptozoological world had burst, levee gates busted from their hinges and washed away in the force. Every beast Kat had ever mentioned, every monster ever whispered about in the depths of the Internet flooded into the open field of her mind.

They could be behind any of these trees, dragging knuckles, and tails, and webbed feet—

Miranda shook her head, shook out the impossible. *They're not real,* she reminded herself. *Not real. Not real.*

That wasn't phantom growls, or sniffles, or breathings or rustlings, only the collective sound of the leaves shifting.

"I don't believe in you," she whispered aloud.

And then she heard another sound. A quiet, collective whistle.

Like the forest was breathing.

In the bushes ahead, a faint light flashed.

Back and forth it darted, winking at her.

She wiped her eyes and watched the light dance around the leaves—what was it? A firefly?

Another light joined, and another. Soon she counted more than twenty of them. They moved through the bushes, their pathways smooth. Warmth surged in her cheeks, her nose, her fingertips—as long as she was watching the lights, she was warm.

She was okay.

Just a little closer.

She stood, took a step forward, and a twig snapped beneath her feet.

At once, all the lights extinguished, blinking off like they were timed with a switch.

"No!" Miranda whispered, her body plunging back into the cold. She held perfectly still, pleading in her mind for the lights to please, please come back, please . . .

The lights appeared again, one at a time.

This time, when she followed the lights into the bushes, she made her footsteps silent as a ghost's, creeping along behind them, deeper into the forest. She couldn't see her mother's glowing campfire anymore, or the clearing. The lights led her deeper into the darkness, glowing so brilliant, they could be confused for the stars themselves.

Miranda watched the lights, hovering in that place that exists between dreaming and awake. She rubbed her eyes, and suddenly the forest brimmed with new colors. Were the pines always this green? Was there always an amber glow between the limbs of the trees? Was Mount Draco always furiously purple, its white cap of snow visible even in the shadows?

The lights doubled, then tripled, until an entire

congress of them flashed in front of her—how many of them? At least a hundred, and now in different colors—neon greens, hot pinks, tails streaming like sparks off a comet.

Maybe even a thousand? Miranda couldn't tell. Her mind was so far away from numbers, from counting, from the mechanical things she could usually rely on to calm herself—instead her mind was gloriously blank, empty in the most peaceful way. All that existed were these lights, and these trees, and her feet to follow them.

The lights congregated around a tree, a huge, massive yew with a split trunk that twisted up and braided together, like two people dancing and reaching for the moon. The lights swarmed around, swirling and swirling . . .

Then the tree swallowed the lights whole. The forest plummeted into darkness. For three horrible, terrifying seconds, Miranda was in total blackness, and so very cold, and alone, and sad. The lights had taken her will to be happy, her ability to smile, even her desire to breathe.

And then it was over, and the tree exploded with light. Light shot out of every patch of bark, every split in the tree, every knot and wormhole, everywhere.

Miranda had to see what was happening. She had to get closer. On toes that barely kissed the ground, she moved to the tree, and when she leaned over the broken trunk to peer inside, she held in a gasp.

The word popped into her mind, and she wanted

to fight it away, to disregard it, to explain it with other things, other logic. She wanted to deny it so badly, but there it was, right in front of her eyes.

Where she could see it.

Fairies.

They were as real as she was—she could see them, each about three inches tall, and she drank in all the small details. The little bends in their wrists. Their elbows, smoother than any human flesh. The curl of their hair, the way the slightest breeze blew their clothing, their dresses and loose flowing shirts—what were their clothes made of? Feathers and leaves and cobwebs, truly? Miranda took in the delicate crispness of their wings, camouflaged as autumn leaves, and her mind twirled.

She closed her eyes and shook her head. It was a hallucination, a trick of the light, a figment of her imagination. The mulberries—she'd eaten too many. They were giving her this reaction, weren't they, they were firing this dream into her brain.

But when she opened her eyes, they were still there. Still so . . . *alive.*

She stared and stared until she could see their veins, their wrist joints, their collarbones—the lights around their heads pulsed, as if their hearts were beating and the light was just a visual manifestation of this fact.

The fairies lined up in rows, and Miranda finally saw that they were in a little ballroom, made here in the hollow of the trunk, trimmed in gold. Not exactly like the illustrations in that book she'd had as a child—different details, but the same *feeling*.

Somewhere from the forest, music began—not the tinkling, mechanical music-box music she'd heard, but a robust minuet. And not from the forest itself, but from a fairy band there in the corner, playing doll-size instruments—fiddles with bows made with the tiniest of twigs and flutes made of reeds and drums made of mushroom caps.

Everything glowed in goldenrods and warm silvers, undertones of that same brilliant, beautiful white, and Miranda's eyes again filled with tears.

They were happy, warm tears—or were they sad ones?

The fairies danced, lining up and switching partners, impossibly light on their feet. Sometimes they let their gorgeous wings unfurl and they lifted off the ballroom floor, spinning. Their dance lines then had texture not only in their symmetrical lines, but also up and down in the air.

Miranda didn't know how long she stood there, watching and listening. She didn't know if the fairies were aware of her, or if they cared about the giant human face, wide as the sky, leaning over the tree trunk as if it were a wishing well. But she watched them dance until a pair of brass trumpets sounded and the music died away. The fairies turned their attention skyward, where a lone fairy descended, perhaps from the moon itself.

This fairy wore a white dress, much simpler than any of the other fairies' gowns, with a rustic leaf crown around her head. Her wings were a monarch butterfly's, harvest gold and webbed in black, pointed and beautiful.

The queen.

Miranda's books had been relocated to the garage years ago, but she hadn't forgotten—she could never forget.

The queen floated down and a whole fairy cavalry followed from the darkness, a group of ten fairies in chestnut armor and acorn helmets.

The fairy queen lifted a drum and beat it.

Again, she beat it, and this time, the ten armor-clad fairies pulled out their own drums and beat on them, their own wings spreading long and wide against the stars. Over and over they beat the drums, faster and louder and faster.

They all rose in the air together, following their queen, who still beat her drum as steady as a heartbeat, and they flew in a great circle, dashing away from the tree.

And Miranda raced through the darkness behind them, greedy for their light, hungry for their warmth. She couldn't stand to be alone. As they flew in their strange single-file parade, every leaf that their light touched turned gold, or red, or orange, and crisped until it curled on its branch.

The fairies were doing it, she realized as she crashed through the understory—changing the seasons. They were responsible for every gilded leaf Miranda had seen in the forest, every reddened vine, every fallen beechnut . . .

Maple leaves turned scarlet, spruce needles shriveled and fell off the trees, pinecones dropped to the forest floor like grenades. And suddenly Miranda was no longer rushing along the ground to keep up; she was swept up above with the fairies, lights swirling around her—Miranda *was* the light. Drums beating around her—she *was* the drums.

She closed her eyes for a moment—the light was too much—and she laughed.

Her hair—it swirled up above her head. She was no longer shivering, no longer lonely, or scared, or sad, or angry. She was floating, flying, falling—did it matter which one? Her body shook, her teeth chattered—but it was warm as summer here with the lights, with the fairies.

Did she fly through the entire forest with them, watching them turn every plant to autumn? Or was it all in her mind?

At some point the drums faded, and she was brought down to a bed of leaves. More leaves were placed on top of her, a patchwork quilt of fall colors. A music-box melody tinkled, faint as chimes in a wind-choked thunderstorm, and she snuggled down and fell asleep.

The forest gave her dreams of white lights and feathers as tall as she was and gauzy wings and packed suitcases and bowls of milk on windowsills that were drained and lapped up, empty by morning.

Miranda was a girl who was so very good at reading shadows.

She could tell from the hallway, even without the light on, which shadows belonged to which things in her bedroom.

She knew the short, scalloped shadows that grew from her shelf belonged to her fairy figurines, the ones she'd collected from yard sales and thrift shops and who watched over her as she dreamed.

She knew the fat hill of a shadow in the corner was her backpack, topped with the textbooks and binders that wouldn't fit into the already stuffed canvas.

She knew the sharp lines on the walls, the places where the darkness fell over on itself, were the posters, the newspaper clippings, the paper relics of a life spent loving and chasing and believing.

She knew the shadow spiking from her dresser was her music box, the one her mother had bought her years ago when they stopped for gas in Montana. The convenience store had been plastered in souvenirs flaunting the Flathead Lake Monster, an eel-like creature who had only a week earlier humped out of the water's surface right in front of a family of waders and swimmers. A popular beast.

But Miranda had chosen the music box, a tidy cream porcelain box with a pair of fairies (of course) with crowns of spring blossoms painted on its top. Even as recently as last week, she would crank it up, open its lid, and listen to its high, tin-bell tune and remember how Kat had scrounged for quarters in her pocket to pay for it. Its very existence in her room had seemed, to Miranda, to be magical.

When she flipped on the light, it was with an almost violent motion.

So this was how Emma saw it, she thought. This is how it had looked to her yesterday when she came over and then left just as suddenly.

Her mother was away at the library, putting the finishing touches on a new presentation for an upcoming cryptozoology convention.

Miranda was all alone.

She had a handful of empty trash bags.

She had a memory and a new craving for fire.

And she stepped into the room and tore it apart.

Everything went. Posters ripped from walls with little care about the delicate corners, about their histories on her wall over the years; those posters had been there longer than some of the hairs on her body. The shadow box of fur bits and backbones—why had she never noticed how creepy it was that she had such a thing?—required a screwdriver. And so instead of yanking that down, instead of wrestling it, she had to fiddle, to unwind, slowly, meticulously, as if she were loosening an old, outgrown heart of hers.

And it was still satisfying.

As satisfying as taking up that music box and letting it fall, deep into the trash bag, knowing she would never see it or hear it or think of it again.

She worked up a sweat, a fever; she didn't turn on loud music, didn't make a ritual of it—this wasn't a cleaning, or a reorganizing.

This was a purging.

The fairy figurines—these made her pause. She stared at them, and they stared back at her, and for a moment she thought, *What if I keep these? What if these are the things I save, out of all of this?*

But an image guided her—that of Emma, the surprise on her face when she had surveyed Miranda's room.

Miranda never wanted to feel that way again, that shame, that curdling . . .

"No," she whispered and into the bag they went, and that was that. She didn't peruse their faces one last time, take a photograph with her memory—she shoved them into the bag and pretended like it didn't hurt when she heard one of them crunch against a hard edge of a picture frame.

For every time I waited next to the window with my dish of milk, she thought, *and saw nothing.*

For every time I chased after a shadow in the green and caught nothing.

For every hollow footprint.

Every time we found nothing. For every nothing.

And when she finished, she looked around the room—clean and white and devastatingly empty. Nothing on walls, or shelves, just bare. A bare bookshelf, even, free from the titles of the things she had fed on as a young girl.

She looked at her new habitat, and she felt . . . different. A new her.

A new skin, a new heart.

Later that evening, when the crickets sang to the stars and the sound of the Critter Mobile playing bumper cars with the curb echoed down the road, her mother peeked in to tell her good night and said, almost wounded, "Bean . . . what did you do?"

Miranda glanced at the blank spaces, where only hours earlier the walls had been coated in dreams—someone else's dreams. Not hers.

"Just thought it was time for a change," she said, and after looking at the bare walls one more time, her mother pulled the door closed, and Miranda was alone in her blank room.

Across the street, a bedroom had gone dark. Emma's bedroom.

Shining through the Roman blinds, the pane of glass, and the ten yards of moonlight between them, was Emma's night-light, rosy pink, the color of dawn and beginnings and hope.

But something had changed between Miranda and Emma the day of the incident with the poop. There had been a brief conversation this morning at Emma's locker, where both girls avoided discussing the incident with a graceless silence—and then, when Emma invited Miranda over after school, Miranda said she was busy.

When Emma asked her for help with history the next day, Miranda said she was busy.

And soon after, Emma didn't ask.

And soon after, Emma didn't stop by Miranda's locker.

And soon after, Miranda could breathe again.

And soon after, Miranda took the plunge and ran for student council president—an ambitious move for a seventh-grader, but friends were not for her. Not while she lived in this house, with this mother. Not with Bigfoot.

But student government. Her extracurriculars. Her perfect grades—those things she could have. Those things could sustain her.

She had lost Emma. She couldn't have her—not in the way she wanted.

But she could maybe, maybe still have him. If she kept trying. Kept putting out tentacles.

And one of these days, he would write back.

And then maybe things could be normal.

21.

Miranda! Miranda, where are you?" The sound of Kat's frantic voice pulled Miranda up and out of the deepest, most drowsy sleep of her life—a hibernation, really.

She blinked, expecting the dawn's light to burst through and jolt her to alertness. But it was still mostly dark, only the breaking of sunrise, a splintering of faint colors and a canopy of gray clouds above the foliage of the forest.

"Miranda, wake up." Kat shook her shoulders. Miranda tried to keep her eyes open, tried to push away the leaves serving as her blanket. But her makeshift bed was so cozy, and she hadn't slept past dawn since before sixth grade.

"Miranda. You're in a patch of poison oak." Her mother's voice floated above her; Miranda's arms were too heavy, otherwise she would have tried to catch it, catch the sound of her mother saying her name, catch it so she could hold it tight.

"Five more minutes," Miranda murmured.

Kat placed her hand on her daughter's forehead. "You're burning up." She lifted Miranda like a baby, and Miranda clutched at the leaves. *No, no, I don't want to leave the lights!*

Did she say this out loud? Or think it?

Or scream it?

"The moss!" she cried now. "The moss will eat us— don't fall asleep, Mom."

Moss on the forest floor, moss along the nurse logs, moss on the branches and on the boughs and on the birds. Moss growing between the leaves and between the crowns of the trees and then there was no sky and no stars, there was only moss.

A dream or a memory?

Or a story?

Had her mother told her this monster already? A story of moss, like a fairy tale of a sleeping princess and a curse and a monster of moss that covered the kingdom in its tiny colonies.

"If we close our eyes, it'll take over. It's taking over everything—" She thrashed once, and as her eyes fell open she saw the green, the green, the green . . .

She was dimly aware of arms lifting her, arms holding

her close, arms carrying her through the forest, back to the campfire, where she was nestled into the lean-to shelter and covered in pine boughs, and then Miranda could feel her mother fitfully sleep next to her through the last dregs of morning.

Miranda drifted in and out of consciousness—whatever that was before, back under the leaves, back in the lights—that wasn't sleep, that was something better than sleep. It had been so peaceful. Like she didn't even exist in that sleep—didn't have a mother driving her crazy, didn't have any pain or thoughts or worries. Didn't care about footprints. Didn't care that her father had really and truly left. Didn't care that he had meant to.

"He's really gone," Miranda murmured.

"Shh." Kat pet Miranda's back, shushed her when she groaned.

Somehow Miranda nestled into the pine needles, breathing in the faded scent of her mother's cotton-candy lotion, and found a true sleep.

When Miranda woke, it was measurably chillier than the day before.

She yawned, shaking the pine boughs off her legs. Her skin tingled, burned in between her fingers, around her neck, down her back.

Kat was kicking dirt into the fire pit, which brought a

gloomy disappointment to Miranda's bones—with every last ember extinguished, the woods were once again unfriendly.

The morning was dark, the sky accented by rain clouds folding over on themselves like bundled wool. The air was muggy, thick enough to drink. Miranda offered a raw "Hey," to Kat, a greeting and an apology, to test the waters.

Kat kept working, pulling a row of pine nuts from the fire pit, where they had been roasting. "How's the itching?"

Miranda's fingernails were digging into the dry spots on her elbows. "Horrible. What is it?"

"Poison oak. I tried to scrub off most of the oils last night," Kat said, "but in another couple of hours you'll really start to feel it."

Miranda didn't need a couple hours—her skin demanded attention now. "What happened last night?" she asked.

Kat looked Miranda up and down with an expression on her face Miranda had never seen. "You took off. Don't you remember?"

Miranda rubbed the last of the sleep from her eyes. A group of strange fireflies. A hollow tree. Cold so biting, it made her ears ache and her toes numb.

"It's a blur."

"I was worried sick, Miranda."

Miranda. Not Bean.

"I'm sorry," Miranda said with sincerity. "I needed a moment—alone—and then I couldn't find my way, and then—"

Then I followed the lights, she almost said, and suddenly she remembered.

Not lights.

Fairies.

Floating with fairies, riding along in their parade as they flitted through the forest and changed the seasons. She stole a glance at the woods around them—there were new hints that autumn was in full stride, a new crispness in the air. Early morning frost on the tips of the brown branches, dew on the bluebells, moist and cakey soil, highlights of yellow in the berry bushes, like a painter had pressed a brushful of cadmium into the leaves.

"And then?" Kat prompted. "And then what?" She barely moved her mouth as she spoke, and her eyes were distant and puffy.

Had she been crying?

Miranda's heart jumped into her throat. "And then I guess I fell asleep." A dream—that was all it had been—a dream. The kind of dreams only the daughter of a cryptozoologist would have—fairy flights and legends. "My head hurts."

"Probably dehydration." Kat passed over the orange

soda bottle and the purification straw. "We'll drink our fill at the stream before we leave."

It was like Miranda's entire head was stuffed with cotton — like she was still in a dream, still half asleep.

She sipped the water. "How long to the road?"

Kat gave her a handful of pine nuts and a bird's egg, fried in the fire and now lukewarm and rubbery. "We'll get there before dark, if we hustle."

She watched her mother untie the string from the shelter. Something was different about Kat. She was acting like . . . like Miranda. Like how Miranda had been for months now, pushing away, rolling her eyes, scoffing at every word or else zoning out, jetting miles away in her mind just to escape.

Then Miranda remembered the other thing that had happened last night.

Their fight.

Kat's words churned in her brain — about her dad, about how he left, about how he never planned to come back.

The things Miranda had said to her mom . . .

Her fingers were busy itching her skin; if she had another hand, she would have used it to yank out hairs until her eyes stung. She needed it.

"It was a full moon last night," Kat said.

It was so far off topic, Miranda couldn't respond. Kat

waited, storing the last of the pine nuts in an old baggie from her cat bag.

"A special full moon," she said. "A harvest moon."

"Oh," Miranda said.

"Strange things happen during a harvest moon." Kat stood in front of Miranda, star-eyes penetrating her to the core. "Did you see anything strange? Moon dogs? Unicorns? Mud monsters? Fairies?"

Miranda froze, but said flatly, "Nope." The sky above them crackled, the air thin.

A jarring smile from Kat. "You remember that fairy encyclopedia you had when you were little?"

A drop of rain fell onto Miranda's nose. "Yes." Every part of her whispered: be careful, be aware, predators abound.

"Of course you remember it. You looked at that thing until its spine fell apart." She tilted her head. "You remember the folktales that were in there? Fairies who drowned human men. Fairies who stole babies and replaced them with goblins." The corners of her mouth were pulled up, but her eyes stayed steely.

Miranda had never seen her mother like this before, and to hear her talk of fairies swapping humans out for other creatures had Miranda missing their fire even more—its heat, its safety.

She nodded. She could recite those stories like they

were the alphabet—but now was not the time, not when the rain fell in a gentle pitter-patter on their heads.

"There's another folktale about fairies," Kat went on. "I don't know if you've heard it; it wasn't in your book. But there are some fairies who change the seasons."

Miranda's heart gave a pound so loud, she was certain Kat could hear it from where she stood.

"They paint the leaves—pink in the spring, green in the summer, red and orange in the fall, black in the winter. They call forth the sun, and bring the first freeze, and the wind, and summon the fall storms and make the moss soft and green or crunchy and gold." She ran a hand through her hair. "During harvest season there were always humans in the forest—gathering berries to can for winter, hunting game—so there'd always be someone who spotted a fairy, and when they did, everyone around them knew. People could tell."

I hallucinated them, Miranda told herself over and over. *I dreamed them up. They weren't real.*

"We should get walking," she said.

Kat leaned even closer, and Miranda counted the elusive red freckles on her mother's nose, darkened to visible from the last two days outside. "In the stories," Kat nearly whispered, "someone would come home, and their eyes would be glowing like lamps. Or they would get a glittery patch of skin somewhere—on their cheeks, maybe, or the backs of their hands. But those rare stories where a person is lucky enough to see an entire fairy, the person's hair changes color."

Miranda could feel her mother waiting for her to say something, in that way that only mothers could—the space between them filling up with expectations, each one tangible as a soap bubble, Kat's eyes hooked and waiting.

Such a silence was always a trap.

"Huh. That's . . . good to know," Miranda offered.

Stand your ground.

Kat nodded, as if Miranda had confirmed something. Without a word, she headed to the stream.

As Miranda followed through the soft rain, her hand left her elbow to its own misery for a moment and pulled out a strand from her head, and as she cast the hair to the ground, it caught a weak ray of sunlight and gleamed gold.

Gold.

The strand was gold.

Miranda plucked another hair—it, too, was gold, the color of an afternoon pond, of a lioness's coat, of flax. So gold, it gleamed, nearly white. The color of fairy wings.

Miranda breathed in.

Not real.

Then why did she gather her hair in her hands, bringing it forward so she could see?

Gold. Every strand of it, gold.

Why did she run past Kat, who dipped the empty bottle into the stream, and nearly tumble headfirst into the water to see her reflection?

Gold.

Her hair shined in the drab mist, a beacon. Every color she'd seen last night—the pinks, the greens, the blues, the peaches of the fairy lights—was embedded in the strands. When her hair moved, the colors shifted—a moving, living golden campfire.

"If you remember from that encyclopedia," Kat's voice was crackly with emotion behind her daughter, "most people never see a real fairy. They catch a glimpse of a light they can't explain, or a shadow darting across their windowpane." She sucked up water through her straw. "The more a person sees, the more they change. If someone sees a fairy shadow, they might get a new little twinkle in their eye. One that's visible even in total darkness. But if someone sees a whole fairy"—she touched the side of Miranda's hair, running her fingers through the golden locks—"she might wake up and find that she's grown an entirely new head of hair."

"Fairies aren't—"

"Don't, Bean. Don't do it." Kat shook a finger at Miranda; most of her blue polish had been chewed off. "Don't you dare tell me another lie when the evidence is right there."

301

Not real. Not real. Not real.

"Mom, it was just a dream—"

"You know, you weren't the only little girl who used to stay up waiting for fairies to come visit her window." The rain cascaded down Kat's face like her cheeks were windows, and suddenly she looked just like Grandma Hai: brokenhearted, disappointed. And so very, very tired. "You'll notice all my hair is still black."

"Mom," was all Miranda could say, but her mother stood, her boot pressing right into the giant hole where Miranda had ruined the footprint the night before.

"Come on," Kat said. "Maybe if we hurry we can get ahead of the storm."

Miranda's new golden hair hadn't grown to cover the bald patch, but she couldn't stop her hands from pulling out hair after hair after hair. Enough to spin into thread. Enough to make everything go away for a moment. And then another moment. And then another.

She walked behind her mother, gold hair sopping against her face and forehead. There had to be some logical explanation. Her hair had been bleached by the sun, she reasoned, but even she knew this was far-fetched. *An entire head of jet black hair, made golden in a day by the famous Washington sunshine?*

The lights . . . they were tricks on her eyes, distortions of the fog in the night—so many tricks this forest wanted to play on the unsuspecting humans, so many things that seemed to be one thing but were actually something else. But even as she thought it, she knew there was no fog on earth that could produce such color, such movement, such tiny little people with wings—

Why couldn't she admit the truth to her mom?

Why couldn't she admit it to herself?

Why was it so hard for her to *believe*?

22

Miranda's lips hurt.

They were chapped, and sunburned, and every rain-drop that fell on her face slid down into the cracks and stung.

Her body hurt.

Her calves screamed for a hot bath, her feet were blistered and chafed in her boots, her back ached as if she'd hung a thousand streamers for the Fall Fling in the school gym.

The Fall Fling.

What if she didn't make it back in time to finish preparations?

What if she let everyone down?

What if she was remembered as the worst student body president in the history of the school?

Her head hurt.

The walking, and the worrying, and the wondering if they would ever make it back to safety—those thoughts, combined with the tension between her and her mother—it made her temples pound and her brain want to snooze.

To go back to sleep, and dream through these difficult hours.

They hiked. For hours, they hiked—Miranda had no idea where they were, but the colors around them changed—from autumn's bold, gilded spectrum to a gray, bleak, dead area where the trees spiked black against the sky and the ground was littered with dusty old twigs zapped of color, and now, back into the green.

"Look!" Kat opened her arms wide. "Moss! We're back on the right track now."

Yes, the moss, the moss—Miranda felt dizzy as she searched the forest for any space that wasn't grown over with, dangling with, *infected with* green.

It bunched on tree branches and felled logs once, twice, three times over, making the world look blurry. It hung over ponds, brushing the still water like a maiden's hair.

It's only moss, she had to tell herself more than once. Still, she flicked her head over her shoulders, back and forth, watching for movement in the shadows.

At a bend in a tea-colored stream, Kat filled the bottle and passed it to Miranda; Miranda knelt in the mud and caught her reflection in the water—the golden hair made her glow. The human incarnation of a butterfly, a sunbeam.

She caught her mother peering down at her; Kat looked away, her eyelids fluttering like wounded birds.

Oh, for heaven's sake, Miranda thought. The second she got home, she would buy a box of hair dye.

Then Kat would stop looking at her like that.

Then Miranda could forget any of this ever happened.

"Bean! Bean!" Kat jumped to her feet and pointed, farther down the stream. "Look!"

Miranda looked—and immediately wished she hadn't. Not one, but *four* footprints this time, giant ones, sunk into the muddy bank, filled with rain. Five toes the size of sausages, a curved heel, a series of ridges and valleys like humanoid skin.

Not an animal.

Something else.

They stepped in procession; she could follow the path where they led, if she wanted to. She didn't want to. She wanted to stomp and twist and writhe until they were erased—but Kat had already seen them.

"Oh, yes! Yes, yes, yes!" Kat jumped up, punching the wet air with grimy fists. "A *succession*—this is it, Bean, this is it! These prints are fresh—within the hour. There's a Bigfoot nearby!"

Miranda's stomach curdled.

Kat placed a gentle hand on her back. "Are you okay?"

"No," Miranda answered honestly, nearly laughing at how easy it was to say it, even with the heat of panic and fear curling down into her toes. "No, I'm not—what made this? Who has a foot this big?"

"Who do you think? Big—"

"No," Miranda said. "No. There's no such thing as Bigfoot."

"Wow, Bean." Kat shook her head. "You held a giant owl feather. You rode on the back of a river fish the size of a Volkswagen. You saw the thrum trees—you touched the bark. You *touched* it. You heard the moon dog howling—*you saw a fairy and now your hair is gold!* How are we supposed to find Bigfoot if you can't even believe your own eyes?"

"We're not supposed to find Bigfoot!" Miranda shouted. "We're supposed to waste three days camping, and hiking, and working through the steps of the scientific method—and then we're supposed to fail! You're supposed to give it all up! You're supposed to admit it's all nonsense!"

A peal of thunder struck, and then there was a great silence. Like the wind was gathering itself, and the trees were holding their breath.

Kat removed her glasses, cleaning them free of mud smears and smudges, and looked at Miranda, unblinking, her eyes naked and gleaming without the lenses to shield them.

Miranda knew she was unhinged. Knew she was coming unspooled. But it was time. She had practiced saying this for days, now. Practiced the right combination of gentleness and firmness, the right words. But now that the moment was here, she went for blunt: "I found the bills."

Her mother frowned. "What bills?" She seemed genuinely puzzled, which annoyed Miranda to Pluto and back—of course Kat had already forgotten. Of course she'd put them out of her mind.

"The bills in the silverware drawer, Mom—the stacks and stacks of unpaid bills—how could you let them pile up like that?"

"Those are nothing," Kat said.

"So the red stamps across the front of the envelopes are nothing?" Miranda wished she had them here to hold up, like a mirror, for her mother—how could Kat remain so cool, so calm? Not a hint of shame that someone had found her secret stash of ignored responsibilities. No shame at all that she'd been caught being a terrible adult.

"Relax," Kat said, and Miranda tried not to boil. "They use that red ink to scare you. We're fine."

"You should be scared!" Flames stoked Miranda's insides, threatening to devour. "You didn't even read them—do you know what they say? They will kick us out of our house unless we pay them. Do you understand? We will be homeless!"

"Hey, Bean?" Kat broke a cranberry-and-chocolate granola bar in half. "I've got it taken care of."

A mother saying, "I've got it taken care of" to her daughter should be a source of comfort, should be the final words needed for a daughter to push a situation out of her mind, flop onto the couch, turn on the television, and escape from the problems of the grown-up world—but Kat had said she would "take care of the lawn," and when the blades of grass got tall enough to house a family of raccoons, Miranda had to beg the neighbors to borrow their lawn mower.

Kat had promised to "take care of the library books," and six weeks later, Miranda went to the library to do homework and the librarian took away her card in front of everyone because the books were still in the back of the Critter Mobile.

Kat had promised, at the beginning of every trip, that they'd find something. "We're close, Bean, I can feel it"—how many times had she said this exact thing, and then they'd come home with nothing?

The granola bar still waited in Kat's outstretched hand; Miranda pushed it back toward her mother. "You got a loan?" She was suspicious. "Or you talked to the credit card companies? The bank?"

"I told you, I'm taking care of it." Kat tried to hand her the granola bar again. "Will you eat this, please?"

"With a grant, or what?" Miranda wanted specifics.

Kat sighed and dropped her hand before the granola bar got soggy in the rain. "I know our trip got derailed, but we're close, Bean! Look at these footprints—this is the closest we've ever been, and when we do find Bigfoot, we'll have the money to—"

"How?" Miranda's voice was shredded, corroded from the weekend of shouting and crying and hiking. "How will you do this? You think the world will pay you for some stray hairs? A plaster of another footprint? You have a house payment. You have bills. You have me." She had tipped over the abundance of things she felt about her mom, things she wanted to say—that Kat was irresponsible, that Miranda felt like her childhood was taken over by her need to be the adult in the house.

How could you let it get this far?

How could you choose Bigfoot over me?

"You have to find a new job," she said to her mother. "When we get home, you have to give up all this—this make-believe—and act like a real grown-up!"

"How can you say that?" Kat said. "After all these years—how can you call it make-believe?"

Miranda set her jaw. "Because it's true! Bigfoot isn't real! Every qualified scientist says so."

"Scientists don't know everything, Bean!" Kat said.

"How would you know?" Miranda spat. "You dropped out before you got your degree!"

Kat was calm as she replied. "Some things you don't have to go to school to know. Some things are true whether your professors say so or not—why can't you trust me on this?"

"Why can't I trust you? You're really asking me that?" Miranda was a loosed arrow, a boulder rolling down a hill and gaining momentum. "What about our bills, Mom? What about the foreclosure notice? Can I trust you to take care of those? Or maybe you believe they'll just magically go away—"

"Hey!" Kat snapped, and the sound echoed off the pines. "You don't get to lecture me on how I do things."

"Doing things like shoving unpaid bills into a silverware drawer to forget about them?" Miranda forgot about being lost in a forest; she forgot all they had endured in the last two days. The only thing that mattered now was firing shots.

Being right.

Winning.

"Have you ever once gone without food?" Kat said. "Or clean water?"

Miranda paused. "No."

"Have you ever started a school year without new shoes, and new clothes, and a new backpack, if you wanted it?"

"No, but—"

"I have kept a roof over your head your entire life, Bean. I've busted my butt to make sure you never go without a thing." Kat's voice was sharp enough to fell a tree. "To make sure you have the kind of life I want my daughter to have. And what I'm hearing from you now is you don't trust me to take care of this situation?" She clicked her tongue. "You think this situation is bad? I have been through much worse, and I've made it to the other side kicking and punching. So show a little respect, huh?"

"I've gone without things." Somehow Miranda kept her hands to her side, though her head itched, every little hair volunteering to be pulled in a chorus. "I've gone without Grandma. I've gone without friends. And I've gone without Dad."

Gutted. Open and raw and out of words.

"Oh, Miranda." Kat placed her hands on Miranda's shoulders; Miranda was shaking too hard to push her away.

"He left, and now he's off in California with his start-up, and I'm stuck here with a mom who thinks if you shake a forest hard enough, Bigfoot will fall out."

As soon as she said it, she knew it was a mistake. She'd said too much.

Too many tentacles.

Kat closed her eyes. "How? How did he find you?"

"I found him." The rain fell, and Miranda explained

how she searched for him online—how she's been search-ing, and writing to him, every week for years.

She didn't explain how she searched for him all the time—in spare moments, in spaces after midnight and before dawn, whenever she felt rootless and weightless, whenever she felt less than perfect . . .

Her face burned when she admitted she'd sent him e-mails.

Kat, who been listening patiently, cleared her throat. "What did you say? In your e-mails?"

"Just—I just told him who I am. Told him about my camp. About school. About me." A lone tear rolled down her cheek. "I just thought—that if he knew me, if he knew what I was like—maybe he'd want to come back."

There it was. The stupidest thing she believed.

And then she let herself cry, and her mom let her cry, and the rain fell harder.

"And what did he say, Bean?"

There it was, at last—the splitting of her heart in two: "He's never written back."

Kat brushed Miranda's cheeks clean of rain, clean of tears. "Bean, I—I have to tell you something." She lifted a fingernail to her mouth, about to chew it, then gained control and dropped it back to her side. "I got a phone call from him. Six months ago."

"He called you?" Was Miranda hearing her correctly, or was the rain distorting her mother's voice?

"His marketers for the start-up quit his account. Investors were dropping like flies. He needed money."

"Dad asked *you* for money?" Miranda's stomach opened wide enough to sink a ship.

Kat nodded. "He had to pull out of his partnership. He sold his spot and his fancy apartment and his car, and he moved—"

"Where?" The word burst from Miranda like a gunshot. "Where'd he move?"

Kat paused.

And Miranda felt as teeny as a fairy, as insignificant as a pebble.

"Oh, he's about an hour away from us," Kat said. "He was going to try to get a job at the hardware plant."

"And he didn't ask—he didn't want—"

The last thing Miranda saw before she fell into her mom was those star-eyes, shining with pity, and then she was pressed against Kat, and she lost the forest; all that existed was this shoulder, this arm, the place where they connected. A shoulder that would never leave her.

Miranda's mind spun through the new information— her father was not a business tycoon; he was making parts for flash drives and cell phone batteries, and was an hour's drive from those stupid gnomes on their front porch.

An hour away. One hour.

Less time than a movie, less time than first period.

314

A single stone on her back, heavy enough to drown her.

"I'm so sorry," Kat whispered, her lips pressing the words against Miranda's golden hair. "I'm sorry."

"It's okay." That was the kind of thing you said in moments like this, wasn't it?

"Bean, I want to tell you—"

A growl.

The most terrifying sound Miranda had ever heard.

The sound of a black bear, a monster, snarling its satisfaction over finding its long-lost prey. The smell of it behind them, that stink of wild animal, its musk and its fur, damp in the rain.

They didn't wait for it to tear out of the bushes, they didn't argue about what to do next.

They ran.

23.

Stand your ground, stand your ground, stand your ground.

Miranda's own words rang through her ears, but even she was too terrified to do anything but go. You're not supposed to run from bears; you're supposed to stand your ground, make yourself tall, shout and scream and kick to make them realize you're a fighter—but Miranda ran.

This doesn't mean anything, she told herself as she scrambled around the spiking branches of a downed fir. *This is pure instinct, to flee a predator. This doesn't mean I think—it doesn't mean I believe—*

The river! There it was again, a sure sign that they were headed the right way. They followed it upstream this time—running, running—and then there were the falls, and the reservoir with the strange things shaped like feathers and there, near the water's edge, Kat yanked Miranda behind a row of boulders.

"Shhh," she whispered—as if Miranda needed the prompt to remain silent. She would have stopped breathing, stopped her heartbeat altogether, if it meant they would be safe.

She strained for any sound of the bear, but heard nothing over the noise of the falls. Her legs began cramping, her heart beat a drumline.

Kat pulled Miranda into her side, her arm a surprisingly heavy comfort—Miranda's nose caught the last vestiges of her cotton-candy lotion scent, buried beneath layers of sweat and dirt.

Her pulse slowed.

Is that why she really ran? Out of instinct?

Or was there a teensy-tiny part of her that still wanted to believe?

"Mom—" she whispered, and Kat held up one finger, lifting her head above the boulders to peek around.

An angry roar sounded above the crash of the waterfall, and Kat grabbed Miranda's hand. "Come on!" she cried, and around the lake they ran, through the swampy shore, their feet squishing in the mud. The bear chased them through the hazy rain, and Miranda's brain shook out the final panicked questions—

What if this is it?

What if we survived the last two days in the woods only to be torn to shreds by this bear?

What if this is how we go?

"Follow me!" Kat did not bolt into the trees, but scrambled up the wet, mossy rocks of the falls, next to the rushing water, hiking to the top.

"The Internet said bears are supposed to be good climbers!" Miranda said. She couldn't help it—this was how her brain operated. See a problem, make a list, find a solution.

A friend is shocked by her mother's collection of scat, Miranda cuts her out of her life completely. A solution.

"I want you to forget that. Forget everything you read or think you know," Kat said. "I want you to just climb and leave the rest to me."

Miranda let her mother help her up, and the two of them made their way up the narrow path, all muscles required to keep from slipping.

Below, the bear arched up on two legs, scrambling up the rock behind them—it had slowed, but did not stop its pursuit. Above them, the storm crashed, the rain bucketing down.

With every rock Miranda pulled herself past, she thought about everything that had happened in the last forty-eight hours. Standing on the road beside the busted Critter Mobile, the strange forest sounds and knockings and hoots. The black bear bursting into the ranger's house, chasing them away from the cabin and all their plans. The heap of litter and mud in the river. The howl of a far-off feral dog. The strange lights in the moonlight, and the forest switching to autumn in a single night, and her golden hair.

Footprints in the mud.

All these things, she thought, had perfectly logical explanations.

The black bear was simply territorial.

The garbage pile only looked like a fish.

The moon dog was just a wolf, and the fairies . . .

The fairies were the result of dehydration, exhaustion, and near-starvation. Or she had eaten a hallucinogenic berry, and imagined it all. Her hair was just sun-bleached, and the drive home to the impending wintertime would coax it to darken.

And anyone could have made the footprints — another animal, a hiker, a prankster looking for giggles.

But sometimes, she thought as she watched the bear climb higher and higher, his black eyes flashing with frustration and anger — sometimes logic wasn't enough.

Sometimes the answer was simply, "That's the way that it is."

No bear was *this* territorial. No bear had a memory like this.

The garbage raft had dived—it had swum down, bucked, moved, because it was alive.

She had touched a dying tree with her hand and she had held a heart-eating bug on her finger.

Those howls last night around the campfire hadn't been from wolves or feral dogs; Miranda had never heard anything like them before.

Her hair . . . well, if the sun hadn't bleached her hair—and deep down she knew it hadn't—then something else had turned it gold, made it shine, made it shimmer.

And the footprints—what were the odds that someone would trek out to the middle of a national park—miles and miles from any trail—and plant Bigfoot tracks, on the off chance that someone might find them? Might believe they were real? It defied logic.

It all defied logic.

Some things were true, whether you believed in them or not.

Her father left. And he wasn't coming back.

And that was the way it was.

"Mom," she cried, over the din of the falls. "What does it want?"

"I don't know!" Kat was frozen—above Miranda on the rocks, she was like little-girl Kat, wide-eyed, only getting a taste of how dangerous the world would be.

"In the stories!" Miranda said. "What do they want in the stories?"

Kat stared at her, stunned. "What are you—"

"Werebears," Miranda went on. "Is there a plant they're supposed to eat to change back, or a spell we can say, or . . ." Did she sound ridiculous? She didn't care. "Tell me! Tell me a monster, Mom, a creature—a werebear!"

"Water," Kat finally said. "They submerge themselves in water, and they morph right back to their human form. In the stories."

Both of them looked back as the black bear carefully placed his paws on a slick rock, its balance steady. It was getting faster now.

"Keep going, Bean," Kat coached. "Just keep climbing."

Higher and higher they went, all the way to the top of the waterfall. Kat made it first, to where the river rushed off the slope.

Miranda was only a rock behind. From this high up, she could see all the way to the border of the forest, where trees sputtered and slowly turned into buildings, and the highway curved like a snake out of the park, paving a gray road all the way home.

The real world.

Where they would be heading soon. Back to bills, and school, and student government.

Back to all their old problems.

And she couldn't wait to greet them—as long as she had her mother with her.

Miranda stepped up to meet her mother—and slipped.

321

In a fortuitous reach she grabbed a twisting tree root, saved herself from a topple down the violent falls, all the way down.

"Mom!" Miranda screamed, dangling there, both her hands slick with rain.

"Take my hand!" Kat reached down for her, and Miranda tried, but when she took one hand off the branch, she slipped farther and faster.

"I can't!" Miranda said. "I can't let go!" Her legs kicked, desperate for ground.

"It's okay, Bean!" Kat scrambled back down until she stood on the rocks beneath Miranda, between her daughter and the bear, a fifty-foot drop to the churning white below. "You can let go!"

The bear climbed faster.

"I can't!" Miranda shouted. "I can't do it, I'll fall!"

"I won't let you fall." Kat stood with her arms spread, her face serious. "Miranda! You have to trust me!"

And so Miranda let go, dropping into her mother's arms, and Kat did not even wobble with the weight of her—her mother's legs held firm, her arms cradling Miranda like she was little again, and it was story time, and the night-light was already on . . .

"Look out!" Miranda shrieked, just as the bear reached the rock below them. Its snarl was dripping as it swatted at Kat with fat, glinting, sharp claws.

"Hold on to me, Bean!"

Miranda barely had time to process her mother's words when Kat took a running start and leaped across the waterfall. No looking, no scouting out the best angle, no measuring the distance—just a jump, and a certainty that somehow, they would land safely.

A leap of faith.

They made it to the other side.

24.

They lay there in the dirt, stunned, Kat with skinned knees, Miranda's forehead scratched on a protruding tree root when they landed.

But they made it.

The bear was gone. It had tried to follow them, to make its own flying leap across the falls, and had come up short—beneath them, the water swirled white, no animal to be seen.

Miranda's hair was soaked, golden tendrils now hanging like muddy, rusty snakes. Even sopping wet, it was not blonde, it was not any ordinary hair color, any color that the sun might take credit for. It was decidedly, impossibly gold.

Kat pulled herself onto a downed tree and sat, catching her breath and cleaning her glasses, which had survived the scamper up the falls with only a hairline fracture in one lens.

"You saved us," Miranda said. "Seriously, if it weren't for you, we'd be dead."

Not just the heroic leap across the falls, but all of it. She'd saved Miranda from dehydration, from hypothermia, from hunger.

Kat smiled. "Just doing my job."

"I didn't realize cryptozoologists had to be Olympic-level long jumpers," Miranda joked.

"Not that job," she said. "My other job. Being Mom." She took a slug of water from the soda bottle, splashing some on her face. "Can you walk?"

Miranda's legs were a bit shaky, but she was fine.

Her mother stood. "Let's get you home. You can't miss any more school, I hear."

School. Absences. The leadership camp.

All of it seemed a million miles away.

"Wait." Miranda sat on the dying tree and exhaled a gust of wind. "Mom, about the camp—let's not worry about it."

"What are you talking about?" Kat knit her hair into two long braids, then fastened them into loops below her ears.

"I'll apply for it next year," Miranda said. "Or when

money isn't so, you know . . . nonexistent." Part of her caved in—everything she had been working toward this year, and was she really willing to let it go?

I'm not letting it go, she told herself. *I'm trading it in for something more important right now.*

"Miranda." Kat leaned over her, so Miranda had to strain her neck to look up at her, her huge round glasses, her starry eyes. "I'm going to get you into that camp. Whatever it takes. I promise."

Another promise. Miranda could litter all of Fable Forest with the promises her mother had made and broken—but this one. This promise . . . Miranda looked at her mother, and she believed.

She chose to believe.

"Mom?" Miranda's voice shook. "I owe you an apology. I never should have looked through your mail—or told you what to do with your money. It's your business, and you've always taken care of us—"

"Bean, stop." Above them, two birds preened their wings clean from the rain. Kat lifted her hand to chew a chipped blue fingernail, then caught herself and took a deep breath. "When I opened the mailbox and saw all those bills, I panicked. I kept holding out hope that a grant would come through, or that I'd find something big to sell on the blog . . ."

"Or that Grandma Hai would change her mind," Miranda said softly.

Kat stared at her in bewilderment, then heartbreak. "Oh, Bean, I'm so sorry. I never meant for you to know about any of this. I just let things slip for so long—" She rubbed her face with her hands. "I don't know what I'm going to do. I really—I blew it, Bean. I need help."

When she lifted her head, her eyes were red-rimmed, and she looked afraid. Not running from a black bear afraid, but truly lost. "Tell me how you do it, Bean. When you have something big and scary that you have to do, and you don't know where to start. Tell me how to be more Miranda-like." When she reached out her hand, Miranda took it.

"A list," Miranda told her. "I always start with a to-do list."

Miranda's mind whirred into action like a cold engine waking up for the day, and the possibilities shot out at her quicker than she could speak them—

To-do list:

Sell expensive cryptozoology equipment

Call banks (just in case)

Check online for jobs that are hiring

But she stopped.

Kat stared at something behind Miranda's shoulder, mouth lolling.

What now? Miranda thought wearily. Would it be a bloodthirsty vampire bat or a lake beast or a flying horned monster, or something even more obscure? Everything that's ever existed only in books and minds and imaginations and bedtime stories. *Give me your best—convince me to believe.*

There, just behind the falls, tucked away from sight, was a small cave, protected by the veil of the falls and a natural doorway of ivy tendrils and Spanish moss—if you didn't know it was there, you'd miss it. Leading into the yawning black opening, smashed into the mud, were footprints.

Big footprints.

"Is that—is it—" Miranda's sentences kept stopping and starting like the Critter Mobile on a January morning.

But Kat said nothing, and the moment remained reverent.

The rain fell on their heads as they waited—for what? For something else impossible to happen?

It was Kat who finally said, "Well, maybe we should go inside where it's dry." She was asking Miranda for permission, for confirmation that whatever was about to happen, Kat wouldn't lose her. Not physically—but rather, that this Miranda, this version of her, wouldn't slip away as soon as unbelievable things began happening.

Miranda nodded. "Until the rain lets up." Whatever happened in that cave, she would stand by her mother.

Into the cave they crept—first Kat, then Miranda—slowly, cautiously, the clamor of the falls muted. It was dank, muggy, a wet dog smell permeating the air. The rocks carved back, shaped by tiny water droplets over the millennia. It calmed Miranda to see the daylight on the other side, to know they could run straight out if they needed to.

Kat was nervous. Miranda could see her mother's knees threatening to buckle as they stepped, like they could buckle any second. She popped her knuckles over and over, and when she looked back at Miranda, she didn't even smile, just nodded.

Halfway across the cave, Kat stopped.

"Mom?" Miranda whispered.

"I—I can't believe it. It's really here," she whispered back.

Miranda shuffled next to her and saw it.

A nest. Prehistoric-looking, somehow. A mess of hair, and twigs, and feathers, tucked against the rock wall, large enough to house a mother pterodactyl and her eggs. Scattered beside the pile of twigs were long bones, little rodent skeletons, poop, dried branches of leaves, and footprints.

More footprints.

"This," Kat said, "is a Bigfoot nest."

Miranda inspected it again with this new definition. "I think I read about these," she said. "They fashion these nests for daytime use, and defecate around them to mark territory." *Ridiculous,* a voice inside her hissed.

Go away, she told it.

She stepped away from one such pile, and around her the light shifted. A new shadow cast on the wall above the nest.

Miranda froze.

Breathing. She could hear breathing.

Behind them, in the entrance of the cave, something stood, breathing.

Something huge and wild and real.

"Mom," she whispered. She could have counted the hairs on the back of her neck.

Kat reached for Miranda's hand, but the motion died unfinished; she was stupefied.

The shadow on the wall materialized, clarifying itself—an outline of a two-legged creature, standing tall, watching them.

Waiting.

Heat flooded Miranda's body, even in the chill of the damp.

"I have to," Kat said to no one. "I have to." As slow as a figurine on a music box, she turned around, spine curled, her head bowed. When she faced the entrance of the cave, she lifted her eyes.

"Miranda," she whispered. "Look."

Every cell in Miranda's body seemed to pound against her muscles. She couldn't move. "No."

"Please," she said. "You have to look."

"No. I can't." If she looked, she'd never believe it. Her

brain would feast on every small detail, analyze them, catalog them, and figure out why she wasn't seeing what her eyes told her she was seeing.

If she didn't look, maybe she could keep on believing.

Her mother linked her arm in Miranda's, one of them facing the shadow and one of them facing the thing that cast it, and they stood there, Kat staring at the thing — whatever it was — and Miranda waiting.

Miranda, a girl who was so very good at reading shadows.

After a weekend in Fable Forest, she knew so many new ones.

A massive, many-limbed shadow dripping with black, icicle-like daggers — that was a western hemlock, covered over in moss.

A fat cloud of a shadow, squat against the ground — that was a salmonberry bush, its roots drinking from the nearby stream.

A tiny trumpet shadow — that was a mushroom.

A shadow that darted, and moved, and became a light — that was either a fairy, or else something flying over the wide-eyed moon.

But this.

This was not an oddly shaped rock. This was not a misshapen tree branch, or a gnarled nursery log, or a flock of birds, or anything that she could explain away with logic.

There was only one thing this shadow could be.

"Okay, Bean," Kat said. "Time to go. Now."

"What—what's wrong?" Miranda pulsed with adrenaline.

"Nothing—it's just time to let it come back home. Keep your head down, stay quiet," Kat said, "and take small steps. Here we go." Her arm in Miranda's, she led her daughter across the cave to the other side of the falls, the curious nest and the shadow on the rocks fading as daylight blurred their figures.

Was she really going to do this? Walk out of the cave without looking, without turning around and seeing this thing she'd spent a lifetime searching for?

But seeing wasn't believing. Believing was seeing. Miranda's last chance to look, but she kept her eyes on the sky and let the darkness swallow the mystery behind her.

The storm had thinned, and the sun peeked through the clouds. Gray turned to rose, turned to white, turned to blue. From here, near the top of the falls, they could see the distance to the road—they could see the road. Not a far walk at all.

Miranda let her arms drop shaky at her sides, her legs loosening one at a time.

But her mother gripped her shoulder, wobbling, and her hand was like concrete. "Bean, that was . . ." Her chin trembled, her eyes spilled over.

"Mom . . . Are you okay?"

332

"He was right there." Miranda could see the heartbreak in her eyes. "He was right there, but no one—" She swallowed. "No one will ever believe me."

Miranda slipped her hand in Kat's; her fingers brushed against her mother's jagged, bitten nails. Different nails, but those same, curling pinkies. "I believe you."

Kat's lips twitched, but still the tears streamed down her cheeks. "We found him once," she said. "We'll find him again, right? When we have a camera? Something to prove it?"

"We don't find Bigfoot," Miranda reminded her. "Bigfoot finds us."

And then her mother came back—she grinned, and said, "That's my girl."

25.

Their walk back to the road was quiet. Not the kind of quiet that was deliberate, that required concentration to sustain. That kind of quiet was a weapon, one Miranda had employed many times. No, this was the clean quiet of exhaustion, and of resolution. The quiet that came when there was nothing else to say, or everything else to say—a million things to relearn about each other, but they had a lifetime ahead to figure those things out.

For now, it was enough to just walk side by side.

The one time Kat did speak was when they passed a tree, and even with the moss and the memory of that night of terror, they both recognized the way its trunk was braided—it was the hollow tree they had crawled in when they first ran from the bear.

From the werebear.

"We're close," Kat said.

Sure enough, after a while, the ranger's cabin came into view, and beyond it the black asphalt river of the road, ordered by a bank of dark green laurel bushes. The cabin looked exactly as it had when they'd first come upon it—garage open, mud-splattered blue truck parked inside, the wooden frame of the screen door fixed back into place. Just as they passed it, the front door opened.

Ranger Pat stepped onto his porch, buttoning a flannel shirt over a hairy bare chest. Even from the bottom of the hill, it was clear he looked awful—like he hadn't slept in days, a fresh lawn of whiskers on his face, a stupor across his eyes.

"Shall we go ask for his number?" Miranda teased.

Kat laughed. "I think he's been through enough this weekend."

Her mother kept walking, but Miranda watched the ranger for another moment before she followed.

What was she looking for, exactly? A lingering detail, an untransformed bit of ear or muzzle or fur? Tendrils of wet hair, still dripping from his plunge into the falls?

Any of these could be easily explained through logic—wet hair could just be from a shower. A patch of fur could be a spot of stubble he missed while shaving. An ear could be a snarl of hair.

But she was searching for something. Something to make her believe.

Something to make it easy.

"Bean?" Kat called, and Miranda ran to catch up with her.

She'd never know for sure, and that was okay.

Along the road they walked, and then there it was, the Critter Mobile. The rundown, rust-covered van was an embarrassment, a thorn in Miranda's side when it was parked in the school pickup zone, but right now, she was weak with happiness to see it—wagging tongue and all.

"Good," Kat said. "It's still standing." She patted the hood and the driver's side window slid down an inch, like it always did.

Miranda opened the passenger door. There was her notebook on the seat, filled with schemes, plans, lists for this weekend, which had really boiled down to one giant task: convince her mother there was no Bigfoot.

She flipped through the pages.

Get Mom to quit her monster hunting

Find Mom a new job

Pay the bills

All of these were things that did not belong on her to-do list. Not anymore. Not ever. They were beyond her control, beyond her jurisdiction, and so she let them slip out of her grasp and blow away, leaves in the wind.

Kat squeaked open her door and got into the front

seat, which still made a fart sound when she sat. "You ready to get out of here?"

"We're still out of gas," Miranda pointed out.

Kat was about to answer when someone knocked on Miranda's window.

She shrieked.

A tall woman waved, a white baseball cap smashing down her curly blonde hair. "Katerina Cho?" she said through the glass. About seven other people crowded behind her, holding various equipment—a boom stick, a light on a pole, a couple of cameras.

Miranda spotted the silhouette of a lurching monkey-man with dragging knuckles embroidered on the front of the woman's cap, and her stomach fell off a cliff.

Oh, no.

The tentacle.

Kat opened her door. "I'm Kat Cho."

"Oh, thank goodness you're still here! We thought we'd missed you, but then we saw the car, and we knew— this has to be the writer of the famous *Bigfoot Files*!" The woman extended a hand through the open door and shook Kat's vigorously. "Anyway, I'm Alison—we spoke on the phone? We're so excited to have you be part of the show!"

Miranda reached up and pulled out a gold hair—even with all these people here, she yanked one out. She had to. She couldn't breathe.

"Sorry, what's happening?" Kat said.

"I'm the one who called you," Miranda blurted. "I'm her daughter. Mom, I'm so sorry! I—"

Alison passed Kat a manila folder. "A mother/daughter segment. Perfect. I love it. These are your nondisclosure agreements, your safety waivers, and your humiliation clauses—"

"Humiliation clauses?" Miranda repeated.

"You release us from any psychological damage, real or imagined, that comes as a result of being a guest on our show," Alison recited carelessly with a bit of an eye roll. "And you give us the right to cut the raw footage as we see necessary—even if this excludes actual events that transpired that would have otherwise portrayed you in a 'positive' light." She made air quotes around the word *positive,* and suddenly Miranda understood: it was a document that gave them the right to embarrass their guests.

"If you don't sign, we can't air your footage," she finished.

Kat was bewildered. "Footage of what?"

"We'll have plenty of time to go over the paperwork after we film," Alison said. "Joe, let's get them rolling—I want a shot of this car." She stifled a laugh as she surveyed the Critter Mobile, nudging the tongue on the bumper with her shoe. "This is fantastic—did you get it done just for us? Who'd you get to do this?" She jotted a note on her hand.

"Are you reporters?" Kat asked.

338

But Alison had nonstop momentum in conversations—honestly, she was worse than Kat. "Are you excited for the big hunt today? Are you feeling lucky?"

Miranda scrunched down in her seat.

"You looking for hair samples? Or footprints? Or wood knocking?" Alison went on. "Last week we interviewed someone who says Bigfoot is shocking people now—with lightning powers, or electromagnetic fields, or something." She laughed, a twitchy, birdlike sound that disappeared as quickly as it had come on. "Anything at all that you've got, we're ready for it."

Miranda sank lower and lower with every word Alison said—her neck compressing into her back, her back compressing directly into the seat. What had she done?

Her mother, surprisingly, kept her cool. Her smile looked like the smile Miranda wore for school—a false one, controlled and calm. "Let me just speak with my daughter for one second," she said, "and then we'll be out."

"Guys," Alison was saying to her crew as Kat shut her door. "Make sure we get plenty of shots of the daughter rolling her eyes—you know, just as she described it: 'tortured teen dragged along against her will . . .'"

Kat stared at the steering wheel. A crisp brown leaf landed on the windshield, its tips frosted.

"Is that who I think it is?"

Miranda took in a breath. "Mom—"

Kat snorted. "You really did think of everything."

Miranda closed her eyes. "Yes, it's *Bigfoot Bozos*. I'm so sorry."

"How did they find us?" Kat asked.

This was going to be difficult. And painful.

"I e-mailed them," Miranda confessed, "and pretended to be you. I told them you would be looking for Bigfoot at Fable Falls this weekend."

Guilt hollowed her out, made her naked and raw, all her mistakes laid bare.

She had no idea she was capable of such cruelty.

"Why would you do that?" Before Miranda could respond, Kat answered herself: "I mean, I guess I shouldn't be surprised. I know this is what you think of me."

Miranda's old instincts flared up, the instinct to bark, to talk back, to wrestle her way out of this situation with words. Possible justifications came to her—this was a show for people who believe in Bigfoot, wasn't it? Wasn't that a perfect description of Kat Cho? Someone who believed in the impossible?

"I just wanted you to see yourself the way the world sees you," Miranda admitted in a tiny voice. "I wanted you to stop being like this and start acting normal."

"Normal," Kat repeated. "What does that even mean, normal?" She could hear in her voice the weariness of someone who had been combating that word all her life. "Normal, like a mom on television who wears a pastel apron and has pot roast on the table by six?"

"No," Miranda said. "Of course not."

"Normal, like one of your friends' moms? Emma's mom?"

Miranda's throat tightened—how did she know?

"What does that even mean, normal?" she went on. "I'm your mom, Bean, but I'm also a person."

The hurt Miranda had caused her mom this weekend—all of it paraded through her mind, ugly-toothed and sharp-clawed—running away from the campfire, scaring her mother enough to take years off her life. Smashing the footprint near the stream, stomping Kat's hopes down into the mud.

Tantrum after tantrum. Eye roll after eye roll.

Inviting herself on this trip in the first place, inserting herself in her mother's business, then manipulating it all to go her own way—how could she ask her mother to be normal when she herself wasn't even in the neighborhood?

"You know," Kat said, "when I was a kid, I used to think the same thing about my mom. 'Why can't she be normal?' And now look at us. My mom and I don't even talk anymore. Not really."

"Please," Miranda whispered. "Tell me how to make this right."

"I'm sorry, Bean. I can't give it to you. I'll never be able to give you normal." Her star-eyes glittered, her face shining. "But I can give you something else."

Without warning, she opened her door and climbed

out of the Critter Mobile. "All right! It's showtime!"

"What are you doing?" Miranda scrambled out behind her.

"Who's ready to find Bigfoot?" Kat called. "Today's the day. I can feel it!"

"Camera!" Alison motioned to her crew to move in, putting her headset into place.

"Let's go find him!" And before Miranda could undo the terrible mess she'd orchestrated for her mother, Kat led the crew away from the road and back into the forest — back toward the reservoir, the waterfall, and the odd nest in the cave.

Off to share her biggest, most important secret with people paid to destroy it.

26.

As soon as the cameras rolled, Alison stopped her rapid-fire blabbing. She scribbled notes on her hand, and occasionally ordered one of her cameramen to film Kat at a certain angle, or change their focus, or capture a spiraling shot of the canopy above as famed Bigfoot finder Katerina Cho led the group through the thicket.

The three cameramen did a strange dance as they walked, twisting around to get Kat at different angles: up close, from a distance, from the side. They never spoke, their choreography already solidified into habit — but then Miranda had seen the show enough times to know these men were pros at getting what they needed from people like her mother. They knew exactly how to make her look million-dollar ridiculous.

Now that the curtain had been stripped away, Miranda no longer thought the show was entertaining, harmless fun. Alison was now a vulture who preyed on people like her mom—regular people who chose to see the little bits of magic that the rest of the world ignored.

How could Miranda have ever thought *Bigfoot Bozos* would be her savior?

"Bigfoot is usually nocturnal," Kat explained to the cameras, "but recent evidence has led scientists to believe he could be evolving to a daylight routine . . ."

Alison listened intently as Kat talked on and on, and for a moment Miranda's heart held itself still for joy—Kat was definitely better-spoken and more engaging than most of the people usually featured on the show. Was Alison actually finding herself interested? Convinced?

Then she spotted the glance shared between Alison and the guy holding the boom stick. Pure mockery in their smiles, cold laughs ready to tumble out. How many times had she had that same look in her eye? Miranda considered this with a cringe, and her heart released the hope that this could turn out okay, and away it flapped.

Whether or not Kat was converting anyone, she was nevertheless engaging. Miranda found herself mesmerized as Kat spoke, even though she'd heard all of it before—Kat was really good in front of the camera. Really, really good. A lifetime of nonstop talking, countless public speaking engagements, and years of crafting enchanting bedtime stories for her daughter had trained her so well for this type of thing.

What if Mom looked for a job incorporating this skill?

What if she could narrate movies, or commercials, or audiobooks?

The idea hit Miranda's mind like lightning —

What if she could teach?

Not just an odd class here or there at cryptozoology conventions —

What if she could be a professor?

She always loved teaching at her conferences — people sitting through her lectures and then still asking questions, still wanting to know more — and maybe teaching could give her the validation she craved so badly. The things Miranda had never been able to give in the way she needed them.

It wasn't a fix to their immediate problems. It would take years to fix those, especially if Kat kept creature hunting on the side. Kat would have to figure it out — and Miranda would have to let her — but if Kat was interested, Miranda could help her look at college applications when they got home. It was an option. A possible career — one that could incorporate all of Kat's passions and skills: public speaking, education, biology, cryptozoology.

"And of course, we can test this theory by making our own knocking sound." Kat banged two sticks together. "An intermittent rhythm is best to mimic —" She cut herself off and lunged for the base of the closest pine. "Look at this!" she cried. "Do you know what this is?"

She reached down with her sticks, crossing them to scoop up her exciting find—poop.

"Mammal scat," she said to the camera. "See the ridges? That's from the intestines of a large biped. An omnivore, by the look of the undigested grass." Her face glowed as she leaned forward and—Miranda grimaced—sniffed the small pile. "Yes. This is it. Bigfoot scat." She grinned right into the camera, radiating energy.

Alison and the cameramen, too, beamed excitement in waves. It was ratings gold and they were lapping it up like ravenous cats.

Miranda winced as she anticipated the memory— Emma's face when Kat held up the white paper sack of poop, the sound of the front door shutting behind her—

But the forest didn't dip down into Miranda's mind and pull out this memory for her to relive; it let her be. It kept it for itself.

Kat set down the sticks and the scat, and as she tucked her hair behind her ear, she winked at her daughter.

Then Miranda understood.

Kat was overdoing it on purpose. Hamming it up for the camera.

Giving Alison exactly what she wanted.

But why?

Why was she acting like such a . . . for lack of a better term . . . a Bigfoot bozo?

"That scat was fresh—we must be getting close." Kat led the crew through the trees. In a few hours, they'd hear the faint rush of the falls, the chittering of the goldfinches.

Kat would lead them to the rocky cavern behind the waterfall, and the cameras would devour it all—the cavern, the nest of sticks, the rodent skeletons . . .

And if there was an appearance from the big hairy ape man himself . . . well, maybe Kat would get her validation as a cryptozoologist after all. Every wildlife explorer in the world would be begging her to be their guide.

But Kat changed direction, pivoting away from the falls and the reservoir, so they were parallel to the road again.

Where was she going? Why wasn't she leading them back to Bigfoot?

This was her big chance, her moment to show everyone that he was real, that she had accomplished the impossible, and everyone who had ever laughed at her was wrong.

If it were Miranda, she would have done anything to prove she was right.

Kat stopped. "Do you hear it?" she whispered. "There." She pointed at a hawthorn bush, flanked by two ancient pine giants, and the leaves shook.

Miranda's pulse jumped.

"This is it," Kat said. "He's right . . . in . . . there . . ."

"Slow down—we're in black bear territory . . ." Alison kept her eyes on the hawthorn bush, her smile gone.

Was Kat really about to make two Bigfoot sightings in one day? Miranda wanted to puff up in pride for her mother, but instead she crumbled—how could she have ever doubted her?

The bushes trembled again, and Kat yelped, grabbing her thigh like something had bit her. "Ouch!"

Alison yelped, too. "What, Cho? What is it?"

"I don't . . ." Kat inched closer to the bush, then cried out again. "He zapped me!"

Any fear Miranda had melted away.

Zapping was a Bigfoot theory that had floated around in the last few years—the idea that Bigfoot manipulates his electromagnetic fields to disorient prowlers—and Kat hated it. She thought it was one of the most absurd things she'd ever heard. "This is supposed to be science!" she always said. "How would Bigfoot have any kind of thermal regulator? These people are drinking beer too close to their bug zappers."

Something had to be pretty absurd if even Kat found it far-fetched.

"Ow! Ow!" Kat slapped the back of her neck, dancing around as if invisible hornets swarmed.

The cameras captured it all—a fine performance, if a

bit dramatic. But then again, this was exactly the kind of over-the-top nonsense this show's viewers craved.

But it was not at all representative of the real work required for this job. Miranda could acknowledge that now. Cryptozoology required fortitude. Resilience. The strength to keep going even when no one believed a word you said, when the world told you that you were ridiculous.

To keep going even when your own daughter called you ridiculous.

The bushes rustled again. Kat stood back, bracing for the big reveal.

"Everyone stay calm," she warned. "Large animals can smell your fear."

The hawthorn leaves shook, and the whole forest seemed to pause, listening—even Miranda held herself still, waiting for the universe to prove itself unpredictable and unknowable for the second time today.

And out ran . . . a squirrel.

27.

Alison was kind enough to send one of her crew to the nearest gas station. He returned with a can of gasoline, two water bottles, and two club sandwiches, a day away from expiring. Kat and Miranda didn't care. They gobbled them up.

At some point Miranda saw herself in the rearview mirror of the white production van—a hollow-cheeked, dirt-smudged, sunken-eyed wild girl with snarled hair the color of glitter.

"Student body president." Miranda pointed to her reflection, and Kat snorted.

"Let's get a photo for the yearbook," she said.

While the crew had packed up their production van,

Kat signed all of Alison's paperwork with her own green sparkly flower pen from her cat bag.

"We don't choose the segments for the show until we've reviewed them," Alison said, "but I'll tell you now — you can plan on being featured. This is good stuff."

"Yes," Kat said in a dreamy voice that wasn't completely hers, "we were so close."

Miranda couldn't miss the cruel laugh in Alison's eye. "Yes. Absolutely. So close." She shook Kat's hand. "We'll let you know the airdate. Oh, and your checks will be processed and mailed out within two weeks."

"Checks?" Kat looked at Miranda, but Miranda had no idea.

"All our cast receives a small compensation for your time," Alison said, pointing to the provision in the contract. "If your segment turns out to be longer than a minute, you get a bonus."

And then they left.

Kat could count on that bonus — her footage was going to be a season highlight.

Miranda couldn't believe it; perhaps they'd be able to save their house after all. All thanks to Bigfoot.

After the squirrel had popped out of the bushes, chattered angrily at the humans, and scampered to a snag in a nearby cedar, Alison had breathed a sigh of relief. "Okay. I think we've got everything we need."

She'd wrapped up their session with a quick interview

351

against the Critter Mobile, where she asked Kat if she would ever give up the search.

"How could I stop now? He's out there," Kat had said, and her star-eyes glittered beneath her smudged, cracked glasses. "He's just waiting until the time is right. Then he'll show himself."

"What about the overwhelming lack of evidence?" Alison had prompted.

Kat had furrowed her eyebrows. "What are you talking about, 'lack of evidence?'" she'd said. "There are hundreds of eyewitnesses every year. People see Bigfoot dashing through trees, walking through their campsites, spying on their farms—"

"But that isn't reliable scientific evidence," Alison had said. "That's just people."

Kat had looked right at Miranda, and smiled her same old Kat smile. "If you can't trust people, then what can you trust?"

Exhaustion now gnawed at Miranda's bones. She climbed into the front seat of the Critter Mobile, in a daze as Kat poured the gas in the tank and checked the rest of the fluids, tasks she hadn't known her mom knew how to do.

Miranda decided this would be the last thing she ever assumed about her mother.

Kat got in the car. "Well, what do you know." She

angled their copies of the contract so Miranda could see her swirling signature. "Looks like I finally earned some money with my Bigfoot nonsense."

"Mom," Miranda said. "Why did you do that?"

Kat adjusted her mirrors. "Isn't that exactly what you wanted me to do?"

Miranda's cheeks flushed, and her eyes burned, ashamed.

Kat took Miranda's hand. "You said you need proof to believe. So anytime you start to have doubts, I want you to watch that episode of *Bigfoot Bozos*."

"Mom," Miranda said, "after what happened behind the waterfall, there's no way I'll—"

"I'm not talking about believing in Bigfoot," Kat said. "I'm talking about believing in me."

Something inside Miranda collapsed, folding in on herself.

"Anytime you have doubts about how much I love you," Kat went on, "I want you to watch that episode. Watch me make a fool of myself. And remember that I would throw it all away for you. All of it. You wanted evidence, you got it."

A sob escaped Miranda's chest.

"Miranda," Kat said. "I love you. More than anything. More than Bigfoot. Believe it."

"What's that thing you always say?" Miranda said.

"Some things are true, whether you believe in them or not."

Kat smiled. "Let's get home."

"If we still have a home." Miranda was only half joking. The other half of her pictured cruising down their street, pulling into their driveway, and seeing a terrifying sign across the front door—a foreclosure notice—relinquished to the bank.

She pictured searching for solace in Kat's eyes, and finding it.

She pictured stripping their possessions down to the essentials, packing the Critter Mobile to its limits, and driving away to . . . somewhere. Anywhere.

The truth was it didn't matter where they ended up.

Home was wherever Kat was, and that could be near the shapeshifters in New Mexico, or the wendigo in Canada or the lake monsters of the north. Sleeping under the stars in a different forest every night.

Or it could be in their same old house with their same old gnomes and their same old stack of bills and their same old problems. It didn't matter.

"All right. Time to hit the road. Just you and me, Bean."

As Kat pulled the Critter Mobile off the shoulder, Miranda's eyes followed a bizarre bug darting across the windshield—what was it, a thrum? Or a moth? Or something else entirely?

Miranda thought she knew so much—but this was a

better way to view the world. Full of possibilities, instead of certainties.

It took going all the way through the forest—looping down a river, through a mountain, and into the old growth of a national park—to be able to admit she was wrong.

"Just you and me, Bean." The first time Kat had ever said that was the day her dad left, when Miranda stood in the driveway and her mother had wrapped her up in a hug so tight, she couldn't breathe.

But as they drove out of the forest, she imagined a different scene.

A stormy morning, her mother sitting in a hospital bed holding a tiny daughter swaddled in a white blanket, little heart-face staring up at her helplessly, curiously. "It's just you and me, Bean," Miranda imagined her mother saying, and the baby is silent, studying the mother's face, searching it for evidence of love.

Somewhere out there, Bigfoot might be tromping back to his nest. Somewhere else, another creature—unknown yet even to the cryptozoologists—might be crouched between a pair of trees, watching through pine needles as a group of humans set up a tent for a night of s'mores and stargazing.

And somewhere even farther out there, her father might be thinking of the daughter he'd left behind.

Or he might not ever think of her again.

But here, right here, was the mother who loved her, the mother who'd fight for her, the mother who would always help her fly when she needed to take a blind leap into darkness.

Just me and her.

A hot summer night in Humboldt County, where the water in Bluff Creek whispers over the logjams and debris like a child with secrets, and an eight o'clock sun finally began its somewhat stubborn descent, letting the moon have its share of the hours, and the cryptozoologists gathered around the fire.

It was a familiar lull, one that happened every night during these hunts—there reached a time when the light was too drained to search by, but it was still too early for the infrareds or the night-vision goggles.

Somewhere out there, the cryptozoologists declared, the creatures were doing their twilight dozing before they would venture back out into the world, and so the humans might as well make merry and eat s'mores.

"Is Bigfoot nocturnal?" Miranda had asked this on more than one occasion, and everyone gave her a different answer. "Yes, definitely, there's too many reports of night knocking." "No, absolutely not! Think of all the eyewitnesses who've seen him in stark sunlight." And, her favorite answer: "I sure hope not. No one's gonna believe us if the only photo we have is some dark, blurry shot of him with glowing red eyes—they'll just say it's an oversize possum."

Her own mother had thought the question was delicious. "All these little details, Bean . . . Don't they make you all the more excited for when we finally find him?"

Yes, they did. It had filled Miranda with firecrackers to think of it. It had made her too excited, too twitchy to stand without pacing. And so she sat, cross-legged, bouncing her knees in the dirt where she was, beneath her mom's chair. She had already roasted her marshmallows to gooeyness—then she had sandwiched them between two chocolate cookies and bit into sticky, sugary bliss. Her mother pushed another log on the fire, the flames belching, then settling

At eight years old Miranda was usually the youngest one. A few of the other cryptozoologists brought their kids sometimes, when weekend visitations coincided with creature hunts, but most of the time, she was the only one. These adults never asked about school. They never asked what she wanted to be when she grew up. As far as they were concerned, she was the same as them, only shorter. The very fact that she was out there with them equalized her.

The search equalized them all.

As soon as everyone had turned into silhouettes, the sky on fire behind them, Uncle Bob had started.

"I was eighteen," he said, "walking home from a girl's house. Decided to cut through the neighbor's farmlands. This was down past Twin Falls, by an offshoot of the Snake, and I shuffled through their cornstalks and the hairs on the back of my neck stood right up. I turned around, and there it was, right across the river, staring at me in the moonlight." Uncle Bob widened his eyes when he looked at Miranda, as if he had been possessed, made to relive the very moment. "Something slimy, something on all fours. I remember it had a frill around its neck, like one of those old-fashioned Shakespeare collars—and it shook itself, like a dog gone swimming, and cold river water flew off the frills in little drops." The fire hissed. "By the time I realized what I was seeing, it took off. I came back with a flashlight and a camcorder, but I only found tracks frozen in the mud."

A newer addition to the group, a woman with dreadlocks, went next. "I heard magpies fighting one morning, right before my twins were born. The birds would do this, squabble over the rights to the watermelon rinds and coffee grounds that spilled out of my neighbor's garbage cans. I rolled myself out of bed and opened the window to yell at them, and—and I saw this little leathery thing, the size of a squirrel, crouched on the top of my fence posts, shoving all the food from the bird feeder into its gob as quick as it could, which made the magpies screech—" She shook her head. "Then it scampered up the tree and I stood there, gaping, wondering if I was still dreaming."

One by one, they had all shared their tales—their origin stories—and Miranda's eyes burned as the campfire brightened against the darkness. The circle had been sacred, it had been unbreakable, made of the deepest secrets and the darkest fears and shames and doubts, cruel as Mondays, and hopes as blue as the planet. It had been a setting, this circle, like any other—as palpable to be inside as a school or a car or a living room. Miranda had clung to that feeling with all her heart—this feeling that she was in the midst of something special—something that all the mainstream outlets had rejected, but that was how it was, wasn't it? The world sometimes took a bit longer to catch the things that were the most true.

"What about you?" someone had prompted Miranda's mother. "Why are you here?"

Miranda had shifted. Had her mother ever made such a confession here, in this group? The moment split, as if with lightning, into another thought: Had Miranda ever even heard such a story from her mother? She'd heard so many tales of her mother's creature sightings, she couldn't pinpoint which one was first. Couldn't line them up in a timeline, her mother's oldest monster with her newest. Usually her mother found other things to do during the confessionals, Miranda realized now—making cocoa, fussing with supplies, standing guard while subtly listening, starry-eyed.

But tonight, the magic must have overwhelmed her. Holding a cup of cocoa close to her lips, blowing across the rim so the steam wafted up in clouds, Miranda's mother spoke.

"I was little—I don't know how old exactly. Four or five?—young enough that I shouldn't have gone off alone, but I did. Vacationing with my family here in California—not far from here, actually—and I snuck off to the lake, where I waded in, only up to my knees at first, and then I took one more step and slipped right in." She laughed at the shock of such a memory—at the fact that she almost drowned. "I fought to keep my head above water, but I'd walked right off a ledge and my feet couldn't find the lake floor beneath me. When I looked up through the water, up past the beach and the rocks, to the tree line, and—I saw him."

Even Miranda had been silent. She knew her mother had once fallen into a lake as a kid—which was why her mother made her take a course of basic swimming lessons one summer. But she had no idea that the story of the lake was this story.

The story.

"A figure, dark—even against the dark brown of the tree trunks—and taller than any person I'd ever seen," her mother went on, "walking parallel to the lake's edge. But I sank all the way down and lost sight of it, my arms flailing, and I probably would have drowned." The firelight was golden in her eyes, filling in where the pupil was black. "But something pulled me out. Something strong—something with massive hands. It reached down into the water and dragged me back to the shallows. When I finally came up, when I swallowed air, it was gone. There was a pathway of trampled bushes, a quiet in the sky after the birds settled. A smell."

The others had murmured; they all knew that smell, the scent of muted skunk, of mountains, of leaf grit and matted fur and sulfur.

"And footprints. In the mud. Footprints leading down into the water, and footprints leading out."

Miranda shivered.

"No one believed me," her mother went on. "Not a single person. When I told my parents, they dismissed it. 'You were underwater,' they said. 'The lake distorted what you saw.'"

Again, the others had whispered to themselves—they all knew those kinds of comments, those kinds of dismissals.

"'It was only a tree branch, blowing in the wind, it was

only a bird, or a bear, or a shadow.'" Her mother smiled. "That must have been a huge bird, then. And they still couldn't explain what pulled me out of the water. But you know what? I didn't know the lake dropped from a foot deep to four—the water wasn't dark or murky. Clear water, and there was still something unknowable. Something hidden."

The fire crackled, and she finished with, "It seems wrong to think we know everything. There are things all around us—things we see, things we don't. That's why I'm here."

All else slunk away, and Miranda was left with only the reverberation of her mother's words on her vertebrae, trickling down her spine like raw egg. It was a story of a sighting, but it was more than that—it was testimony.

In the reverence, no one dared speak. No one would for some time, to let the stories that had been told float up past the trees like smoke, into the atmosphere to join the stars.

Eventually Uncle Bob pursed his lips against the ocarina he kept on a string around his neck, his tinny, ghostly tune chasing after the stories, blowing over the creek, and the valley, and possibly even over Bigfoot himself.

Miranda nestled close to her mother, warm and snug and sleepy, and also wide-eyed at the wonder of this world, this wonder that she shared with everyone here like a giant blanket.

"I didn't know that," she raised her face to tell her mother. "About that day at the lake."

"Well, Bean," her mother said, cupping Miranda's face in her hand, "that's the whole point, isn't it? There's so much we don't know."

Miranda tilted back against her mother's shins. Soon the coziness would dissipate, and the evening would shift into gear. The cryptozoologists would break into groups to set up for their night detections—armed with infrared tools and cameras, they would hide in the trees and bushes like soldiers. Even after a full day of scouting and hiking, their hope would keep them awake and fed.

"Tell me a monster," Miranda murmured, her eyelids falling like heavy velvet, the taste of marshmallows faint in her mouth.

And her mother wrapped them both in a crocheted quilt, the cool night air still finding its way into Miranda's skin through the holes in the links—but it was welcome. Everything about this night was welcome.

Her mother's voice was part lullaby as she started, "There is one—some say he has antlers the size of an eagle's wingspan . . ."

The last thing Miranda saw before she surrendered to her dozing was a shadow, dark against the distant green of the trees that bordered the mountain's rocky exposure, lumbering between the trunks, and she fell asleep with a smile on her lips and a secret of her own.

THE BIGFOOT FILES
- A Blog for Believers Everywhere -

The Nature of Discovery

Good morning, believers!

Today I want to write about something that's been on my mind quite a bit lately. A different creature — the coelacanth.

Coelacanths are a plump, lobe-finned fish with thick cosmid scales and oversize white eyes and small mouth. They are primarily found in the Indian Ocean and Indonesia. For those who aren't aware, they were thought to be extinct until a museum curator, Marjorie Courtenay-Latimer, discovered a specimen in the net of a South African trawler.

From her diary: "I saw a blue fin and, pushing off the fish [piled on top], the most beautiful fish I had ever seen was revealed. It was five feet long and a pale mauve blue with iridescent silver markings. . . ."

It's obvious to us now that the coelacanth is a living fossil — we've all grown up hearing the legend of its rediscovery in biology courses and on nature documentaries. But Latimer had a hard time getting anyone to believe her.

365

The taxi driver initially refused to cart her and her five-foot, slimy, stinky fish carcass from the dock to the museum.

Her colleagues laughed at her or ignored her. When the university verified her findings, her male superiors tried to take the credit.

As Bigfoot believers, we are laughed at. We are ignored and our research is mocked, unless we find something substantial—then it is taken over by the so-called real scientists and we are left in the woods with our plaster molds and our shadows.

When you feel discouraged, Bigfoot tribe, or exhausted, or overwhelmed by the world's cynicism—by their refusal to believe—come here, read Latimer's entry, and imagine how you will feel when you finally find it.

When you find something.

You're so close.

I believe you.

And I believe in you.

BELIEF

A strange shadow lurked down the road and stopped with a noxious belch in front of the house with the gnomes on the porch.

It was the Critter Mobile, its antlers on the roof rack draped in moss, its bumper tongue disheveled and stuck with burrs. Miranda couldn't tell if her mother had pressed the brakes or if the car had died right as they drifted into their driveway, but either way, she sank back into the seat, four days' worth of relief coming into her body at once.

"We're home," she breathed. The sun was setting, the light rosy and clear.

"And we didn't even need a hatchet." Kat unbuckled her seat belt and turned sideways, looking at Miranda. Her hair was loose, calm around her shoulders. Her capelette had unraveled during the drive and so she shed it, looking small in an oversized T-shirt and shorts. Her nibbled nails were their natural color, the blue polish all chewed or chipped away.

But in the fading sunset, Miranda saw a sparkle on Kat's cheek, the glitter from some old swipe of blush or gaudy eye shadow that the forest hadn't wiped clean.

Or perhaps it was like Miranda's hair, still golden, even as they sat outside of their very normal, very mossless house. Perhaps the sparkle was proof.

"What do you say we unpack," Kat said, "and then order a pizza?"

"Perfect." Miranda swung out of the Critter Mobile and stopped cold.

There was an unfamiliar car parked on the street, and on their porch, among the gnomes, her grandmother stood, her expression unreadable.

It was an odd thing, Miranda thought, how you could look at one face and see many different people.

This woman was her Grandma Hai, the wrinkles around her eyes and mouth entirely her own—earned, no doubt, by the exhausting, stressful years of raising a child and then losing her. The stress of choices sweeping them both to opposite sides of the river. The stress of the empty e-mail inbox, the stress of the phone that never rings. The stress of having to explain over and over to people, "Yes, I have a daughter; no, we don't speak."

But Miranda also saw her mother's features on that face, and as she studied her grandmother, a feature or two of her own reflected back.

Three generations in one solemn, scared face.

"Miranda," she said with a definitiveness that was the opposite of Kat's flighty-sparrow voice.

Kat came around the Critter Mobile cautiously, like she was approaching a wild animal. "Mom? What are you doing here?"

"Where have you been?" Grandma Hai said. "Your daughter calls Thursday night, tells me you need help. Then I call and call and call, for three days, with no answer! So you're alive—I'm glad to see it." She turned back to her car.

"Wait!" Kat ran forward, blocking her mother's door. "You—you were worried about us?"

"Of course I was worried!" Grandma Hai bit her lip. "Katerina, I—I want . . ."

Part of Miranda wanted to slice through the tension, barge in and save her mother, save her grandmother, save all of them. But it was not her place. Not her job to fix this. They needed to do it on their own.

Kat made a sound that was like a little kid laughing and a choking sob, all at once. "Mom," she cried, "I'm so sorry." She hugged Grandma Hai, and Grandma Hai hugged her back, and the two of them stood there, entwined, while Miranda watched.

Across the street, the lights were on at Emma's house. A light in Emma's bedroom.

"I'll be right back," Miranda said.

And she crossed the street like it was a whitewater river cutting through a mountain, and the only way to safety was barreling through to the other side.

She knocked on the door and put her hands to her side. In the twilight, the bay window was like a mirror—would Emma recognize her with her new golden hair?

Miranda stared harder at her reflection in the window, at the way her eyes seemed brighter—almost as if there was a star or two in there, gleaming against the darkness.

Did she even recognize herself?

What if, what if, what if?

Enough, she thought. For now, she could balance here, on this edge of uncertainty, and she could live among the wonders and the potentials and the what-ifs.

Because what if you never stopped wondering?

What if instead of saying "I know," you learned to ask questions?

What if instead of closing doors, you opened them?

What if you decided to believe?

The deadbolt sounded, and Miranda's heart beat staccato. But when the door opened, Emma was smiling. "Hi," she said, surprised.

A tentacle.

"Hi."

And just like that, Miranda leaped.

What if?

ACKNOWLEDGMENTS

My sincerest, warmest thanks to everyone who helped me write, edit, and produce this book.

A thank-you to my early readers, my brainstormers, and my cheerleaders, among them Melanie Conklin, for always reminding me I can do anything I want; Julie Falatko, for being so generous with your energy and time, always; Heidi Heilig, for your patience and your optimism; and Claire Legrand, for being there every single day and holding my hand when necessary. Your insights and words of encouragement pushed me through the seemingly impossible task of writing and rewriting this book, and I am so grateful for each one of you. We have the coolest jobs.

A massive thank-you to those who helped me research this project's setting, particularly my brother. And thank you to the brilliant proofreaders at Candlewick, who made sure every detail of this weird little book was just right.

Thank you so very much to my shimmering publicist, Jamie Tan, for making me look good; my cover designer, Matt Roeser, for making my book look good; and all the others at my wonderful publisher. I am so lucky to work with all of you.

To my agent, Sarah: Five years now we've been working together, and I have learned so much from you. Thank you for your wisdom, your guidance, and your ever calm, ever straightforward ways.

To my editor, Kaylan: How did we survive this? How did we burn this down and rebuild it and live to tell the tale? I will never get over it, and I will never forget your steadfastness, your fortitude, and your gumption. And you were right. You know that, right? You were so, so right. I want to write books with you forever. Let's make a million more (on a realistic, responsible time frame).

This book was born from a hodgepodge of strange ingredients, and yet without a single one of them, it would cease to be what it is now. And so thank you, Pixar's *Brave,* Snow Patrol's *A Hundred Million Suns,* Joel McNeely's score to the Tinkerbell movies, and Tibble Fork Reservoir in American Fork Canyon.

Thank you to my family—my mother in particular, who encouraged me and my odd little fairies and taught me how to be a parent. Thank you to my siblings—I am so happy we had one another for everything that's happened in the last three years. Thank you to my husband for his patronage and his adoration, and to my daughters, Finley and Clementine—there is nothing I wouldn't do for you. I love you both a giant hairy Bigfoot.